DAUGHTER

OF

DESTINY

BOOK ONE OF GUINEVERE'S TALE

NICOLE EVELINA

DAUGHTER OF DESTINY

Nicole Evelina

© 2016 Nicole Evelina

Lawson Gartner Publishing
PO Box 2021
Maryland Heights MO, 63043
www.lawsongartnerpublishing.com

Printed in the United States of America
First Printing 2016

ISBNs
978-0-9967631-0-3 (print)
978-0-9967631-1-0 (e-book)

Library of Congress Control Number: 2015953097

Editor: Terry Valentine
Proofreader: Cassie Cox, Cassie Cox Editing
Cover Design: Jenny Quinlan, Historical Editorial
Layout: The Editorial Department

1. Fiction 2. Historical Fiction 3. Historical Fantasy 4. Myth and Legend 5. Arthurian Legend

To Mom and Dad, with all my love

And to Bryan Vilmer and Dr. Benjamin Moore,
for teaching me to love writing

HIGHLAND PICTS

LOWLAND PICTS

DALRIADA

STERLING

FIRTH OF FORTH
TRAPRAIN LAW

ANTONINE WALL
DAMNONII

VOTADINI
LOTHIAN

FIRTH OF CLYDE

STRATHCLYDE

SELGOVAL

NOVANTE

HADRIAN'S WALL

IRELAND

SOLWAY FIRTH

CARLISLE
CAMELOT

BERNICIA

RHEGED

YORK

NORTHGALIS

MIDLANDS

GWYNEDD

POWYS

ANGLO-SAXON
TERRITORY

DYFED

CORBENIC

AVALON

SUMMER
COUNTRY

DYFNAINT

CORNWALL

PROLOGUE

I am Guinevere.

I was once a queen, a lover, a wife, a mother, a priestess, and a friend. But all those roles are lost to me now; to history, I am simply a seductress, a misbegotten woman set astray by the evils of lust.

This is the image painted of me by subsequent generations, a story retold thousands of times. Yet, not one of those stories is correct. They were not there; they did not see through my eyes or feel my pain. My laughter was lost to them in the pages of history.

I made the mistake of allowing the bards to write my song. Events become muddled as ink touches paper, and truth becomes malleable as wax under a flame. Good men are relegated to the pages of inequity, without even an honest epitaph to mark their graves.

Arthur and I were human, no more, no less, though people choose to see it differently. We loved, we argued, we struggled, all in the name of a dream, a dream never to be fulfilled. Camelot is what fed the fires that stirred us to do as we did. History calls it sin, but we simply called it life.

The complexity of living has a way of shielding one's eyes from the implications of one's role. That is left for others to flesh out, and they so often manipulate it to suit their own needs. To those god-awful religious, I have become a whore; Arthur the victim of a fallen Eve; Morgan, a satanic faerie sent to lead us all astray. To the royalty, we have become symbols of the dreams they failed to create and Arthur is the hero of a nation, whereas to me, he was simply a man. To the poor, we are but a legend, never flesh and blood, a haunting story to be retold in times of tribulation, if only to inspire the will to survive.

We were so much more than mute skeletons doomed to an eternity in dust and confusion. We were people with a desire for life, a life of peace that would be our downfall. Why no one can look back through the years and recognize the human frailty beneath our actions, I will never understand. Some say grace formed my path; others call it a curse. Whatever it was, I deserve to be able to bear witness before being condemned by men who never saw my face.

It ends now. I will take back my voice and speak the truth of what happened. So shall the lies be revealed and Camelot's former glory restored. Grieve with me, grieve for me, but do not believe the lies which time would sell. All I ask is that mankind listen to my words, and then judge me on their merit.

PART ONE

Isle of Glass

CHAPTER ONE

Spring 491

One more step, and there would be no turning back.

I glanced hesitantly at Viviane, who waited in the belly of a small boat at the edge of the gray-green lake. A slight breeze lifted her long, dark brown hair around her face to frame the crescent mark of a priestess tattooed on her brow. She stood patiently, one pale hand on the scrolling prow of the boat, which curved like a swan sleeping with its beak nestled under its wing. The vessel seemed to disappear in her wake, the other end obscured by a dense fog that rolled and curled in a sinuous dance that made it impossible to see what lay beyond. The air was thick with the heavy, choking fumes of the tar that turned the boat black, protecting it from the waters that lapped incessantly at its base and sides.

I looked down at my reflection; the gentle current pulled at the image of a girl hovering between youth and womanhood, fists balled nervously into the fabric of a green dress, wisps of black hair escaping from a long, tight braid flung over her left shoulder. She looked back at me with uncertain eyes, not emerald as they should be, but nearly black in the odd half-light where the spring sunshine gave way to the dower mists.

Who are you? she seemed to ask.

I wasn't sure how to answer.

If I stepped aboard, I was no longer Guinevere, daughter of King Leodgrance of Gwynedd, but Guinevere, acolyte of the Goddess. The boat would take me to Avalon, away from the only life I had ever known and into a place of great mystery. I remembered my nursemaid, voice full of awe and reverence, describing Avalon as an earthly paradise—a holy place of temperate breezes and unending sunshine, where disease was unknown and crops needed no tending to produce a bountiful harvest each year without fail. Some of our servants even believed the hillsides teamed with faeries, dragons, elves, and all manner of mythical creatures that only came to ordinary mortals in their dreams.

Now I had to make a choice. Did I wish to go this place and learn to control the visions haunting my waking hours, or return to the familiar security of my home at Northgallis, despite the constant threat of Irish raids?

As if in answer, my sight clouded over against my will and a devastated seaport village arose before me, an unfamiliar place. My inner vision did not see the attack, but the aftermath lay before me as though I were there—the burned-out hulls of overturned ships, bodies being carted to the countryside by black-robed mourners for burial, crumbling houses laying bare the broken lives within.

I clenched my eyes closed, but the images remained, and they would come again, as they had so many times before. There would be no respite anytime soon if I didn't go with Viviane and learn from the priestesses on the isle how to control this ability, this gift—as my mother called it—that I regarded as more of a curse.

Taking a deep breath, my decision made, I willed myself to lift my right foot, clad in a thick leather boot against the last of winter's chill, from the sand and place it in the boat. I took Viviane's cool, reassuring hand and let her help me aboard. She untied the mooring from a dock shrouded in fog and sank a thin pole into the invisible water. The boat glided smoothly across the lake, which scarcely seemed disturbed by its passage. As we moved, the world around us became even more engulfed in mist, until the shore was swallowed up and we floated in a land of milky vapor.

My stomach tightened. Had I made the right choice? What was I getting myself into? I was only eleven years old, not yet mature enough to foresee how such a decision might affect my future life and still enough of a child to already miss my family terribly. I fidgeted with my tunic as worry swam through my mind. What if the priestesses did not like me, or worse, what if the darker rumors were true?

I bit my thumbnail apprehensively as I thought about what I had heard—the priestesses were keepers of powerful magic that could influence the weather, bring forth life from the barren, or curse the wretched with unspeakable suffering, according to their will. Most common folk considered the priestesses harmless, but a vocal minority cowered in fear, regarding them as dark seekers of unnatural forces who, according to a few accounts, chose to roam the countryside in animal form, transforming back into humans only to cause mischief. What if they were right? What would these women do to me? I shivered at my own horrible imaginings of bloody sacrifice and evil magic.

No, I would not choose to indulge in such dark tales. Viviane had been nothing but kind to me, so I was determined to believe the same of the rest of Avalon's inhabitants. I'd made my choice; now I had to see it through.

Straining to see beyond the mists, I tried to perceive the path Viviane followed with ease, navigating through the maze of sandbars and other perils as only a trained priestess could. Nature had provided a perfect ward against those who would do harm to the inhabitants of the isle. Like the tides that responded to the urgings of the moon, every morning, the mists rolled out across the lake, cutting off access to the uninitiated; each evening, they contracted around the Tor, the tallest, most sacred hill on the island, providing a thick blanket of protection to those who slumbered in the darkness below.

Eventually, the boat stilled and Viviane lifted the pole into the boat, a trail of water dribbling after it. She gave a sharp whistle, which was answered a short distance in front of us. I nearly toppled over as the boat was heaved forward by unseen hands.

⁂

Once ashore, the veil of mist thinned and I caught my first glimpse of Avalon. The land dipped lower as my eye moved inward from the lake. The shoreline gave way to damp marshes, slim clusters of reeds, and wetland grasses in which stately silver herons and colorful kingfishers played and hunted for fish, heedless of the activity around them.

Mountains and low hills veiled in shadow appeared brown, purple, and gray on the far horizon, acting as a screen separating

Avalon from the outside world, while directly in front of me, the sun shone brightly on a cluster of buildings, giving their white-gray stone a radiant appearance. Beyond them, the sun warmed colorful gardens and vast green orchards that in a few months would be heavy with fragrant fruit. Farther to the east, a soft, cool breeze stirred tall golden grasses in the open plains, and shadows played hide-and-seek with the sun on the outskirts of tall forests of oak, ash, elm, and other sacred trees.

To my right, the sacred Tor loomed above the flat land, its humped shadow reflected in the still waters of the inland lake encircling its base. A spiral path wound around the hill, and nine pairs of evenly spaced pillars marked stations along the way. As my eyes traced the pathway upward, I was surprised to find the summit was ringed with standing stones, the two taller portal stones capped by a horizontal slab, much like the Druid's circle several days ride to the east.

I was immediately caught up in the buzz of activity generated by the throng of brightly clad women preparing for some great event. A few younger women dressed in robes of forest green helped secure the boat, while young and old alike scurried up and down the stairs of a tall, stately columned building, and others carried supplies to the long, flat houses that lay adjacent. I marveled at their organization. In the flurry of activity, none seemed to lose sense of her purpose. Even my father's army could not boast that.

Viviane followed the line of my eyes and smiled, her blue eyes twinkling. "These are your sisters now, Guinevere. They will be your only friends and family for many years. You will be introduced to them later. Come."

She took my hand and showed me into one of the flat houses near the gardens. I met a short dark-haired girl, who I guessed to be one or two years older than me.

"Mona, this is Guinevere, our newest candidate. Guinevere, Mona will help you become acquainted with the isle," Viviane said by way of introduction.

Mona gave me a welcoming smile as Viviane departed. Then, with a fluid gesture, she ushered me inside to a small bedroom where I washed the dust from my hair, feet, and skin and changed into a pure white gown, just like the one Mona wore.

Snatching up my discarded traveling clothes and a ball of soap from the bedside table, Mona strode across the terrace overlooking the lake. She was halfway down a gently sloping hill before she paused then turned, a small frown creasing the otherwise smooth skin between her eyes.

"This way," she said, beckoning before she wound her way through a series of herb, vegetable, and flower gardens. She walked along the edge of an apple orchard to a clear, softly flowing stream.

I remembered hearing that waters such as those were rumored to heal every illness and even grant eternal youth. I glanced about in awe. Were the stories true?

Mona handed me my tunic, which I held dumbly. I watched as my tan cloak turned the color of freshly tilled earth as she submerged it in the water. She wrung it out, laid it flat against the surface of a large, smooth stone, and began running the fragrant lavender soap over the material, working it into the fibers with her fingertips.

I was utterly transfixed. At home, we had servants and slaves who took our soiled linens and then returned them to us clean. I had never thought to question how it happened.

Mona looked up at me with eyes as dark as her hair, the ghost of a smile playing at her lips as if she could read my thoughts. "Go on," she said encouragingly, gesturing toward the tunic I still held balled between my hands. "You will have to learn to clean your own clothes. You will have only three tunics, two for daily use and one for rituals, so take good care of them. You will need to learn to mend them too, but that is a lesson for another day."

My heart twisted at the thought of having to do menial labor, and the better part of me wanted to refuse. I opened my mouth in protest, but Mona's gaze silenced me. I knelt down beside her and plunged my tunic into the stream. I gasped, not expecting the water to be icy cold. Mimicking what Mona had done, I lifted my dress out of the water and twisted the sodden lump of material between my reddened fingers, nearly drenching myself in the process.

Mona grabbed my hands and pulled my arms out straight. "Hold it out, away from you," she instructed, "unless you want to take a bath at the same time." She giggled, not unkindly, at my ineptitude.

I spread out my dripping tunic on Mona's chosen rock and began to soap it. She looked at my hands with curiosity, no doubt wondering why they resembled the rough, callused hands of a warrior in training instead of the smooth, silky skin of most noblewomen. I could sense the unspoken question she was too polite to ask.

"My mother," I began, throat constricting with emotion as I pictured her face, "has been training me to wield a sword since I was old enough to feed myself. She is a Votadini from the lands far to the north. It is a tradition of her homeland that all the women of the tribe be trained to fight alongside their men in battle."

"Are you good at it? The fighting?" Mona's interest came through as pure excitement.

I dipped the frothy material back into the water, fighting the current and the leaden heaviness of the cloth as I tried to rinse it clean. "I thought I was," I said quietly, disappointment slowly creeping into my voice as I spoke, "but I could not even defend myself when we were attacked. I nearly lost my life, but my mother saved me."

Mercifully, Mona asked no more questions. I told myself it was all in the past now. No acts of violence were allowed on the isle, so I would have to let go of my training and the horrors of the day it failed me, just as I would have to relinquish my noble rank.

By the time we completed our task, it was late afternoon. Instead of taking me back to the house where I had changed clothes earlier, Mona guided me through the maze of trees to a long, single-story building of white-gray stone, one of the ones that seemed to glimmer from the shore.

"This is the House of Nine," she explained on tiptoe as she draped my wet garments over a sturdy branch of white-barked birch about half a foot above her head. "If the Lady deems you a worthy student, you will live here with me and seven other girls. We are all about the same age." She glanced over her shoulder. "That is Grainne peeking out from the doorway."

The golden-haired girl shrank back momentarily at the sound of her name, seemingly embarrassed at being caught spying on us, but then she came bounding toward us like an excited puppy.

Trailing hesitantly in her shadow was a small brunette girl who exuded peace and calm in equal amount to Grainne's energy.

"You must be Guinevere," Grainne said by way of greeting. But before I had time to reply, she asked, "So is it true you were kidnapped by Irish raiders?"

"You told me they were landless tribal outlaws." The smaller, dark-haired girl scowled at Mona before introducing herself as Rowena.

"Then you must have misheard me," Grainne shot back. "I said no such thing."

For a moment I couldn't respond, shocked they had been gossiping about me before I even arrived.

"In the House of Nine, there are no secrets," Mona whispered in my ear. "We know every scrap of one another's business."

Grainne and Rowena looked at me expectantly, clearly waiting for my answer.

"Well, I yes," I began. "I was attacked—"

The tinkling of a soft bell cut me off. Viviane appeared in the doorway and bid us to follow her.

"Where are we going?" I asked, unsure of what activity might begin when the sun was fast sinking below the horizon.

"To meet the Lady of the Lake," Viviane answered.

 споре эгое

Viviane escorted us into a massive temple-like building that lay open to the lake and world of mists beyond, and she led us up a set of steep stairs. How silent the structure seemed to be, although the air around us vibrated with a low hum. After passing through a small foyer, we entered a large square room with ceilings as high as the tips of ancient oaks. As my eyes adjusted to the light, I began to make out figures in the room behind us. At first they appeared as phantoms without faces, but after a moment, we were surrounded in a semi-circle by a crowd of women dressed in brightly colored gowns of forest green, pearl white, and the same ocean blue Viviane wore. She led me to stand in front of a throne-like chair at the far end of the room.

The wall behind the chair was lined with pots of sweet-smelling incense, its lazy haze blending with the orange flames from rows of candles that glowed like the midday sun. From the ceiling hung brass containers of fire, probably fed by small charcoal bricks. Craning my neck, I peered between the curious women to my right, just catching a glimpse of flower petals floating on the surfaces of bowls of water surrounded by scores of seashells on a small table. In the opposite window, the one facing east, bronze wind chimes adorned with feathers hung limply from their strings, silent due to the lack of a breeze. Glancing over my shoulder, I was startled to see the Tor framed perfectly in the doorway behind us. All of the elements—earth, air, water, and fire—were represented here, all in perfect balance.

As the moments trudged slowly by, I grew increasingly uncomfortable. Everyone seemed to be staring at me as if I came from another world. A few whispered to each other, no doubt talking about me. I began to nervously twirl a strand of my hair in order to combat the sickening fear welling up inside me.

"Guinevere, stop that." Viviane swatted at the fingers knotted in my hair. "It does not befit a student of Avalon to fidget like a child," she said, her voice sharper than I'd ever heard it.

I dropped my hand to my side. Just then, a small wooden side door creaked open, and I jumped in fear. The murmuring ceased as every woman in the room snapped to attention at once.

An aged, stately woman emerged from the dark interior room and took her place on the throne. Her hair was a rich auburn streaked with heavy bands of gray, her face lined and furrowed from many years of living, but her eyes were bright and perceptive, like a hawk's. She wore a blue gown similar to Viviane's but decorated with intricate spiraling patterns. A single glittering crystal bobbed from a silver chain around her neck, and a thin silver circlet rested on her head, just above the mark that signaled her rank as High Priestess—the three visible phases of the moon drawn in blue ink. Her crown mirrored the mark so that the waxing and waning moons peeked out from her hair on either side of an opaline full moon.

As I watched, awestruck, every woman in the circle around us, including Viviane, dropped to one knee in unison and touched the thumb of her right hand to her forehead, lips, and heart—the same gesture my mother had made to Viviane when she arrived at Northgallis. As one, they whispered, "May the Goddess grant me wisdom, may the God govern my speech, and may my heart be filled with their love."

I looked around nervously, unsure if I should do the same, and fumbled a slight curtsy instead.

"Her name is Argante, but always address her as Lady," Viviane whispered.

The old woman smiled slightly at my attempted reverence but then just as quickly resumed her serious disposition. "Viviane, for what reason have you gathered us here?" Her voice was stern and authoritative.

Viviane stepped forward and nudged me toward the Lady.

"Sisters, I have brought with me a new candidate to be counted among our number." She placed a hand on my shoulder, turning to address the woman on the throne. "Most blessed Lady of the Lake, this is Guinevere of Northgallis, who wishes to be named a servant of the Goddess."

Viviane had warned me on the journey here that in Avalon, when speaking in general, all the goddesses of our people were collectively referred to as the Goddess, and likewise, all the gods as the God. Avalon welcomed people of many tribes and traditions, each with their preferred deity names and mythologies. This way, they avoided confusion and arguments over exactly which deity was being referenced or whose gods were better. Here, all were equal and, except on feast days sacred to a specific deity, all were worshiped according to individual preference. Personally, I favored the horse goddess Rhiannon, worshiped in my homeland, and the sun god Lugh, patron of my mother's Votadini tribe.

Argante's eyes met mine with an all-knowing gaze that pierced my soul and laid the entire contents of my being out on the floor for her examination. As her eyes searched mine, I trembled and said a private prayer to my gods, terrified she would find in me some imperfection, some reason to send me back to my father in shame. Argante reached forward, placed a hand on my brow, and my eyes involuntarily snapped shut. Moments passed in silent darkness, and then wood creaked as she sat back in her chair. When I opened my eyes, she appeared pensive.

The women in the assembled crowd shifted their weight restlessly, and tears began to prick at the back of my eyes. I feared this lengthy pause was a sign of disapproval; surely if I was pleasing to her, the Lady would have made it clear without delay. I searched the air between us for Viviane's hand, and she gave mine a gentle squeeze before leaving me once again on my own.

"This child is pure of heart," the Lady said at long last, her voice far-off and intense, as if it was not she who spoke, but someone greater through the medium of her voice. "Her innocence and faith please me greatly. I see in her no duplicity or capacity for betrayal, only a strong desire to love and serve. In her blood the sight runs strong, and she will be for Avalon a great asset." She paused, and a slight frown played on her lips. "However, she will not ascend to greatness on this isle. Another crown sits on her brow, one that will secure the safety and prosperity of many, but at a great cost, both to herself and to those she holds dear."

A whisper of concern ran through the circle as I knitted my brows together, trying to puzzle out the meaning of her words.

"But that is the future and its lines are not writ in stone, only hinted at by an uncertain sight interpreted by the human heart." Argante looked at me lovingly now, seeming much more human, her voice softer. "Do not fear what is to come but embrace it, following the Goddess's voice—which you shall not fail to hear in your heart—and trusting she will lead you on the right path. Guinevere, you have been chosen by she who created life itself and now you must prove your devotion by stating your intent. Why have you come to the isle of Avalon?"

I shifted my gaze to the floor in embarrassment, unsure how to reply.

"Answer from your heart," Viviane whispered.

I raised my eyes to meet the Lady's. "To serve the Goddess, who has protected me since before my first breath." My voice issued forth strong and clear, as if propelled by a will other than my own. "My mother promised me to this isle in thanksgiving for our safe deliverance from her difficult labor. Now I fulfill the vow she made eleven years ago."

In truth, this was my fate, but I purposefully neglected to mention my visions in such a public arena. Argante likely knew about them already, and I feared the judgment of the others.

Argante nodded in understanding. "Honorable as that is, it does not compel you to stay. Do you come here free of coercion and choose to remain here of your own will?"

"I do."

"Look around. The women gathered here are your sisters. Do you promise to treat them as such, harming none and living in love and trust so strong that you give freely of yourself when needed and accept their aid when offered to you? Will you treat each woman as you would treat the Goddess, your own mother, or yourself?"

I looked out over the sea of strange faces. "I will."

Argante caught my gaze and held it, impressing on me the seriousness of what she was about to say. "Know that the vows you now take are not binding and you may be released from them at any time, should you so desire. They are, nevertheless, a promise, and you will be held to them by value of your word, as it is your source of honor."

Uncomfortable, I wanted to look away but could not break her gaze.

"Do you vow to serve the Goddess and God with all of your mind, heart, and soul and preserve your maidenhead until such time as you take your final vows or part ways with our community?"

I swallowed, sensing the sacrifice required in assenting to these terms. "I do."

Argante smiled at me with all the warmth of a doting grandmother and leaned forward to kiss me on the forehead. "Welcome to the sisterhood, Guinevere."

CHAPTER TWO

Summer—Winter 491

*L*ife in Avalon—a life equal to, rather than above, everyone else—was more difficult than I expected. I cried
myself to sleep for a month.

No amount of protesting, tears, or will power could change
the orders dispensed daily by the Lady's authority. Argante had
no time for temper tantrums and flatly ignored them. Complaints
only ended in a sentence of silence for the remainder of the day,
and if I refused to obey a command, I found myself without sup-
per or barred from the evening's ceremony, a great humiliation in
this sacred place.

When my attention wasn't fully focused on the task at hand—
such as when I was helping to clean our communal living quarters
or learning to cook a palatable meal—I found myself longing for
home. As my parents' only surviving child, I had rarely been away
from them, following in their footsteps to learn how to rule the
kingdom I would one day inherit.

But now I faced years without their love and attention, and I missed everything. Sparring with my mother and male cousins had been replaced with chasing the other girls across the hillsides and racing to climb trees. Quiet evenings learning new embroidery patterns by the firelight with my lady's maid were replaced by solemn rituals I barely understood. I even missed sitting with my parents at council meetings, where the western lords would lament High King Uther's inattention to their kingdoms now that he was focused on the invading Saxons. Those practical lessons in politics and governance now gave way to endless language and writing classes, which were followed by studies of the lore of the gods and practice of how to worship them on each of the eight great festivals.

Every morning began with sunrise salutations on the holy Tor. Then while the other girls scampered off, laughing and joking, to their lessons in familial groups, I followed Viviane to her quarters for private study. It was unusual for a first-year student to learn control of the sight—that usually came after a series of tests designed to assess our mental preparedness—but given my situation, Viviane thought it best for me to begin with that skill.

"You will not be able to give your other studies full attention if your mind is clouded with visions," Viviane explained on our first day.

That had been several weeks ago. Now I was used to the pattern of each lesson, although that didn't stop my hands from shaking as I washed my face and hands in the cool, clear water collected from the white spring. Sitting with my legs crossed beneath me, I closed my eyes and took a series of deep breaths, focusing my attention on my heartbeat.

I dreaded these meetings. My fear was in part because I knew they were separating me from the friendships I was trying so hard to forge. Even though they never showed it, I heard the other girls' spiteful whispering that I was getting preferential treatment. But even more, I feared the painful memories and horrifying images that each session unearthed. Even when the visions were unrelated to me personally, the experience left me feeling raw and ragged.

"Tell me when you feel the sight coming on," Viviane directed, her voice gentle and musical like the tinkling of bells.

She had already taught me the signs preceding each vision—the disorienting feeling like I was floating above my body and the now-familiar tingling in the center of my forehead, the very spot all priestesses were marked upon their consecration.

"Now," I exclaimed, the area between my brows prickling.

She settled to the floor behind me, her voice almost directly in my right ear. "This time, instead of replacing what you see with a pleasant memory, as we have done before, will the image to go away, simply because you desire it to."

At first, I thought I was succeeding because I couldn't see anything. But before I could draw my next breath, I was reliving the day my mother and I were attacked in the woods near North-gallis, the moment that had led me here. My mother's scream rang in my ears as they descended on us, a pack of foreigners with strange markings on their left forearms. I tried to defend myself, but there was an arm around my throat, crushing my windpipe. I was dragged from my saddle onto another horse by one of the men. My arms were wrenched behind me, leaving me defenseless. Even now, the stench of his skin filled my nostrils.

"I can't. It isn't working," I cried to Viviane, only half aware what I was seeing was not real. My panic rose with the pace of my breath.

Viviane placed a hand on each of my shoulders. "Yes, you can. Imagine the scene collapsing in on itself like folded cloth. When that is done, frame what remains in an open doorway. Shut the door tight. You can even lock it, if you like."

I concentrated on the vision as it played out before me, my mother and captor battling with me trapped between them, their blades clashing dangerously close to my nose. Slowly and with much effort, I covered the scene in reams of gray wool, first over my stunned captor, his face eternally contorted by the last thing his eyes saw—my mother's sword buried in his stomach. I folded that in over the memory of my wounded mother, blood streaming from gashes in her arm and side. One more fold to make that image disappear, and I slammed shut the door of my mind. Now there was nothing but the chirping of the birds outside Viviane's walls.

I opened my eyes in relief, still panting from the effort.

Viviane's pale eyes searched my face. "It is over. It may take some time and you may have to repeat the exercise, but eventually you should be free. As long as you keep that door closed in your mind, the vision should not trouble you again." She put an arm around me.

I reached behind me to complete the embrace.

"In a few years, I will teach you how to open your mind without letting that memory back in, so have no fear. For now, it is probably best to shut off the channels of the sight until you can control them."

Laughter echoed outside as the women moved from one task to another, interrupting our private moment. Viviane poked her head out the door and waved to Mona.

Turning to me, she said, "You have missed your Ogham lesson for today, but I have no doubt you will catch up. Off with you." She shooed me out the door.

I followed Mona to Argante's hut where we would learn from her great wisdom.

৩ৰ ৩৯৹

My days began to pass quickly. Spring gave way to summer's heat, and we spent nearly every pleasant day outdoors, getting to know every inch of the island and learning to feel the subtle shifts in energy as the seasons progressed in their endless cycle. Romping through the forest and over the hillsides, we were taught to identify every herb and flower that took root in the land and how to use it in healing.

Today, however, we stood in a large rectangular garden spread out behind Avalon's main cluster of buildings. Tiny blooms of chamomile magnified the sun while tall reeds of dill nodded their hairy stalks and seeded starbursts over thick carpets of fragrant thyme and marjoram. In the far shadows of the wall, foxglove bells stood sentinel over purple-winged wolfsbane, perky clumps of larkspur, seductive nightshade, and other herbs not meant for untrained hands. Those were the herbs of the Goddess, which, like her power, could bring life or death, depending on the intent and skill of the one using them.

While every one of the herbs cultivated here could be found

growing wild across the isle, this garden kept the most commonly used ones near to hand, in case of emergency. It also served as a teaching ground for new students.

On the opposite end of the garden, a tall, thin girl with bright red hair and skin like fresh cream was pointing at herbs as Viviane named them off, a test we each took to determine who could advance to more complex lessons and who still needed more study.

I toyed with the finger-like fronds of a fern whose name would forever be etched in my memory. It was the only one I had misidentified. Unfortunately, had the situation been real, my mistake would have killed the recipient. Viviane was displeased, to say the least, and there was no question she would tell Argante. I was desperate to win their approval, so this setback troubled me deeply.

I eyed the girl engrossed in the test, who was now squatting over a spray of tiny pink flowers at Viviane's feet. "I wager she is right on each," I muttered to the girls waiting impatiently with me. "She always is."

Rowena snorted. "Herbs come as easy to Morgan as does breathing."

"But she's part fey, so she has an advantage," Grainne chimed in.

I narrowed my eyes at the bright-eyed girl with wavy, golden tresses. "You don't really believe that rot, do you?" Although I thought I detected a slight lilt in Morgan's voice when she spoke, I didn't think for a moment she was part of an ancient, mystical race from across the sea in Ireland. I had been living with Morgan for months now, during which time she had proven herself very much mortal, although she would be loathe to admit it, content as she was with her reputation for Otherworldly perfection.

"Oh yes." Grainne scooted closer to me, leaning in as though confiding a great secret, and the other girls inclined their heads to listen. "One of the old priestesses told me Morgan has lived here most of her life, but no one can remember her coming here. There was no boat ride through the mists for her; she just appeared." She made a popping sound with her lips.

I looked back at Morgan, noting with a pang of jealousy the blossoming approval on Viviane's face as they moved from plant to plant. She was outshining me again.

Everyone seemed to have their own theory about Morgan's origins. Other whispers named her the lone survivor a slaughtered tribe, or worse yet, a changeling or the abandoned offspring of some unholy union. But more than likely, the tongues which told such tales were simply jealous of Morgan's intelligence and aptitude in the magical arts, if not of her great beauty. I assumed she had been promised to Avalon much like myself, or taken out of kindness from the arms of a mother who could not care for her.

"No, I think she is very much human." I turned back to Grainne. "I just wish she were more forthcoming. I never know what she is thinking, and that unnerves me."

Grainne smirked as a placid, lightly accented voice floated over my shoulder. "I think it is unkind to speak of others outside their presence."

I whirled around. Morgan had materialized silently behind me, her slate blue eyes flashing. Maybe Grainne was right about her otherworldly bloodlines.

An amused smile played on Morgan's lips. "Viviane told me to tell you we all passed the test."

The others whooped and hooted with joy.

"There is only room for one favorite among us," Morgan quietly added to me. "That title is mine, and I intend to keep it. You'll have to try much harder if you wish to best me."

✍ ✍

As summer wore on, Morgan's declaration of dominance ate at me. I was used to getting my way unchallenged, and to make matters worse, I was also used to being the best and brightest of the cohort my mother instructed back home. So I was ill-equipped to endure my rival's constant assertion of superiority.

At first, I took the passive route, hoping she would be satisfied, forget me, and move on to hating someone else. I let her think she was superior even when I knew my skill to be greater and frequently resorted to false flattery, but Morgan saw through me every time. To truly win her over, I would have to openly admit my inferiority before the rest of the House of Nine, bowing and scraping like a slave before her master. That was the one thing I would not do, and she knew it.

So our competition slowly became a battle of wills. We found tiny ways to trip one another up or gain advantage—petty things like toppled ink pots, missing vials of herbs, and well-timed pinches that forced one another to break the solemnity of ritual—childish pranks we thought went unnoticed by anyone else. That is, until one day in early winter when Argante asked us to remain with her after our lesson ended.

We were learning the basic tenants of law, which at our early level consisted of memorizing categories of possible dispute—property, contracts, and crimes—along with their corresponding value or punishment. After eight months of study, we could easily recite the equivalent value of a cumal of rich farmland versus one of poor, rocky soil, or how to determine the honor price owed to a father for a bride. While not as exciting as divination or as entertaining as learning epic bardic poetry, it was equally important. Someday, as priestesses, we might be called upon by kings or lords to settle matters of law they did not want or were unqualified to decide themselves.

Argante had just returned from such a journey, where she'd adjudicated several cases for the new lord of the Summer Country, a young tribal prince named Malegant who, according to rumor, had managed to overthrow his own mother, as well as kill or subdue nearly a dozen siblings who contested his right to the throne. The resulting kingdom was a blend of three previous tribal holdings, and peace was tenuous at best. He'd had the foresight to call on Argante for aid, and she had been using some of the examples from his court to instruct us.

"I have called you apart from the others because I have a special case to present to you, one I would normally pose only to advanced students. I believe because of your superior skills and wit, you will rise to the challenge. Imagine yourselves the judges of this scenario. A man takes a second wife—"

"Does that happen anymore?" I asked, not realizing I had voiced my thought aloud, until Argante pinned me with an outraged expression that answered louder than her voice ever could have. I'd better not interrupt her again.

"A man takes a second wife," she repeated. "His first wife is displeased and kills her. Is she to be held guilty or not?"

This situation was a matter of tradition, one told in bardic lore from ages long past, before the coming of the Romans, so we were familiar with the idea, even though our studies had not yet reached that level of complexity.

"Does he have sons? When did the murder take place?" Morgan asked.

"Ah, now you are getting to the heart of the matter." Argante gestured with her index finger as she spoke. "He had no sons, and the murder took place two days after his second wedding."

Morgan wrinkled her brow. "Then no, she is guilty of no crime and no punishment should be given. If the second wife dies within the first three nights of marriage, then the primary wife is held blameless, regardless of her actions."

"The primary wife would have to pay a fine to the victim's kin, whether or not she was within her rights," I corrected Morgan.

Argante turned to me. "And if the second wife's family seeks vengeance?"

"If the family takes revenge, they do so at their own peril, unless they hire outlaws to do their bidding," I answered.

"And why is that permitted?" Argante asked Morgan.

"Because outlaws are not held to the same code as those with tribal ties. The only way to impose the law on a band of outlaws is to hire your own, and even then, they may turn on you."

"Exactly." Argante nodded and clapped her hands together, pleased. "Now what if the husband kills the first wife out of anger for her act? How is he to be punished? Is he put to the sword, or does he pay a heavy fine and enter slavery for a number of years? Or is there another alternative?"

Morgan and I looked at one another, puzzled. That was well beyond our ken. I decided to keep silent.

Morgan attempted to form an answer but never made it beyond stuttering, "I-I-he..."

Argante fixed us in her solemn gaze. "I did not expect you to know the answer. You see, ladies, you have just proven you are equals both in knowledge and ignorance. Stop trying to best one another, and concentrate on your studies. You only hurt yourselves by directing your attention elsewhere. Now go join your sisters."

Morgan was silent as we made our way out the door, but then we moved out of earshot of our teacher.

"We are *not* finished," she sneered.

᷄ᷟᷗ

Hours later, in the deep stillness of night, I woke with a startled gasp, one hand pressed protectively over my racing heart, the other clamped in a fist at my side, still holding my one piece of home—a small wooden dog that had been my going-away present.

Sometimes the door of my mind would not stay shut. Most of the time it was locked to even gales, but in my weaker moments, just the slightest whisper of a memory was enough to release the lock and let the sight slip in like a winter draft.

Fighting to see through the cobwebs left behind by my nightmare, I sat up and gazed around at the other girls sleeping soundly all around me. Rowena was facing me in the next bed, a slight smile upon her lips, one arm tucked beneath her head, the other thrown carelessly above it. At least I had not woken them in my fright.

I lay back down, focusing on my breathing as the snow swirled outside the window facing the Tor, blanketing the isle in a glimmering cape of white. Slowly, I went through the steps of shutting my mind to the sight, trying to forget the terror that came with it.

That was one of the strange things about visions that came unbidden. Even after the images faded, the emotions they conjured remained. Tonight it was the bittersweet dregs of the Holy Grail, with its sanguine promise of peace offset by the rumbling threat of destruction. This was a dream that had haunted me for as long as I could remember. I suspected it was my confession of this dream, more than my recurring visions or my mother's vow, which had prompted Viviane to bring me here. The Grail was one of Avalon's clandestine treasures, and anyone who knew of it belonged here, safe behind the mists.

I shivered and drew the blanket closer around me. In the months that had passed since I came to Avalon, my visions had dwindled in number and more time elapsed between them, but they did not cease as Viviane had hoped. Argante told me they probably never would but echoed Viviane's promise that with training, I could control them. However, she warned that I would never be totally in control. Weakness, she said, was the strongest trigger, even for a woman of many years like herself. Each one of us, just by being alive, was subject to its many whims. Even with all the training Avalon could provide, illness, fatigue, or even strong emotions such as love or fear could render us powerless to the sight.

I bit my lower lip, trying to decide what had prompted this dream. I was healthy and my initial fear of life on the isle had faded, so that left one possible trigger—some strong emotion. Even without much thought, I knew what it was. Hatred. It burned in my belly even as I turned the previous day's events over in my mind. Morgan's refusal to let go of her quest for dominance over me, even after Argante's strict admonition, set me on edge. I was done fighting, but Morgan never would be, at least not until she saw me trod down once and for all.

Suddenly, a sound as soft as the tease of a feather captured my attention. I lifted my head slightly off the pillow. It came again, more distinct this time, a small cry almost like the mewing of a kitten. I lifted myself onto my forearm and scanned the beds. One was empty. Wrapping the heavy fur blanket around me, I followed the sound, my bare feet swishing softly on the cold floor.

I could just make out a small figure hunched on the thick white rug in front of the fire. As I drew nearer, I recognized Mona's silhouette.

I crossed my ankles and sank down silently beside her, wrapping my arm and half of the blanket around her. She nestled into my embrace like a baby bird beneath its mother's wing. Neither of us spoke, for we both knew the source of her grief. Whether by design or malevolent coincidence, Mona had been named after a holy island off the coast of my father's kingdom of Gwynedd, which had been home to the Druids before its inhabitants were slaughtered by a power-crazed Roman governor, an event she frequently relived in her dreams.

When I first joined the House of Nine, I thought her a banshee, but by now, I was so used to her screams in the night that I usually turned over and went back to sleep whenever she woke me. But something was different tonight. Maybe it was because of my own nightmare, but I wanted to keep watch with her, to hold her until her tears ceased and she finally succumbed to sleep.

After a long silence, Mona spoke, hiccupping through her tears. "I asked Argante today why I am cursed."

"What? Why?"

"By the nightmares, I mean. She told me the sight works differently in every person. Some can see the future, while others are given the gift of seeing distant things as they occur or, in my case, long after."

"But I still do not understand. It seems pointless to repeat the same events over and over again, even if only in our minds." I stroked her hair, gazing off into the distance as I thought of my own visions and felt anew the frustration of reliving tragic events and portents without any understanding of why.

"That is exactly what I thought, so I asked her what value there is in seeing the past. She did not really answer me but went into one of her lectures."

"What did she say?"

Mona shifted around so she was facing me. Distracted by her story, she had finally stopped crying. She adopted a dignified pose and mimicked Argante's regal voice, quoting her while being careful not to wake the others. "'How can we ever plan a better future if we do not learn from our past? If you burned your hand but did not remember the pain, how would you know not to touch the flame again? It is the same in battle or politics. If no one remembers the successes and failures, then our lives are but one pointless circle with no hope that future generations will advance. Knowing someone's past gives special insight into their motivations, which is much like being inside their minds. Do not discount the gift you have been given. If you develop it properly, it is a blessing that could prove very useful.'"

We were both silent for a moment.

"How very"—I searched for the right word—"cryptic. Do you feel any better?"

She shook her head. "Not really, but at least I know Argante sees potential in me, in my condition. What is that?" She pointed at the object clutched in my left hand.

I opened my palm, having completely forgotten I was holding anything. In it lay the small wooden carving of a dog. Peredur, the young son of my lady's maid, had given it to me as a farewell present on my last day in Northgallis. It had been a gift from his own father to help him conquer his fear of the dark. My palm was still etched with its imprint, made as I was clutching it in my sleep.

"This"—I gave Mona a squeeze—"is a magic wolfhound. He protects you from all your fears. I have been sleeping with it to combat my homesickness, but maybe you should keep him for a while."

Mona took the toy from my hand and examined it in the firelight. "I think he is one of Ellen's own," she said with awe, referring to the goddess of all journeys, even in the land of dreams.

"He doesn't appear much of a protector," interjected a bored voice from the dark depths of the room.

We both turned. Morgan stood in the shadows, her blanket trailing after her like a cape.

"Considering you are both awake, I would say he is not doing his job," she said, sitting down on Mona's other side.

"And what is your excuse?" I countered, annoyed at her interruption of a private moment.

Morgan narrowed her sleep-ringed eyes at me. "Who could sleep with the two of you chattering away like squirrels?"

"Have you been listening long?" Mona asked, a mixture of embarrassment and distrust in her voice.

"Long enough. I-I came over to ask you a favor." Morgan inclined her head to Mona and pursed her lips, as though unsure if she should go on in my presence.

"You could simply ask, if you want privacy," I pointed out to Morgan. I rose, leaving my blanket with Mona. I would take the one from her bed. "Good night, Mona. I hope you feel better."

She waved the wooden dog at me. "Of course I do."

I padded back to bed, slowing my pace just enough to catch a hint of Morgan's request.

"I heard what Argante told you. Will you try to see my past? It would mean very much to me to know where I come from."

Mona's voice lost its edge and once again radiated her natural warmth. "I don't think it works that way, but I will try."

I pulled Mona's blanket around me as I padded back to my bed, pondering this turn of events. So the rumors were true. Perfect little Morgan had a weakness after all—she was an orphan, at least as far as she knew. That meant she had no kin, no tribe to return to, no life save that which she had built on this isle. She was utterly beholden to the whims of Avalon. No wonder she was so anxious to secure her place as favorite daughter.

Well, she would have to fight me for it. I knew it was wrong, but I couldn't help but smile inwardly at the possibilities and plot ways to use my newfound knowledge to my advantage.

CHAPTER THREE

Autumn—Winter 493

Two years came and went in the ceaseless rhythm of sacred festivals and lunar cycles. In the House of Nine, change began to unleash its unsettling force as bodies began to blossom. The Goddess saw fit to give Morgan ample curves, while I had little more than budding breasts and barely perceptible hips beneath my gown. But my moon time came first, and with that sacred milestone, I was finally able to trade my white robes for the forest green of a second-degree initiate.

Were I still at home with my mother, a different kind of ceremony would have marked my entrance into womanhood, one which had been passed down from mother to daughter for countless generations among the Votadini. I imagined my mother at her mortar and pestle, crushing leaves of woad, adding them to a tiny steaming cauldron of water, copper, and other substances which she would not divulge until I had a daughter of my own to mark, then carefully straining the liquid to produce a dark blue ink. I imagined myself lying facedown in her chamber at the new moon as a cluster of thin, sharp bones like teeth slowly pricked the symbol of our tribe, a horse whose body formed an endless knot, into the flesh of my left shoulder blade. She would lovingly bandage the tender flesh and embrace me, now officially a woman of our tribe, though I lived far from our ancestral home.

But those were the memories of a person I had chosen not to become. My life was here, in Avalon, among the ranks of the acolytes struggling to understand our new roles in ritual and study. We were learned, but not yet masters, and stood as assistants to those who trod the path of the Goddess before us. Gone were the carefree days of childhood; we now had to adjust to the growing demands of adulthood and increasingly complex temporal and spiritual studies.

A sharp autumn breeze shook the tips of the fiery oaks and rustled our gowns. We were supposed to be concentrating on the circular boards in front of us, carefully set with gleaming crystals in a purposeful formation, but my mind kept drifting to my friends back in Northgallis. We were all nearing marriageable age now, and they would be preparing to leave their childhood homes for the beds of powerful men they barely knew. At one time, I would have envied them, but now I was grateful to be here, learning about one of Avalon's most sacred forms of divination.

As Argante had explained it, Holy Stones originated with the Druids who had ruled our tribes long before the Roman eagle made her nest on our shores. Comprised of two sets of twenty-one stones aligned in a triangle formation facing off across an empty field, it was primarily used to predict the outcome of battle and advise clan leaders of strategy. Stones with different properties were used to represent troops—footmen, archers, or cavalry—protecting the two most important pieces: the king and the queen. The battle or situation in question was simulated using these stones, performed over and over as the seer received strategic advice from the gods. Once the best strategy with the most positive outcome was determined, the Druid would advise his or her leader.

Although capturing the king was the point of the exercise and the only way victory could be claimed, the queen—a red stone symbolizing the Goddess, lifeblood, and the power behind the throne—was the most important piece. Known by names such as the Sovereignty Stone or Lady Fortuna, the queen was the only piece that could move anywhere on the playing field. The queen also had the ability to sacrifice herself to save the king or "heal" captured troops and return them to the board, but no more than three times in any game. The only piece that could actively capture a queen was the opposing queen.

Outside of Avalon and the Druids' isle, Holy Stones was primarily a game of strategy for the wealthy and well-educated, and few knew its true power or purpose. Some of my earliest memories were of playing this game with my father. He often played it as a way to clear his mind when he needed to think. The tenderness and patience with which he'd taught his "little warrior" how to protect the queen on an oak board with polished gemstones was as clear to me now as when it happened.

Today, however, it was more than a game. We were learning how to use this seemingly secular cover to reach out to the world beyond the lake and its marshes to gather information useful in advising those in power. We had each been given a different situation and were now asked to play it out and relay what strategy would most benefit our ruler.

I was paired with Morgan. She sat across a long wooden table on which rested five sets of boards. In our scenario, High King Uther faced a challenger to his supremacy—one of his own lords from the Midlands who had recently allied with the Saxons.

Morgan and I faced off just as they would have but played out our moves and counterattacks with stones instead of lives. We had taken about an equal number of each other's troops, and I was waiting for her to make her next move. To my right, Grainne and Mona were moving their pieces at astonishing speed—forward, back, off the board, and on again as each of their queens asserted her healing power—eyes unseeing, concentrating on the visions that directed their every move.

"Are you going to make a decision before the sun goes down?" I asked Morgan.

"Be quiet and let me concentrate. I can't help divination doesn't come as easily to me as it does to you," she sneered, fingers vacillating between two groups of stones.

I was about to retort that the sight often passed from mother to daughter—an admittedly cheap dig at her unidentified maternity—when Argante drifted in our direction, checking on each pair's progress.

"Remember, ladies, true power, true skill is not about doing one better than one's sister. All things thrive in balance, and for that to be maintained, each must focus on what she is best at and on her own destiny, not that of her sister."

She was speaking to the whole group, but her chiding glance was clearly meant for me.

Argante noticed Morgan's hesitation and paused behind her, placing a gnarled hand on top of the one Morgan held in mid-air. "Stop for a moment, Morgan. Do not try, just be. What you see before you is not a wooden plate and scattered stones, but two armies on the field of battle. You are the war goddess Morrigan, directing battle through the eyes of her ravens perched in the tree-tops and awaiting the final outcome. You know the strong and the weak. You call some to glory and others to death. Breathe deep, and tell me what you see."

Morgan's eyes became distant, but I did not need to hear her words to know what images flashed before her, for I saw them too. On both sides, the soldiers were badly wounded and tiring fast. Blood streamed from gaping holes in chests and abdomens or congealed into dark patches around slashes to faces and limbs. Some collapsed from their injuries while others fought on without an eye, an ear, and even a hand. Beneath the soldiers' feet, the ground was thick with bodies.

I suddenly understood this was the turning point. The next few decisions would determine the outcome, whether the troops returned victorious to their wives, died in battle, or ended their days as slaves to foreign masters.

Morgan's hand shot out, and she advanced an archer, putting him in firing range of my foot soldiers but also leaving him unprotected.

It was a decoy. The move was meant to draw my attention to the obvious kill and away from her increasingly vulnerable king. If I wanted a prolonged siege, I could have stayed back, picking her men off one by one, but I saw an opening. Her right flank was weak, and I surged forward, ignoring her archer. In this state of heightened awareness, I knew it was better to sacrifice a few troops to protect the many.

The unexpected onslaught threw Morgan, who struggled to keep pace. She eventually faltered, leaving me free to replace her queen with mine and, in the next move, capture her king.

We both sat back, breathing heavily. The visions had cleared, but my head buzzed with the exertion. Around us, the afternoon was advancing, the declining sun making the crystals scattered about our boards gleam merrily in the last gasp of day.

"Very good," Argante lauded us. "You have both done well. Remember, when we practice this way, one of you must always lose. But when you use this method of divination in real situations, be sure to control your sight so that you may see both your best advantage and your enemy's every weakness. It is the only way to assure victory for your side."

Morgan threw her an acerbic glare, clearly displeased about losing, but fortunately for her, Argante had already turned her back.

"Guinevere, I would like to speak with you in private." She guided me to the shade of a nearby oak, leaving Morgan to sulk at the table. "I did not make this known, but each of the scenarios I set before you was a real battle, one I could use to measure your skills because I know the tactics that were used, as well as the outcome."

Argante leaned heavily on her cane. "The battle you and Morgan just completed was the one exception. We received word last night that King Uther was contemplating just such a move against an insurgent and wished to see the possible outcomes before advising him. So we set our two strongest seers in opposition—you and Morgan—and you have given us the key to the battle. Because of the number of casualties you anticipate, I will warn him to avoid any confrontation whatsoever. If he is foolish enough to defy my advice, at least I can tell him how to come out alive. Congratulations, Guinevere. You have just saved the life of your king and many of his men." She patted my shoulder and hobbled back to the table, leaving me to contemplate her words in stunned silence.

૭ૐ ૭ૐ

Morgan towered head and shoulders over me now, having shot up like a weed over the last lunar year, and she took no small pleasure in being able to literally look down on me. Mona too had grown, though she was still considerably smaller than Morgan, while it appeared I was destined to mirror my mother in petite stature. Even Grainne, so child-like in appearance, was slightly taller than me. Though I felt like a dwarf compared to them, I was glad to share the Neophyte Hall with those women. The rest of our sisters from the House of Nine had already left us, bound for marriage or ministry in the outside world, a world I scarcely remembered though I had called it home less than three years before.

A year and a day—that was all that remained before our period of study ended. After that, the Goddess could summon us at any time to the mysterious ceremony that preceded our final vows. We all intended to remain on the isle and serve the Lady here, but that was not entirely in our control. If our families wished to have us back, they could call for us, or if Argante became aware of a need for our skills, we could be sent anywhere in all of Britain.

As an uncertain future loomed before us, we made the most of our time together, taunting and teasing, fighting and laughing as though we were related by flesh and blood.

Late one winter morning, Argante was summoned to High King Uther's court in Carlisle by a rare personal invitation. Although she rejoiced at the king's choice to consult the keepers of ancient wisdom in such turbulent times, the chill weather had taken a toll on her health, so she appointed Viviane as emissary in her stead. Late season snows still clogged the passes and trails of the Mendips, which led north out of Avalon, so Viviane sent word that it would be several weeks before she could safely undertake the journey.

To fill the time between, Argante commissioned a tapestry for the king in praise of his wise decision to include Avalon in his circle of closest councilors. The motif chosen was representative of the mysteries of Avalon, the very same mysteries Uther himself had sworn to uphold many years before when he took the Druidic oath upon his initiation into their mysteries. In this way, the tapestry would be not only a gift; it would also serve as a reminder of the old ways in a court increasingly populated by unsympathetic Christian priests.

It could have been woven on one of Avalon's many looms, but Argante insisted the tapestry be hand-stitched in ancient decorative tradition. She decided such a task would be perfect for the neophytes, and so Grainne and Mona were given the assignment of preparing and weaving the base fabric, while the elaborate embroidery would fall into the more dexterous hands of Morgan and myself. We worked for what felt like months, and as winter warmed into early spring, our labor was nearly complete.

The evening before Viviane was to leave for the northern country, only two blocks of sewing remained. The pattern was rapidly taking shape, my tired hands sewing what remained of the Goddess's gown. Next to me, a stool sat empty but for multicolored threads brushing the floor as Morgan had left them hanging the night before. Only one of the God's feet and the grass on which he stood remained to be sewn; an hour or two more of stitching, and her wearisome job would be done.

But Morgan was nowhere to be found. She had disappeared not long after breakfast and never showed up to complete her task. Where could she be? Not for the first time, I found myself resenting her ability to do as she pleased with little or no consequence.

I will likely be the only one to note her absence as long as she comes to the evening's ritual on time. One thing is for certain, I will not do her portion of the work for her. Let her feel Argante's wrath for once. It would only be fair.

The sun was just beginning to slip below the horizon when I buried the final knot in my section. Breathing a sigh of relief, I snipped off the excess thread and sat back, admiring the results of our work. Finally, it was all done, except for Morgan's block. I stretched my aching arms, pinched out the candle flame, and made my way toward the door, intent on resting before the twilight ritual.

I didn't even make it out the door before Morgan came rushing up the stairs, face white, hair flapping wildly behind her.

"Morgan, kind of you to make an appearance. Do you not think you are taking quite a risk? Many threads demand attention, but little time remains."

She threw a biting look in my direction in response to my

mocking. "If you must know, *Guinevere*"—she said my name like it was bitter to her tongue—"I came to fetch your help."

I feigned surprise. "*You* are asking *me* for help?" I started toward the door. "You made your bed, Morgan; now you must sleep in it. I will not aid you one stitch."

Morgan's hand clamped around my arm, forcing me to face her. "No, you silly cow, I do not need your help with the sewing. Ailis has found her way up a tree near the lake and cannot get down again."

How did Viviane's young daughter manage to climb up a tree? There was little time for speculation. Viviane would have all our hides if her only child were to suffer any misfortune.

"Where is Viviane? Does she know?"

"I don't know. I came here because you were closer—"

I didn't wait around to let her finish her excuse. My feet carried me swiftly across the plains of waving grass to the shore of the inland lake. I scanned the trees lining the water's edge. Sure enough, there was the sobbing lass, a tiny version of her mother save for her auburn hair, clinging to a tree branch that stretched its fingers out over the lake.

Morgan had been right to summon help. Ailis had not yet learned to swim, so if she fell, she would drown. And from the vise-like grip she had on the bobbing branch, I guessed she did not have the dexterity or courage to back down the tree either.

"Ailis! Ailis, stay where you are. I will come and get you."

The girl did not respond, only continued to wail.

Without a second thought, I scampered toward her, plowing through the foliage that separated us. The base of the tree was surrounded by clumps of tall plants with spiked stems and tooth-like leaves, whose berry-like purple and green flowers appeared harmless from a distance. Only now that I was standing in them, arms and legs prickling like I was being attacked by bees, did I recognize the plants for what they were—stinging nettle. No doubt I would pay for my good deed later with an itchy rash.

Grumbling to myself that I should have known better—it *was* one of the plants we'd had to identify in our first herbalism test—I climbed up the tree, using the outcropping branches to support my ascent. I inched forward, wincing as the skin pricked by the nettles was irritated by the tree bark, until I had the wailing child in my arms and we were once again safely on the ground.

Even before I set Ailis down, the tiny poisonous teeth hooked into her dress told me she had been playing in the nettles long before I arrived. Not wanting to expose anyone else to the irritating plant, I bathed Ailis in the lake, hoping the water would lessen the severity of her outbreak. As her tears slowly subsided, she began to tell me about the colorful songbird that had caught her attention, inspiring her to scale the tree to have a closer look. Once she was dry, I returned her to Viviane's care, but only after making her promise never to do such a thing again.

The sky was almost completely dark by the time I neared my quarters, so I would not have enough time to change my clothes before the ritual began. As I passed the weaving room, I heard Argante speaking with Morgan and peeked my head in to see her reaction to my earlier work.

At first, I could not understand the distress and concern etched in Argante's face. But then I looked down and saw its source. All of my long hours of stitching had been ripped out of the hanging as if I had never completed them, and the lower left corner—Morgan's block—was burned, pieces of blackened thread and crumpled cloth the only testaments to the tragedy. Nearby, a soot-stained taper lay in a pool of wax, as if someone had franticly flung it away from the tapestry.

"What happened here?" I asked incredulously, crossing in front of Morgan to finger the thread that made up all my missing stitches.

"Your irresponsibility caused this girl's work to be ruined," Argante growled coldly. "That is what happened here."

"What?" My astonishment echoed off the stone pillars and silent loom.

"When I came in, some of the ribbons were hanging down from your block, dancing precariously close to the candle flame," Morgan explained, picking up a charred thread as evidence. "I tried to intervene, but a gust of wind tipped the flame, igniting the cloth. All I could do was put it out." Her wide blue eyes were filled with innocent astonishment.

My blood boiled. How dare she blame this on me! Did Argante really believe that story? Surely she could see through Morgan's lies.

Struggling to contain my rage, I faced Argante. "But that is not . . . I am certain I extinguished the flame—" I began, unable to collect my thoughts.

"No, I will hear no excuses from you, Guinevere," Argante cut me off. "Look at you, scraped and covered in dirt. If you had been here doing what you were supposed to be instead of cavorting through the hills, none of this would have happened."

I listened to her berate me in utter shock. So that was how it happened. Morgan needed a way to blame her absence on someone else, and the child's peril proved a convenient means. She might even have encouraged Ailis to climb that tree. Now she was turning her thoughtlessness on me. I had to make Argante understand.

"Lady, please listen to me. I did no such thing. Morgan—"

Argante turned on me with steely eyes. "I said no more!" She clasped her hands and surveyed the burned material. "The damage is unfortunate, but it is repairable. As you know, Viviane leaves at first light for her meeting with the king, so all the work must be completed by then. Guinevere, you will stay here and mend what your carelessness has ruined, as well as complete your allotted portion of the embroidery. Morgan will assist me in tonight's ritual in your place. In addition, to ensure you learn to take your responsibilities seriously, you will scrub the sanctuary stairs in the morning."

I opened my mouth to protest once again, but Argante ignored me and walked away, as did Morgan, but only after casting a wicked grin in my direction.

So that was it. I had no choice but to endure Morgan's punishment while she plied everyone else with lies. *Damn her!* I raged inwardly while I completed the tedious work. The moon rose and set, the stars shone brightly and paled into dawn, and all the while, my heavy eyes squinted at endless rows of stitching until at long last, the final thread was knotted and hidden away.

Argante woke me with a gentle pat just after sunrise. I had no memory of falling asleep, but she said I had done so a few hours earlier. She inspected my work, nodding approvingly as she ran her fingers across the needlework.

"Your stitching is well done," she commented, inspecting a complex pattern.

I began to pack away the spools of thread. Slowly, I became aware of Argante's silent gaze and looked up.

"Where did you get those?" She gestured to the trail of red, inflamed blisters that wound their way up my arm.

Involuntarily, my face flushed. "Yesterday, after I finished my sewing, Morgan came rushing in, telling me Ailis was trapped in a tree and in need of my rescue. I rushed to help her without paying heed to the plants at its base. It is—"

"I know what it is," Argante said, clearly irritated. "Most of Ailis's body is covered in blisters. At least now we know where she was exposed to the plant." The old woman sighed. "Now if you will excuse me, I need to speak with Morgan." She stopped in the doorway and turned. "Mona has gathered all you will need to tend to the stairs. In the meantime, make a poultice of sorrel and mud to apply to your rash. It will help relieve the itching."

৵ৎ৹৵

When I arrived, bathed and medicated, to complete the last part of my unjust sentence, I was surprised to see Morgan leaning against one of the pillars at the top of the stairs, her expression as sullen as the gray, frostbitten morning.

"Morgan? What are you doing here?"

She shot me an icy look. "Always so innocent, aren't you?" She pointed toward the pail and bristle-brush sitting at her feet. "I, too, am to play scouring maid today. And I suppose I have you to thank for that. Am I right?"

I raised an eyebrow at her and dipped my brush into the bucket. "If anyone is to blame, it is you. Why did you burn the material, Morgan?"

She turned away, toying with her own brush. "I have no idea what you are talking about."

"Yes, you do. Why did you do it?"

She ignored my question and raised her voice in a mocking, sing-song tone. "High and mighty Guinevere, daughter of the great King Leodgrance. Are you afraid the hem of your gown may be dirtied by a little hard work? Nothing less than perfection for you, oh pristine one."

Her sarcasm stung. I flung the brush back down into the bucket, sloshing soapy bubbles at my feet. "Do you really think me that much a fool? Have you learned nothing about me in the last three years? I have no fear of hard work—no one here does, or she would not survive." As I advanced on Morgan, my mind briefly flashed back to my first washing lesson with Mona. "But unlike you, I would never betray my sister just to make myself look better in Argante's eyes."

A wicked smirk spread across Morgan's face. "Is that so?" she asked doubtfully. "We shall see. But bear this in mind, *my lady.* Not everyone has had your privileged life. Some of us must do what we can to survive."

"Survival at the cost of others is cruel," I retorted. "Although I suppose I should expect that from you by now. Perhaps it isn't your fault, since you had no parents to teach you respect."

Morgan turned on me with the venom of a viper. "I had twenty priestesses as my mother and the Archdruid as my father. Avalon is *my* home. Not that my upbringing is any concern of yours. As for what I may or may not have done, someone had to put you in your place. I cannot help it if you finally saw your inferiority to me and cannot live with the consequences."

With that she turned and began scrubbing in the opposite direction, the conversation closed.

As the silence became a wall between us, I could only wonder what her next move would be and how I would suffer for it. I had, after all, exposed her greatest vulnerability. If I knew one thing about Morgan, it was that she would not let such a deep insult go unpunished.

Chapter Four

Spring 495

In early spring, when I was barely fifteen, during the impossibly cold nights on which the ewes gave birth, they came for me—nine priestesses of the isle. I needn't be told what was about to happen; I had waited four long years for this night.

As I followed behind the solemn procession to the top of the Tor, I tried to recall the tales told of the initiation of a priestess. No one who had successfully passed the tests had ever spoken of them, for they were sworn never to reveal the secrets to the uninitiated. Still, rumors followed every initiation ceremony, and before the crescent was set onto the new priestess's brow, tales of horror and adventure floated through the House of Nine, leaving the young ones petrified yet excited at the prospect of one day bravely facing the unknown challenges.

As we passed through the entrance to the circle of stones, the other priestesses emerged from the shadows into the flickering torchlight to surround us. I knelt before Argante, who seemed this night to be more goddess than woman.

"Guinevere of Northgallis, you came to these shores a child seeking to become a servant of the ancient ones. Now, as a woman, is that still your wish?"

"It is."

"Know then that the gods require great sacrifice of those sworn to them. Before you may give your life to the Goddess and the God, you must prove yourself worthy of such an honor."

She stepped aside, revealing the altar stone, which was laden with symbols of earth, air, water, and fire. I knew then that, like the Druids, I would be tested by each of the elements.

"A priestess must be able to feel and manipulate the energies around her. Draw from the clouds rain which will soak the land with healing waters," Argante commanded.

The clear night sky stretched out beyond the Tor, stars winking defiance from the heavens. To an outsider, it would seem preposterous to try to make a cloudless sky rain, but I had enough training to know nothing was impossible.

I took a deep breath, willing the roots of my being downward, and closed my eyes, drawing the power of the Tor deep into myself until the very heartbeat of the earth was within my veins. I raised my arms, and the naked branches around us shivered. Concentrating on the void before me, I turned nine times sunwise, faster and faster, willing the energy up through my feet and out of my hands. The wind increased with each turn, so that by the time I opened my eyes, the stars were obscured by thick clouds. I brought down my hands with force, and raindrops followed. In the distance, a crack of lightning was answered by the peal of thunder.

Argante nodded. With an outward sweep of her arms, she commanded the rain to cease, though the clouds remained. She led me back over to the altar stone where a brazier burned brightly in the center.

"With power comes great responsibility. I ask you now to demonstrate your trust in the gods you serve by reaching into this fire and withdrawing a coal without fear."

I swallowed hard. We trained for many hours to be able to accomplish this task, one which signified our ability to let go of ourselves and place the needs of others before our natural inclinations. My hand shook as I reached toward the fire, but I willed myself not to feel the burning heat. *Fire is only a spark fed by air. I am much more—a being of spirit above all.* The heat grew more intense as I reached toward the coals, coloring my skin a deep scarlet. But instead of burning me, it traveled around my hand with comforting warmth, as if I was wearing a thick, protective glove. With a final prayer, I grasped the coal, which weighed heavy in my hand but bore no more heat than a sun-drenched rock. With a sigh of relief, I presented it to Argante, unharmed, and set it down on the altar stone.

Argante's face remained impassive. "Your success is a sign of great fidelity, and I am pleased. As one final scrutiny, I bid you prepare the sacred brew from the fruits of the earth that will draw down the Goddess into this mortal frame, that you may swear your vows directly to her."

Facing north, I looked down at the altar stone, on which one of the priestesses had strewn a variety of herbs. I knew some of them were not part of the sacred drink meant to induce a trance, so my ability to complete this task successfully was crucial.

My mind flickered back to the garden and my first test of herbal knowledge, where I had made a fatal mistake. What if

I did something wrong and accidentally poisoned the Lady of the Lake? Would they slaughter me right here, using my blood to atone, or merely banish me from the isle to live my life in shame?

I cast aside the herbs I knew to be a trick and set to work grinding the others, separating valuable buds from deadly leaves. Water from the white spring bubbled in a small cup placed over the brazier. I added the herbs and a heady, sweet scent emerged, a clear sign I had done well.

Viviane strained the liquid and gave it to Argante. She drank, swayed a little while speaking the words of invocation, and then seemed to shrink and disappear into the force that inhabited her body.

I blinked. Her hair had transformed from gray into a lustrous auburn, and her skin was now smooth and unlined. On each side of her stood a ghost-like white horse as insubstantial as smoke, snorting puffs of fog from their nostrils and pawing at the ground, forming tiny clouds beneath their hooves. This was the goddess Rhiannon, protector of my tribe and line.

Holding their reins in one hand, she reached out to me with the other. "I am the Great Mother, she who is at once Maiden, Mother, and Crone, mistress of the silver moon, she of a thousand names, who holds the powers of life and death at her command. Guinevere of Northgallis, do you truly wish to serve me?" The voice that issued from her lips was young, strong, and confident, not the raspy growl that had instructed me all these years. There was no doubt this was no longer the Lady of the Lake, but one far more powerful and ancient.

"I do."

"With full understanding that the vows you are about to make are irrevocable and will forever bind you to my service, even beyond this lifetime, pledge now your life to me."

I knelt, and the words cascaded from my lips without hesitation. "I swear to always obey the Goddess and her consort and to uphold the mysteries of Avalon with all of my being, even laying down my life for them if it is so required. I promise to perform all of my actions with love and trust in the Goddess's guidance, as I am now her earthly representative. Above all, I pledge to love and serve the Goddess and God even through my dying breath and to respect all forms of worship that give them honor."

The goddess stepped forward and placed a kiss on my brow, on my lips, and on my heart. Rhiannon raised my chin to face her, placing her hands on top of my head. "Receive now the blessings of the Great Mother and arise a priestess of Avalon."

When I looked up again, a young man stood in her place. His hair was radiant like the midsummer sun, eyes as blue as the sea. In his left hand he held a spear, and on his right forearm rested a shield. I knew him immediately to be Lugh, the sun god of my mother's people.

"You have pledged yourself to my service, daughter, and for that I commend you. Though I cannot promise you a life of joy, I can promise you one of merit. Seek my wisdom, and you shall not fail. Be blessed, child of the Votadini, and be clothed a priestess of Avalon."

He bent down and placed his lips upon my forehead. Heat like the kiss of the sun shot through my being, and I closed my eyes to shield them from the radiant light. What seemed like an instant later, I opened them to find the sky already brightening to soft orange and pink through breaks in the clouds.

The god and goddess were gone, but I was far from alone. Surrounding me were a circle of priestesses. As the sun began to color the eastern horizon in a pale glow, my forehead, lips, and heart were anointed with rose oil, and with great ceremony, the blue robes of priesteshood were wrapped around my shoulders.

The women laid me face up on the altar stone. I welcomed its cold, solid surety after the ethereal nature of my tests and vows. Argante was still under the influence of the sacred drink, so Viviane bent over me, chanting softly in an ancient language as she set about marking my brow with the crescent tattoo. Our mark was the waxing crescent moon, a sign of ever-increasing power and growth, but as I struggled to remain motionless under the biting tips that created the shape, I wondered if that was simply wishful thinking.

I shivered with sudden cold that had nothing to do with the icy stone. Viviane sighed and put a firm hand on me, bidding me be still, but I barely noticed. I was remembering Argante's prophecy on the day of my admittance.

"Another crown sits on her brow, one that will secure the safety and prosperity of many, but at a great cost, both to herself and to those she holds dear."

Deep down, I knew this moment set in motion forces that would validate her words. What I could not foresee, even with the aid of the sight, was how.

Chapter Five

The new moon following my consecration brought with it a flurry of activity to Avalon's shores. Late one night, the Druid astronomers noted something strange in the sky—a comet, unlike any seen in a generation, soared above a triune of sacred stars. The comet was bright and its tail slender and long, causing it to take on the appearance of a firedrake. It was said that the same sign appeared in the heavens when Britain was in peril before the reign of Uther Pendragon. Because of its prophetic timing, the comet had been known as the Kingmaker.

The reappearance of this celestial sign was taken very seriously, and all unnecessary activity was suspended. The Druids invaded our shores from their own sacred land in an unprecedented journey that made the elders talk of the great wonder that was sure to follow.

For the next two moons, days were spent in Avalon's great library, consulting star charts or speaking with the elders, researching the Kingmaker's last appearance. Our nights were a tireless pursuit of the great star. It had not reappeared since the night following its first sighting, but we all knew it would come again. So that no skill would go untapped, Argante and Merlin, the Archdruid, decreed that Druids and priestesses should work in groups or pairs to pool their knowledge to uncover its meaning. When night fell—except on the full and new moons, when each sex kept to its own mysterious ceremony—young and old alike would fan out in groups to designated sites across the isle where the lines of energy intersected and, with weary eyes, perform their craft.

And so it was on a mid-spring night not long after the equinox. The air was unseasonably warm, the land hushed in drowsy slumber. Creatures of the night sang their soothing lullaby. All across the hillside, small fires twinkled, marking the spots where priests and priestesses tried to divine the will of the gods.

My companion lay on the tall grass a few feet away from me, head resting on his intertwined fingers, dark eyes cast heavenward, while I sat next to the sacred spring, leaning heavily upon a large boulder on its bank.

I studied him with keen interest. Aggrivane was the second son of the great King Lot who ruled the wild kingdom of Lothian far to the north in my mother's homeland. That much Argante had told me before she sent us off into the woods. Over the past several months, I had learned much more about this tall, handsome man. Aggrivane spoke of his dreams of becoming a warrior, dreams that would have to wait to be fulfilled, out of obedience to his father. King Lot insisted he learn the path of peace before espousing a life of violence.

"He told me it would be to my benefit to calm my willful and stormy nature," Aggrivane had explained with a smirk.

I'd seen him for the first time on the day of the Druids arrival. Our paths crossed as he labored to unload one of their boats, and he regarded me warmly with chestnut eyes fringed with thick lashes, the corner of his lips turned up in a self-conscious half-smile.

Just as they were now.

Oh no, he knows I was staring at him. I turned away, and my cheeks flushed with embarrassment. I had believed him to be asleep. Hastily, I forced my attention back to the pool and stared into its depths as if the waters could wash away my humiliation.

Amused, Aggrivane sat up, brushing back his wavy, dark brown hair. "Enjoying the view?" he asked, eyes crinkling with mirth in the way I found so attractive.

He was only teasing me, but I could not bring myself to answer. Words died soundlessly in my throat, and I did my best to shield myself from his penetrating gaze by letting my hair fall as a screen between us. I had no experience with men, so I did not know how to conduct myself in this unfamiliar situation.

"Guinevere, look at me." He seemed remorseful, even slightly hurt I had not taken his joke as intended. "Merlin and Argante sent us here to work together—not to hide from one another. Please, let us make peace." He reached out a hand toward me.

"I am sorry," I stammered, my voice barely a whisper. "It is just. . . we so rarely receive men on these shores. . ."

Aggrivane nodded but said nothing, his look turning pensive.

I feared I had offended him in some way. But before I could give voice to my fears, he came over to sit by my side. His rich, dark eyes searched my face.

"You are a newly consecrated priestess, are you not?" His finger grazed the blue crescent on my brow, only recently healed. His touch was like fire that left a tingling trail in its wake. "Is it true that the comet first appeared on the night you took your vows?"

My eyes widened and I nodded slowly. Few people knew of that. "It is," I replied, more warily than I would have liked. "But I did not see it."

"Of course not." He studied my face with a concentration he usually reserved for the stars.

The intensity of his gaze was making me uncomfortable. Warmth spread from my face to my breasts and was slowly creeping down my torso.

"Perhaps then"—his voice was soft and sweet as nectar—"the firedrake heralds some greatness for you."

A trill of nervous laughter escaped my lips. "I fear you regard me too highly."

"Perhaps," he mused. "Or perhaps not." He smiled sweetly at the thought. He returned his attention to the stars and moments passed in silence before he spoke again. "How long have you been on this isle, Guinevere?"

"I was brought here just after my eleventh birthday, about four years ago."

"How did you come to this vocation?"

"My mother promised me to the Goddess at birth. I was brought here when I started showing signs of the sight." Without realizing what I was doing, I moved closer to him and began to slowly trace the image of a serpentine dragon that wound its way up his dominant arm—the sign of his clan. "What about you?

You said it was your father's wish that you study with the Druids. Do you regret it?"

His eyes followed my hand as he began to gently caress it with his own. Then he let out a slow, deep breath. "No, I do not. My father is a wise man. The path of peace is the best training a warrior can have because it teaches you love and the value of life. Because of what I have learned, I will never kill for sport or pleasure, only out of duty to my king or in self-defense. There would be much less bloodshed if all soldiers were trained to follow the holy path."

The hypnotizing motion of his fingertips stopped.

"And you, my little priestess." He clasped my hand. "Have you any regrets?"

Images of an alternate life—the one I would have led had I stayed with my family—raced through my mind. I saw myself with my childhood friends at play in Northgallis or studying under the watchful gaze of a tutor.

I shook my head. "My life here has taught me to have faith in that which I cannot see"—I found myself leaning into him as I spoke—"in what can only be felt."

We fell silent, lost in the energy that pulsed in the scant space between us. I tried to convince myself that it was the power of the intersecting ley lines, but to no avail. This energy, this blinding, throbbing force drew me toward Aggrivane; in my innocence, I did not understand it, but I was powerless to resist it.

Overhead, a shooting star illuminated the velvet sky. Startled, we both looked up.

Aggrivane's face lit up with a different kind of fire. "It is the first herald," he exclaimed. "Three shooting stars in the vicinity of the triune precede the comet's appearance." Then his face clouded over with disappointment. "Now is the time for us to work our magic if we are to gain access to the answers we seek."

Absorbed in what had passed between us, I had almost forgotten the reason for our nocturnal vigil. Hastily, I slipped out of his arms and over to the edge of the spring, where I peered purposefully into its depths.

The waters shone inky blue and green in the dim light of midnight. In the soft light of the slender moon, I caught a glimpse of the smooth stones lining the bottom. I inhaled deeply, determined to free my mind to the will of the Goddess. A soft breeze caressed my cheek, and I breathed in the heavy perfume of honeysuckle from a hedge somewhere nearby. Slowly, my consciousness sank into the murky depths of the nothingness that separated our world from the celestial plane. Deeper and deeper down I forced my mind, but I still saw nothing but darkness.

Frustrated, I looked up in time to see the second herald paint the sky the color of dawn with its shimmering streak of light. Aggrivane was performing complex mental calculations known only to the Druids, eyes on the sky, darting to and fro in rapt concentration.

I closed my eyes and breathed deeply. I projected my senses outward until the vibration of the Tor behind me pulsed in my veins. I willed myself free of my body and allowed my soul to sink into the void between worlds—into the silent depths of eternity that existed before the Goddess gave birth to the world. Again, I reached the point where visions should start to form, but they did not. I could not seem to pierce the veil.

I cursed under my breath.

Without taking his eyes from the sky, Aggrivane reached out to me. "What is it? What do you see?" he asked, standing to get a better view of the sky.

"Nothing," I replied, defeated.

"Why don't you try one more time?" he encouraged. Without waiting for my answer, he knelt down on the grass behind me, placing his arms around my waist, hands on top of my own.

"But what about the stars?"

He gave a small laugh. "I can see them in the reflection of the water. Have no fear." He pulled me to him and murmured into my hair. "Remember the power that was given to you when you were made a priestess."

His voice was soothing, and I slowly melted into a trance. I relaxed against him and breathed in his scent, the smell of oak and apple wood. Soon my heart beat the same slow, two-note rhythm drumming in his chest.

His fingers intertwined with mine. "You know the power of the Goddess. Invoke her into you and let yourself be free."

The surface of the water rippled with his breath and my vision turned inward; I no longer had need of any sense save that of touch. Everywhere Aggrivane's body met mine, we seemed to be as one, exchanging energy as if there were no bounds between us—no space, no clothing, not even skin. His lips grazed my neck, the stubble around his mouth tickling my skin invitingly, and suddenly the veil that separated me from the spirit world was lifted.

"The third herald," Aggrivane said softly.

His voice reached me as if from a great distance. While the star lit the sky, in the depths of the water danced a vision older than the standing stones. Fires blazed in low pits on the hillside.

A man more animal than human stood on the edge of the forest, naked but for the antlered crown on his brow and the blood painted on his flesh. Above him on a hill stood a woman, also nude, her billowing hair radiant as the sun, her bare breasts mirrors of the full moon that shone in the sky above her.

The woman came to him and bade him to drink from a golden cup, after which she did the same and led him to a secluded grove. There she opened herself to him, and he poured out his seed in the fertile plain of her body.

"The old ways must be kept. Remember the old ways," a chorus of voices chanted in my mind.

I came back to myself suddenly, panting as if I had run the length of the isle, my body held upright only by Aggrivane's arms, strong as the trunks of a pair of ancient oaks. Saying nothing, I spun around and kissed him full on the mouth. He seemed surprised but willing. Too soon, light like the midsummer sun pierced the darkness behind my closed eyes. Squinting, I opened one eye and pulled away.

"The firedrake!"

We both stared in awe at the wonder before us. The firedrake was many times larger than the heralds that preceded it, and even the moon seemed dim in comparison. Its long tail stretched across the sky, led by a fiery head that resembled a snarling dragon. It streaked through the night, accompanied by a shriek that could have raised the ancients from their resting places. Then, just as quickly, it was gone.

ও⊘ ৩ঽ

Merlin gathered everyone together the next morning following sunrise salutations. He sat on the top of the sanctuary stairs, holding court with Argante and Viviane. The other Druids and priestesses gathered around on the steps below. Their voices blended into a low buzz as they speculated on the meaning of the firedrake and the mysterious visions and other phenomenon reported following the comet's appearance last night.

I watched Merlin, in awe of his power of attraction, a gift that flowed as easy as breath. He was a lodestone, able to draw anyone to him when he wished, but equally capable of keeping them away when he willed it. This gift, or illusion, as some called it, never failed to both thrill and unsettle me when he was near.

As Merlin held council with the isle's eldest and most powerful, he appeared perfectly comfortable in his role as the youngest Archdruid in living memory, directing and counseling with the wisdom of a man who had seen six decades, rather than only three. Though he bore great responsibility, his face remained unlined, pale as fresh milk, intense, with knowing eyes the color of the lake. Some said his bright copper hair, which in many ways reminded me of Morgan's, marked his bloodline as descended from the earliest races of our land, those who were part fae and bore greater resemblance to gods than men. Maybe that was where his commanding presence came from. He certainly could inspire fear and awe in equal measure, depending on his mood.

Tearing my gaze away from Merlin, I chanced a glance at Aggrivane, who stood next to me. I was doing my best to hide my nervousness and pretend nothing had changed between us, but we both knew it had. I was finding it difficult to meet his eyes without immediately flushing, but every so often he would catch my gaze and hold it with a smile that made my heart melt. Hesitantly, he brushed my fingertips with his and I nearly gasped at the spark that ran up my arm. Looking up at him with a timid smile, I entwined my fingers with his and bit my lip, bashfully turning my attention back to the activity at the top of the stairs.

Merlin's long red hair shone in the early morning light as he leaned in toward Viviane, the two whispering in an intimate manner. We all knew Merlin fairly well because he visited the isle several times a year to conduct business with Argante. But it was not just her he came to see; he seemed to have a special affection for Viviane, and the two were never far from one another's side when he was here. It was never spoken of, but I strongly suspected Ailis—the girl I rescued from the tree two years earlier—was his daughter and Viviane his wife, though I doubted a legal contract was what bound them to one another.

Regardless of the truth, Merlin never singled out Ailis; he treated her with the same fatherly respect and affection he bestowed on each one of us. No matter how brief his visit, Merlin never failed to inquire about us, as concerned for the welfare of Avalon's priestesses and neophytes as he was for the Druids in his own care. Witty and eloquent, he often regaled us with mythical or historical tales or fanciful riddles, and sometimes even taught us a little of the Druid's lore. As I grew into womanhood, I came to treasure his visits and appreciate the confidence he showed in me, for I viewed him much like a second father and wished never to disappoint him.

Merlin stood, his bright eyes sweeping the crowd as he prepared to speak. "Druids of Britain, priestesses of the Goddess, I bid you good day. And an especially good day it is, for we have the privilege of carrying out Divine orders, beginning this very morn."

All around me, heads turned as neighbor whispered to neighbor, questioning or positing a personal theory on what Merlin's words meant.

"As you have no doubt heard, and perhaps embellished in the retelling"—he chuckled—"many signs and wonders were given to us last night as the firedrake made what I believe to be its final appearance. Alone, your experiences may seem odd and perplexing, but that is because they are but fragments of a greater whole. Taken together, the Lady and I believe they reveal the will of the God and Goddess.

"This we know: from this generation shall arise a great king and so a great sign, the firedrake, has been given to herald his ascent to power. As in days of old, the Goddess wishes this man to be hallowed in both the heavens and on earth, in a ceremony that can only take place on this holy isle between one of her priestesses and the man she deems worthy. This being so, on Beltane we will enact the most holy of rituals ever to be performed—the Sacred Marriage. By coming together in the life-generating, creative act and emulating the love of the God and Goddess, this pair shall assure the great king is wedded to the land—man to woman— priest to priestess—Otherworld to Earth—and the blessing of the Goddess shall be bestowed on him and on our land.

"We know, too, that the Goddess wishes the treasures of Avalon no longer lie hidden in the mists but be returned to the outside world, beginning with the sacred sword. The king will be vested with this symbol of power by the Lady herself when he comes forth to be hallowed."

And so it was to be. The Druids departed our shores for their home within hours, charged with the task of finding this great king before the festival. The priestess who would embody the Goddess would be chosen from our own number in a few short weeks.

I smiled inwardly as I looked around our sleeping chambers that night before retiring. From the expression on many faces, it was clear mine was not the only heart the Druids had taken with them.

CHAPTER SIX

Summer 495

On Beltane morning, all the daughters of Avalon—
young and old—shivered in the chill air as night
slowly gave way to dawn. As we traversed the tender
grass carpeting the plains between the confluence of the white
and red springs, our feet were washed in fresh dew, a silent abso-
lution from the earth herself.

We reached the summit of the Tor in silence and joined
hands, feeling the subtle shift of energy as light broke over the
horizon. This was a sacred day, one of the most holy of all holidays
celebrated by our people. Today was the beginning of summer,
the day honoring the union of the Goddess and God and the fer-
tility of all the land.

On Beltane night, every woman was said to be the Goddess
incarnate and every man the God. Their sexual union reflected
that of the two aspects of Deity, and any child born of such a
union was considered blessed by the gods. However, in rare years
when the Sacred Marriage was performed, those terms increased

ninefold for the couple who invoked the God and Goddess into their bodies in ritual, as well as for their offspring. Today one of us would be chosen, set apart by the Lady to act in her service.

Mona's clear voice broke the silence in a high, worshipful note as she saluted the rising sun in song, speaking the language of our ancestors. We responded reverently and fell to our knees in unison. Mirroring the actions of the others, I ran my palms across the grass and placed them on my face.

"Through the tears of the earth, may the Goddess grant me health and long youth," I quietly prayed, echoing the words whispered by each priestess as she washed.

I glanced over in time to catch Morgan shrinking away as Grainne swiped at her hair, trying to get it wet or dirty—I wasn't sure. I couldn't help but smile. We were all vowed priestesses now, but in many ways we were still children, still prone to the same mischief as the day we came to the isle.

Rising, I turned to face the circle of standing stones that surrounded us, towering twice my height in some places. Somewhere down below, deep in the forest, Aggrivane and the other Druids hunted. I had heard the low blast of their horn as we gathered at the springs. They had their own sacred rites, their own duties particular to this day and to the ceremony that would be enacted tonight. Under the shelter of the oaks, ash, and elm, they fought to determine who would be the Sacred King.

When I closed my eyes and listened, I thought I could hear them chanting and the occasional cry of one being tested. I tried to center myself and send forth my mind to see their progress, but my efforts were interrupted as Viviane and Argante made their way to the center of the circle.

Argante opened her arms wide and addressed us in a tone

of authority. "The Druids have chosen the men from whom will be selected the Sacred King according to the ancient tests. So too have we chosen the one who shall take up the mantle of the Goddess and perform the role of the Virgin Queen." She inclined her head to the copper-haired priestess next to me. "Morgan, the responsibility has fallen to you. Though this is a great honor, it comes at a heavy price. Do you agree to sacrifice your maidenhead in service to the Great Mother and to do so with utmost humility?"

Morgan nodded silently, barely able to contain her excitement.

"So be it then. Come with me." Argante gestured for Morgan to follow her out of the circle. "I will prepare you for the ritual."

Morgan began to follow but then stopped. Slowly, she turned toward me, a triumphant smirk on her face. "Look who is the victor now," she whispered in my ear. "Lineage or no, it seems I have won our little competition after all. While I am taking part in the most sacred of our rituals with the God himself, you will have to be content whoring away your virginity with a common man." She shrugged. "But perhaps that is how it should be. The Goddess never errs, you know."

This, then, was her ultimate revenge—taking the top honor, one that would not be bestowed again, at least not to our generation. I wanted to kill her in that moment, to wrap my hands around her neck or strangle her with the braided rope of her own hair. But Grainne, sensing my tension, held my arms as Morgan gave me one last gloating sneer and swaggered away down the hillside.

I forced my mind back to the present and made myself breathe deeply. "Sweet Mother, give me strength," I muttered, trying to calm the poisonous brew of hatred and jealousy boiling in my belly.

As I fought for control, the first ray of sunlight peaked over the crest of Pen Hill. It shone directly on the altar stone only twice a year—today, the festival of life, and on Samhain, the day of death. Viviane had placed a polished crystal at an angle on the stone and it captured the light, serving as a natural lens to ignite the tinder beneath. From this tiny fire, she lit a series of small white tapers, which were presented to each of the remaining virgins.

As I held mine, I suddenly realized what was to come tonight—the full significance of the candle. It was permission to take a lover, to engage fully in the festival. This flame, lit not by human hands but by the sun, the symbol of the God, was the flame of passion which drew him to the Goddess. Its heat seemed to travel from my fingertips, up my arm, and through my veins, warming my blood. I felt my cheeks flush and my breasts tingle. An unfamiliar stirring below my belly told me I was ready to experience the full extent of the mystery this night would bring.

಄ ಄

As we traipsed through the forest, we sang ancient festival songs and others made up on the spot, gathering wands and flowers, weaving them into garlands and wreaths, bedecking one another and any sacred tree, stream, or well we could find. Some of the Druids had begun drinking already, so to them, everything was sacred and deserving of a floral crown.

"They say the Sacred King is quite a strapping man," Mona said above the boisterous laughter. "Good thing I wasn't chosen for his queen or he'd have crushed my delicate frame." She swept a hand down the length of her slender body to emphasize her point.

"You'll have no such problem from Connor," teased one of the Druids, poking a smaller man in the ribs. "Wiry as a stork, he is."

Connor grabbed the teasing Druid around the neck playfully and pretended to bash in his head.

"Guinevere, did you hear Aggrivane took second?" Grainne yelled over her shoulder to me, never loosening her grip on the man at her side.

"He did?" That meant Aggrivane was the Sacred King's champion, and thus allowed to choose his mate from among the virgin priestesses. It was not as holy an office as the Sacred King, but an honor nonetheless. Suddenly, I was afraid. What if he wanted someone else? Worse yet—what if I, in my innocence, was a disappointment to him? All of my earlier confidence drained away, and I began to wonder if attending the ritual was such a good idea.

"Where is he anyway?" asked a man whose name I did not know. "It is unlike any son of Lothian to miss a celebration."

We continued on, the boys harassing the girls like children and making jokes that on any other day would have been considered lewd. From time to time, a couple lingered behind to steal a few kisses or inspect a grove or meadow and claim it as their own for later in the night.

We were nearing the apple orchards when we crossed paths with another group, Aggrivane among them. He smiled when he saw me and motioned me off the path into a small stand of trees. I followed in breathless anticipation, palms sweaty, heart thumping.

When we were alone, he drew me toward him. I ran my fingers through the thick mass of dark curls at the base of his neck and smiled, breathing in his scent. It took me a moment to notice there was something in his right hand. A golden arrow with a crystal tip shimmered as the wind waved the branches overhead. It was his prize as second.

"I have made my choice," he whispered into my hair, kissing the top of my head.

"And I, mine." I melted into his arms, reveling in a state of pure bliss.

∞§∞§∞

An hour later, the sun was high overhead. The wind had stilled, holding its breath in imitation of the crowd.

At the center of the clearing, the two opponents stood, facing one another on the axis of a great circle drawn in the dirt. On one side stood the morning's victor, a large man who had been transformed into the Oak King, naked save for a loincloth the color of tree bark and the oak leaves twined in his yellow hair. Tiny painted vines and leaves wound their way around his sinuous flesh, tracing the contours of toned muscle in his arms, legs, and torso. His face had been painted green, so his identity was unknown to all but a select few.

Across from him, sweating in fur as white as snow, was the Holly King, a crown of prickly green leaves and bright red berries upon his brow. Merlin, being the last man to hold the office of Sacred King, fulfilled this role. Just as each year light conquered darkness, so too would this newcomer have to defeat him in order to claim the favor of the Goddess and restore the balance of power in the heavens and on the earth.

As I stood at the edge of the circle, Aggrivane's arms protectively encircling me, I caught a whiff of roasting flesh from the stag sacrificed by the Druids, our food at the feast that would follow. I shivered, suddenly aware of the pungent reminder that although this battle was mock, it served a great significance in the cycle of life and death.

Argante stood in the circle between the two men, cloaked in silver from head to toe, the goddess of the stars who directed the wheel of time and decreed all things. She attentively watched the midday sky, waiting for the precise moment between day and night when all things hung in perfect balance.

Looking at her now, I could see no trace of the illness that had kept her confined to her hut the last several weeks. Worried that the ritual might further damage Argante's health, Viviane had asked to take her place, but Argante insisted on fulfilling the role that was her due as Lady of the Lake.

Soundlessly, she gave the signal and glided out of the circle. The two men began to shift, testing one another as in a real duel. As prescribed by the ancient ritual, each man was armed only with a staff made of the wood whose spirit he embodied. Neither was allowed to cross his half of the circle, for it represented the light and dark halves of the year, which twice annually stood in equilibrium but never overlapped.

The combatants poked at one another with their staffs until they reached the center of the circle. Then their branches crossed, crackling and popping as each tried to overtake the other. The sound brought back memories of a forgotten life—a time in my youth when the young boys and I would practice fencing with blunted wooden swords under my mother's direction.

They danced along the center line, bobbing and weaving to avoid each other's swings, while trying to find the weakness in the other, the opportunity to overpower. It did not take long for the stalwart Oak King to topple the lithe Holly King, though Merlin was a much better fighter than I had anticipated. He had a speed and skill belied by his size. Still, that was not of much consequence when he lay supine on the ground, the Oak King's foot resting lightly on his throat.

"The Holly King has died! The Oak King is reborn! The light ascends once again!"

The cry echoed through the isle as the victor helped Merlin to his feet. The time for ritual drama was at an end; the time for celebration had begun.

☙ ❧

In the valley at the foot of the Tor, hundreds of bonfires lit up the night, surrounded by circles of merry priestesses in pale blue ritual robes, Druids in white and royal blue, and nobles loyal to the ancient ways spanning every color in between. Fire was everywhere. It lit up the night and ignited the spirits of the revelers. A handful of men and women made their way through the crowd, twirling staffs with blazing tips, while some brave souls were rolling fire wheels down the hillside into the lake.

Everywhere drums echoed the heartbeat of the earth, whipping us into an ecstasy of wild abandon. Laughter and lively conversation mingled with smoke and the intoxicating scent of ritual herbs, a potion of joy carried on the warm night breeze. A makeshift musical troupe of harpists, pipers, drummers, and singers gathered to play traditional songs of the twelve ancient tribes. Some of the more intoxicated revelers were singing along, while the more sober conversed, told off-color stories, or continued the luck-bestowing tradition of jumping over the smoldering embers from the fire that had cooked the ritual meal.

In the center of the valley was the largest fire, built of the nine sacred woods. Around it, the Archdruid, the Lady of the Lake, Viviane, Morgan, and the Sacred King sat, breaking their ritual fast on the flesh of the fallen stag. The shadows in which he sat made it difficult for me to see the Sacred King clearly, but I could tell that he was now dressed in animal pelts and his face was painted with sacred markings.

While I was watching them, grateful to have claimed Aggrivane as my own but still a tiny bit jealous of Morgan, the drummers shifted to a lively tune. Aggrivane tossed off his cloak and grabbed my hand, easily whisking me to my feet. I laughed and stumbled as he pulled me toward the center of the festivities and we joined a train of dancers whirling between the bonfires. I lifted my skirts in my right hand and struggled to hold on to his with my left as we spun between the bonfires in a dizzying dance of freedom. Faces swirled past—Mona, Grainne, Rowena, Druids I had come to recognize but whose names I did not know—each one seemed more joyous than the last. Finally, the song came to an end, and Aggrivane scooped me up, breathless, in his arms.

"Look." He pointed at the main fire. "The Sacred Marriage is about to begin."

The drums ended on a sharp beat, and silence settled over the valley. The high note of a bell rang out, and the Virgin Queen was led forward by the Lady of the Lake. I would not have guessed it to be Morgan had I not already known. Her face was hidden from view by a gauzy white veil, but her hair flowed softly over her shoulders, blazing brighter than the bonfires, and upon her head rested a crown of spring flowers. A flowing white skirt concealed her thighs from view, but her breasts remained bare, revealing that each of her nipples and her navel had been adorned with paint in the shape of a small blue spiral. After a few instructive words from Argante, she stood barefoot before her consort.

She bestowed her blessing upon the Sacred King, anointing him with the blood of the stag and investing him with the sacred sword of Avalon, the first of the treasures to be returned to the outside world, according to the Goddess's decree. He, in turn, gave her the lingering kiss of knowing, which signaled the start of the most sacred part of the evening.

The couple was blocked from my sight as Merlin and Argante stood in front of them, conducting the rest of the ritual in secret. I could only guess that what was taking place was a magnified version of the ritual the spectators were about to perform in pairs. After the sacred couple was led off to the area reserved for their union, other pairs followed suit, fanning off to secluded groves, caves, and other private areas across the island.

Aggrivane led me by the hand down through the orchard along a winding path, his boots making soft indentations in the dirt in front of me. The apple blossoms breathed their perfume into the air as we passed. My heartbeat quickened with each step.

"Where are we going?" I asked.

Aggrivane chuckled but did not reply.

He led me to a small copse of dense oak trees. Their base formed a nearly perfect circle, roots intertwining deep in the ground beneath. A carpet of soft moss blanketed the base, nurtured by the shade of the branches above. Moonlight filtered down through the leaves, throwing glittering shadows before us.

The grove would have been breathtaking alone, but it had been decorated for the feast. Strings of white hawthorn blossoms hung from the lowest branches overhead, and a rainbow of wild-flower petals were strewn among the moss and ferns, making the grove appear much like a faerie queen's bridal bower.

"I found this place not long after we arrived to await the fire-drake," Aggrivane explained. "It has been my own personal para-dise. I had no way of knowing if you would say yes, but I wanted to make it special, just in case." He scratched the back of his neck nervously as he spoke.

"It is beautiful." I could say no more, emotion choking my voice. That he would do something so thoughtful reassured me that whatever passed between us tonight would be something much greater than lust incited by the festival.

Aggrivane cocked his head to the side as the tempo of the far-off drums shifted. They were softer now, but somehow more insis-tent. He removed his cloak and laid it on the ground before pulling me to him and cupping my cheek in his hand. I was suddenly para-lyzed with nerves, but as I gazed in to his eyes, I knew I was safe.

The thrum of ritual became like a dance as we moved ever closer, drawn in by the steady musical pounding and the pulsing of blood in our veins. His fingertips sent shivers up my spine as he ran them up the length of my body, from hips to shoulders, bringing the fabric of my dress along with them. I reached out a shaking hand to untie his belt and remove his clothing, aided by his more knowledgeable hands.

For a moment, we simply stood, marveling at the sight of one another. Then Aggrivane took a small step toward me, closing the gap between us. Gently, he brushed his lips against my skin in the sacred triune kiss, lightly touching the crescent on my brow, pausing to taste my lips, and trailing down to my heart.

I ran my fingers through his hair, every nerve begging him to remain there, to do what he willed. But mindful of my sovereignty, he looked up, wide eyes seeking permission to continue. I smiled softly and nodded, sending a private prayer to the Goddess to guide me as I trod unknown paths.

His lips closed on my breast, and I arched my back in unexpected pleasure, grateful for the circle of his arms around my hips to keep me upright. As if sensing my thoughts, Aggrivane slowly eased me to the ground, where his cloak waited to enfold me.

He eased himself down on top of me, slowly tracing his way down my body with a litany of kisses and delicate caresses, each one increasing my longing. As the heat of his skin seeped into mine, I lost all sense of space and time, until the boundaries between us melted away.

A quick stab of pain followed as the veil within me was rent and we became one with the heavens and the earth. He was the velvet black of midnight enfolding and embracing me. I was the silver moon that called the tides of our joining and lit up his darkness. Together, we feverishly fought against the coming dawn, only too aware it would tear us apart forever.

ᨆᢙ ᢙᨆ

Far too soon, the pale light of morning began to erase the night. We clung to each other, shivering, unwilling to do what must be done. The ecstasy of the festival had long since faded, and with it, the surety of divine expansiveness. I keenly felt the insignificance of my humanity, how small and helpless I was in the face of the cruel fate that befell all couples of the festival fires.

In the distance, the low moan of the Druids' horn broke the silence.

"They are calling me," Aggrivane whispered, lips grazing my cheek.

"Calling us to part." I said what he did not. Then I kissed him slowly, imparting my unspoken emotions in that single act.

The horn sounded a second time, and Aggrivane reluctantly pulled away.

"Do you see that?" He pointed toward the eastern sky, where a single star still glowed with the fierce brilliance of midnight. "That's the morning star, named by the Greeks for the goddess of love. When you see it, think of me and I will think of you."

"No." I shook my head, wondering how many other lovers were now making that same pledge. "That star is the herald of the dawn that now takes you from me. I don't wish to relive this pain, nor should you. I will think of you on the rising of its counterpart, the one that signals the coming darkness, for it was under that starry veil our love was conceived and consummated."

He held my hands between his and kissed them. "My love, most of the year they are one and the same star. Just as we cannot think of one another without remembering our parting, neither can they be separated. But as you will it, so shall it be. I will think of you when the stars emerge from their daylight retreat."

With one last kiss, he was gone and I was alone in my despair, certain this moment was the worst I would ever experience.

CHAPTER SEVEN

One full moon cycle later, I watched the light slowly drain from the sky as I traversed the seven rings of the Tor with the other women of Avalon. I clung to Aggrivane's parting words as though they would bring him back to me. I was supposed to be thinking of the ritual, but instead I sought out the night star, as I would every night until the end of time.

"Airanrhod, Branwen, Brigid, Rhiannon, Cerridwen, Great Mother," the priestesses uttered in rhythmic unison. The chant echoed off the terraced side of the Tor as we wound our way in and out of its turns, slowly ascending.

"Hear us," responded the acolytes.

The wood chips lining the path crackled underfoot as we passed. We moved like the tide, first closer and then farther away from our destination, which was the summit of the Tor, the center of the labyrinth. Unlike a maze, it had no dead ends or trickery— only a beginning and an end. The complex journey of ascent that began our ritual was meant to free our minds of all care and focus our spirits. When we descended at the close, it would slowly release us from our spiritual state and bring us back to the world.

I pushed all thoughts of Aggrivane from my mind and concentrated on my breathing. Regardless of my mood or mindset when I entered the gate, I always found peace along the way. This walking meditation had been one of the few ways I had found solace during my early days in Avalon. To this day, I marveled at how symbolic the pattern was. As in life, the farther I seemed from the goal, the closer I was, and when I thought it lie just around the next bend, I was at the opposite point.

"Airanrhod, Branwen, Brigid, Rhiannon, Cerridwen, Great Mother," we called.

"Hear us," the younger ones replied.

"Airanrhod, Branwen, Brigid, Rhiannon, Cerridwen, Great Mother."

"Hear us."

I gradually fell under the spell of the chant and lost the ability to distinguish my own voice from the rest. Around me, the rosemary, lavender, and night-blooming flowers that clung precariously to the side of the Tor's rings exhaled their fragrance, coaxed by a gentle nudge from the hem of our gowns. Above, the rotund Honey Moon ruled the clear night sky, sparkling stars surrounding it like dutiful courtiers.

I was so absorbed in the procession that I scarcely noticed when we reached the top.

Across the circle, Morgan's copper hair reflected the silver moonlight with an odd luminosity. By now it was clear she was not with child as was hoped. Still, Argante said the Sacred

Marriage was not a failure; she insisted the Goddess had a greater purpose in mind.

Four of the women raised their arms to honor the elements, then Viviane recited the sacred prayer to the Goddess of the moon. As her last words died out, the wind stirred, fanning the flames of the ritual fire toward the heavens. Argante gave the signal. It was time for the invocation.

Viviane stepped forward and assumed the position at the center of the circle normally occupied by Argante. This was the first time in anyone's memory that Argante had not acted as the mouthpiece of the Goddess. It was not a good a sign. Argante's lingering illness—the one that had taken hold before Beltane— had progressed to the point that she had been carried up the Tor on a litter. She was far too weak to withstand such powerful forces, so Viviane performed the ritual in her stead.

Viviane faced the moon. Morgan and I moved to flank each of her sides, serving as attendants to her every need. Viviane raised her arms, closed her eyes, and the air around her grew perfectly still, as if time had stopped. An ancient chant passed her lips in a language of time immemorial, and her head tilted back as her body received the spirit of the Goddess. Morgan and I braced both of her shoulders, but Viviane shrugged away our hands, indicating she needed no assistance. Slowly, she opened her eyes and turned, regarding each priestess with distant eyes.

"Great Mother, may your wisdom forever guide us." Argante leaned heavily on her cane as she posed the first of the ritual questions to the Goddess. "What say you of this land?"

"*The red dragon is poised to return to the realm of spirit, but another shall succeed him. The hallowed one has received the blessing of the land, and so shall it prosper under his guidance. Although malevolent forces threaten from without, the bear shall be victorious and all shall bow at the sound of his name."* The voice that issued from Viviane's mouth was not her own, but one like liquid silver.

Argante seemed unfazed by the strange reply. "Thank you, Mother." She continued on in the traditional way. "May your goodness be forever praised. What say you of this sacred place?"

"Soon the final passage shall be crossed by one of great power, allowing the lily to emerge from shadow and bloom in the light. An unlikely rose is transplanted to this isle and blossoms in its rich soil. But beware the rose and handle her carefully, for her thorns threaten to pierce the bud of the lily, thus causing the whole garden to die."

A murmur rippled around the circle, but Argante paid no heed.

"We thank you for your wisdom. May your protection be forever on us. What say you of these, your servants?"

"These here gathered serve me well, and I am pleased. But the day will come when sister shall oppose sister, both in this sacred place and without. Loyalties will be tested and betrayed, so heed my warning. That which is birthed in jealousy shall not give life but infect all who draw near. Therefore, act with love and not out of spite. Only then shall you escape the fate the stars foretell."

Silence followed. Around the circle, my confusion was mirrored in all but a few faces. Argante, however, seemed to have comprehended the Goddess's enigmatic words fully, for she leaned against her cane, nodding as if in agreement with what she heard, eyes shining with newly formed tears. Morgan too appeared to have gleaned some knowledge from the prophecy, for she once again bore that sly, cat-like expression that made me suspect she knew more than she let on.

We bid the Goddess farewell and Morgan led Viviane aside to recover from the strain. I was called forward to gaze in the well of seeing. Every month, a different priestess took her turn scrying in a cauldron filled with water from the confluence of the sacred springs. Sometimes her visions elaborated on the prophecy given by the Goddess. Other times they yielded a message that pertained to one or more of the priestesses present, while sometimes nothing was seen at all.

I stood over the cauldron, gazing at my own reflection and breathing deeply, trying to calm myself enough to open my perception. As I leaned forward and exhaled, my breath ruffled the surface of the water, shattering the mirror image before me. A mass of colors swirled in the water, and I sent my consciousness downward through them, into the depths of the dark. I breathed out once again and my hair fell forward, separating the watery oracle from the rest of the world around me. Slowly, my spirit rose up and escaped my body. Smoke-like tendrils of gray mist began to dance on the surface of the water. Then the visions came.

At first, all I could see were shapes, but then I became aware of enough details to know what I was seeing. It was Northgallis. I recognized my father's sign—an eagle with a thistle blossom clutched in its talons—flying high above the watch towers. The sight of the familiar walls made my heart soar, but that joy was short-lived. My father came into view first, unkempt and unshaven, tears etching canyons in his cheeks. On his shuffling heels followed a tall blond man whose ritual robes marked him a Christian priest. My lady's maid, Octavia, trailed behind, scarcely able to stand, so great was her grief.

Bringing up the rear was an honor guard transporting a bier.

The body was shrouded and covered in a black cloth, but I recognized the symbol embroidered on it immediately. It was a knot work horse, the symbol of my mother's clan. Beside the bier, a young man carried a small box draped in matching cloth but bearing my father's standard. It was a baby's coffin; this woman had died in childbirth. Somewhere in the recesses of my heart, I knew who she was, but my mind could not bear to admit it.

The vision splintered to pieces as stabbing shards of light filled my eyes. From somewhere far away, a banshee's high-pitched wail shattered the night. It was only moments later, as my hand struck the cauldron and sent it tumbling to the ground, that I realized I had been the one screaming.

My knees could no longer support me, and my mind threatened to collapse as well. I sank to the ground, heedless of the steaming waters that soaked my skirts. A merciless claw squeezed my heart so hard I thought I would die. I struggled to breathe but could not take in air. Cold, stiff fingers like those of the Death Mother herself pawed at my arms, trying to help me to my feet.

"Guinevere, what is it? What have you seen?" The voices echoed from a great distance.

I swallowed, fighting back the blackness that threatened to engulf me. "My mother—she is dead."

PART TWO

World Beyond the Mist

CHAPTER EIGHT

*A*fter seventeen miserable days tracing old Roman roads north from Avalon with Morgan and a handful of guards, this was not the homecoming I had envisioned. I expected to be greeted warmly at the gates by my family and long-estranged friends, but there was nary a soul present to welcome us home, not even a wandering dog.

Our guards shouted out our arrival. A moment later, the entry doors opened and we were ushered quickly inside the gates with only the merest of polite greetings, as if those inside feared to speak with us. While the others hurried quickly indoors, I lingered in the doorway, drawing comfort from the feeling of protection the thick walls of the fortress gave me.

"My Lady, do come inside."

My thoughts were interrupted by the nasal Midland accent of a blond serving girl who had mysteriously appeared by my side. She tugged on my arm with outrageous familiarity not befitting a woman of her rank. I thought to chastise her for it, but she quickly whisked me away before I could speak.

The fire popped and crackled in the hearth as we stood in the foyer, anxiously awaiting some acknowledgement of our presence. Morgan and I avoided eye contact, still refusing to speak to one another, clinging to the grudge that had begun to fester on Beltane and had only grown worse with time. I still harbored a pit of jealousy over her selection as the Virgin Queen. She had grown secretive and developed a bitter edge in the aftermath of the ritual—I guessed because she had not fulfilled her duty by conceiving a child—using her long-practiced hatred of me as an outlet, never letting me forget she had been chosen and I swept aside. We were only together now because she was ordered to accompany me. I could not wait to bid her farewell.

Time passed slowly, and I began to wonder if my father was even in residence at the moment; perhaps that was why we were so coldly welcomed. Finally, the maid reappeared in the doorway and announced the master of the house was otherwise engaged, but we were all to bathe and rest; my father would entertain our company at dinner.

It was strange that my father would not come to welcome me himself, but it had been many years since I was a resident of this house. Schedules and decorum could change in far less time.

Though I needed no assistance finding my way up to my old chamber, the maid insisted on accompanying me. I planned to return to Avalon after our mourning period, but Argante had insisted I bring a small bag with me. Without thinking, I began to unpack what remained of my life on the isle: a few sundry mementos and the two blue robes I was given to wear when performing my duties as a priestess at births, funerals, and other sacred events.

"Please, my Lady, allow me."

The squeaky, small voice of the maid pulled me out of my memories. For a moment I simply looked back at her, uncomprehending. Then I realized I had grown so accustomed to doing things for myself in Avalon, I forgot the same actions were unthinkable in this world.

Unsure of how to comport myself, I busied myself by admiring the tapestry hanging on the wall above my bed. The hanging depicted a beautiful young maiden befriending a unicorn as a host of faeries and other nature spirits looked on. It was a scene from one of my favorite childhood stories—a tale my mother recounted on many dark winter nights in front of the fire. She and I had just begun constructing the tapestry shortly before the Irish raid and the whirlwind that whisked me away to Avalon. It pleased me to see she had completed it in my absence. I could only wonder if each stitch gave her comfort in knowing she had set her daughter on the path the Goddess intended, or if each dip of the needle pricked at her heart, tormenting her conscience over sending her young daughter so far away.

Alas I would never know; she was not here to ask.

I wiped a tear from my cheek and, without a word to the maid, fled from the room on silent feet, seeking sanctuary, somewhere familiar to get my bearings. Rushes, stone, and dirt passed as a blur beneath my toes, and when I next raised my head, I found myself in the armory.

It was strangely quiet, so I knew I was alone. But if I stopped and listened, I could hear the soldiers practicing not far away.

Their grunts and clamor carried on the wind. For a moment, I even fooled myself into believing my mother's authoritative voice commanded and corrected them, but when I really attuned my ears, I found that Rhys, captain of my father's guard, had taken her place as drill master.

Little had changed in this land of iron, bronze, and leather. Gear for each man was still neatly stacked on shelves against one wall, ready at all times for battle, while scores of javelins, swords, daggers, polished bronze-and-wooden shields, and other weaponry lined the racks. I inhaled, savoring the unique bouquet only the close quarters of an armory could produce—the heavy scent of tanned hides, stale sweat, the sharp tang of polish, and just a little wood smoke from the temporarily silent forge. Strange as it may have seemed, this was the scent of home.

Of course my feet would lead me here; it had been my favorite place as a child. Before I was old enough to walk, my mother carried me as she inspected the equipment. I was fascinated by the glimmer of sunlight on the metal objects that surrounded me, entranced as though in a crystal cave. Later, once I could feed myself, she gave me a tiny blunted dagger, which eventually gave way to a wooden sword when my lessons began. Then finally, only two years before I went to Avalon, she bestowed on me my first real sword, a miniature version of her own. I could still picture the intricately crafted pommel and feel the twists of braided metal in my clenched fist.

I sought out my sword now, as eager for its reassuring touch as a babe for her favorite blanket. In the far corner, the tall chest containing my father's arms and armor stood slightly ajar. But its twin, which had held my mother's fighting paraphernalia, had been removed, as had the small trunk that housed my sword and childhood armor. Dismayed, I picked through my father's things, hoping he had decided to store it all in one case, but I found only his belongings.

Glancing wildly about me, I began searching for the treasure I could not believe was gone. But then I caught my reflection in one of the polished brass shields that hung on the wall and froze. I was not alone after all. Standing behind me to my left was a dark-haired woman. For a moment I thought it the shade of my mother, but when the figure advanced on me, it proved to be very human. Turning slowly, I tried to ignore the cold sweat blanketing the back of my neck at being caught where I ought not be.

"Octavia!" I exclaimed in a sigh of relief. My lady's maid would give me up to no harm. I ran to her side and enveloped her in my arms, suddenly feeling so weak and weary that I had to draw my strength from her.

"Blessed child, you have returned to us." Octavia smiled at me warmly, though her face still betrayed the sorrow in her heart. "Come, let us go outside. This is no place for a reunion."

She led me into the sunlit courtyard, and we stood watching the warriors spar while she insisted on hearing every last detail of my time in Avalon. While I was happy to oblige her with tale after tale, somewhere in the back of my mind I knew we were both simply delaying an inevitable conversation. Finally, in a moment of silence, I could take no more.

"Oh, Octavia," I cried, a surge of hot tears racing down my face. "I wish Mother were here so she could know all that has happened to me." I clung to the older woman's shoulders, surprised at the force of my own emotion. Burying my face in her long black ringlets, I choked on my tears.

"I know. So do I." She placed her hands on my shoulders and tipped up my face to meet her eyes. "But one thing is for certain, she hears you now, and she is very proud of you."

"Do you think so?"

"I know so." She kissed me on the forehead.

I smiled weakly. "Octavia." I licked my suddenly dry lips. "I have to know. The baby—was it my brother or my sister?"

"It was a boy." She hesitated a moment. "That is why your father was so upset. It was the heir to the kingdom he had been praying for. Now it will likely pass to your cousin Bran."

I thought I was the heir to his kingdom. I frowned. I would bring this up with my father when I next saw him.

Octavia saw my puzzled expression and attempted to explain. "Your father has placed a greater emphasis on his Roman heritage, of late. Despite all of the pregnancies your mother lost and babes who died young, your father had always hoped for a son to pass his kingdom on to, so that it would not fall into another lord's—your future husband's—hands upon his death."

I started to protest.

Octavia waved away my rebuttal. "I know your mother intended you to inherit, but Northgallis is a long way from the traditions she endorsed, so your father had a valid concern. Then with the death of the boy child and of your mother, all of his dreams fell apart. You were so far away. He felt he had nothing."

"Nothing?" Anger flared within me, heating my cheeks and quickly drying my tears to an invisible crust. "Is that what I am? Is that why my mother's arms are gone, so that not a memory of her remains? And what of my sword? Have I no say in the placement of my own possessions?"

Octavia clasped my hands in hers and regarded me gravely. "Your mother's sword is buried with her, as is her right of honor. As for yours. . ." She hesitated. "Your father melted it down. He wishes no more training of the kind for you."

I gaped and attempted to interrupt, but Octavia held up a hand to silence me.

"Guinevere, your father is not the same man you left here all those years ago. He has changed so much. Many things, many traditions died with your mother. You must realize that. Take what I have told you into consideration when you see your father, and do not be too hard on him. Have pity on him instead."

The weight of her words lay on my shoulders like chain mail. I could not respond. I had hoped to return to a place of warmth and love, but instead found myself in a house full of perplexing strangers.

Could four years really change so much?

༄ ༄

Late that night, when the candles burned low and all the servants had gone to bed, I padded barefoot along the corridors, searching for my father. He had not shown up to dinner, so Octavia, Morgan, and I ate our meal in awkward silence amid the gaping stares of a handful of servants I did not know. They were obviously curious about me, and more so about Morgan—especially given the tension that sparked the air between us—but fortunately knew their place well enough not to ask questions.

Later, as I lay my head on the pillow, willing the racing questions in my mind to cease, I finally accepted sleep would not come until I saw my father again. He was not in his room and his attendant was fast asleep, so I set out to find him, stealing through halls that seemed much smaller than my childhood memories would have me believe.

The kitchen was abandoned, as was the great hall, so I began to trace the corridors, peeking into unlocked storage areas and long-abandoned living quarters. With every beat of my heart, my conviction grew. I had to see my father, to know that he still cared for me, despite his recent change in attitude. He was my last living link to my mother, and I his. As the thought skittered across my mind, I began to wonder if that was why he had yet to greet me; maybe I reminded him too much of her.

I slowed as I neared a room near the end of the hall on the uppermost floor. The soft flicker of candlelight spilled out through a door slightly ajar. It took me a moment to orient myself and then my heart stopped as I realized where I was. This was my mother's chamber.

I leaned against the wall and closed my eyes, steeling myself with a few deep breaths. Splinters pricked my fingertips as I clawed at the wall and squeezed my eyes tight, fighting back memories of all the times I played in my mother's wardrobe or sat on her footstool while she braided or brushed my hair. She had nursed me in that room through many ailments, insisting I would rest easier sleeping in her bed, with her warmth to soothe me. A shiver shimmied down my spine. She died in that bed. It was only natural my father would be there.

I pressed my lips together and tiptoed over to the door. I

could barely make out my father's silhouette in the pale light of the single candle burning on the windowsill like a beacon, silently calling my mother's soul back to the place she so loved. I took another deep breath. I had thought myself prepared to face my father and all our missing years, but I was not ready to face my mother's ghost as well.

I took a tentative step into the room, knowing my father would soon be able to see me out of the corner of his eye. "Father," I called softly as I approached, not wanting him to mistake me for a specter.

He lifted his head and looked at me, at first unseeing as though I had roused him from a waking dream. Then slowly, comprehension dawned and he smiled, brushing away the tears staining his cheeks. "Guinevere," he breathed. "Daughter, my heart warms to see you."

I raced over to him and hugged him tightly, alarmed to feel fragile bone rather than the hard muscle of the warrior king I remembered. After a moment, he released me, holding me at arm's length and squinting to consider me in the dim light.

"You are not a little child anymore." He sighed.

I reached for a blanket draped over the edge of the bed and wrapped it around my shoulders. "That is true, but even grown women have need of their fathers," I said, climbing up into his lap just like I did as a little girl.

He wrapped his arms around me, as if he feared I would disappear like the smoke rising from the candle wick. I closed my eyes and laid my head on the crook of his neck. His hair, now turning gray, still smelled of the same imported citrus oil that punctuated my youngest memories.

"You look just like her, you know," he said in a small, soft voice. He paused thoughtfully before adding, "I miss her."

"So do I," I answered, tears streaming freely now.

In the silence, I could almost forget the years that had passed, that I was now fifteen and we were grieving the death of someone so dear. I could almost make myself believe I was still the little girl who had climbed into his arms after a terrible nightmare. And in some ways, I was, for this was the worst nightmare either of us could imagine.

"Please don't leave me," my father whispered in an unfamiliar tone of grief. He had always been so confident, so strong, but now he was broken, pleading. "Don't go back to Avalon. I... I need you here."

I pursed my lips, realizing he was right. Unfamiliar as it first seemed, this was my home. "I will stay. You will need someone to keep the servants in line."

He laughed, the first joyful sound I had heard since coming home.

୭୧ ୬ଵ

The following morning, I discovered Morgan had an ulterior motive for making the long journey to Northgallis. Not only was she seeing me safely returned to my family's care in Viviane's stead, but she was also under the Lady's orders to accompany another of our household to her new life in Avalon. Octavia's youngest, Nimue, a small plump girl who had inherited her mother's thick mass of dark hair and her father's haunting green eyes, was expressly requested to return to Avalon as its newest acolyte.

As Octavia and I watched them depart, memories of how quickly I bonded with Viviane came rushing back. If Nimue adored Morgan and clung to her as a mother figure like I had to Viviane, Nimue had little chance of emerging from her period of study with her innocent soul intact. Poor girl. I prayed for her sake she would take to some of the more kind-hearted priestesses like Grainne or Rowena instead. But I dared not voice this to Octavia. She was fretting enough for both of us.

"Nimue is too young. I should not have let them take her yet," Octavia berated herself as she led me down a path over a gently sloping hill to the grove where my mother was buried. "A few more years and she would have been the same age as you were. She would have been old enough, prepared enough to survive this. First I sent Peredur off to be fostered. Now Nimue is gone too. Although I fear I had little choice. Not only did the Lady of the Lake request her presence, I could not very well let her grow up here. Your father would have sent her to a convent before the spring anyway."

I stopped cold at her statement. "What did you say?"

She turned around at the sound of my voice, her pained expression making it obvious she knew she had transgressed. "Guinevere, I have told you your father is a changed man. It is time you knew the full extent."

She led me into the grove of yew trees and sat me down on the soft grass before venturing into further explanation. "Your mother meant so much to Leodgrance that her death nearly drove him insane. For days he would neither eat nor sleep, only sit in her room and weep, uttering only a single word—why?—when visitors came to tend to him. For three days, he refused to allow her to be buried, insisting that she was not really dead. Then the fourth morning, he unexpectedly joined us at the breakfast table and announced she should be buried according to the rites and customs of her people. And so, she was laid to rest here."

Octavia pointed toward the western end of the grove, where a large stone tablet protruded from the bare earth, which was stained red by ochre, a smattering of white quartz stones scattered at its base. The stones and pigment were talismans of the dead to my mother's people, meant to ease the soul's journey to the spirit world.

Slowly, painfully, fearfully, I made my way over to the burial site. Although my mother's burial was performed according to her native traditions, the tombstone that marked her grave was set up by my father in the traditional Roman fashion of his ancestors. It bore the carved image of a slender, long-haired warrior woman in native dress, surrounded by thistles, her eyes cast to the heavens. I ran my hand over the rough surface of the stone, tracing the grooves as if doing so could bring her back again. Beneath the image was an inscription, which began—as all other Roman memorials did—with the words "*Dis Manibus,*" addressing the gods of the shades. It continued, "*Corinna of the Votadini, wife of the king of Gwynedd, daughter of King Cunedda.*" The memorial ended with the traditional Roman attribution naming the deceased's patron. "*Her husband Leodgrance set this up in her memory.*"

I could no longer deny it. My mother really was dead. It was written in stone in front of me for the entire kingdom to see. The world around me faded in a blur of tears, and I dissolved in grief. Eventually Octavia's arm encircled me, her warmth breathing life back into my frigid bones. I looked up, my eyes now parched from so much crying, never more grateful for this woman who, although officially a servant in my father's employ, was also at once my confidant and dearest friend, more like family than many of my blood relations.

Octavia turned toward the fortress, shielding her eyes from the amber rays of the setting sun. "We must return home soon, Guinevere, but I have not yet finished what I wanted to say. I brought you here not only because you needed to come, but so you might better understand your father. You can see in this stone the love he possessed for your mother. After her burial, he was lost like a sailor without a star to guide him. He returned to his habit of sitting in her chamber. He spoke often of the dream that had prompted him to let her body go, though he would reveal its details to no one. We all knew he was still holding on to Corinna in spirit and feared what damage this would do to him. As he would speak to no one else, and your party from Avalon had not yet departed the isle, the local Christian priest was sent for in the hope that perhaps Leodgrance would speak to him."

I bristled at the word *Christian*. I felt no enmity toward them as a group. In fact, they shared the Tor with us, also considering it sacred but for very different reasons. They believed Joseph of Arimathea, a follower of Jesus, settled there after Jesus's crucifixion and brought with him magical relics of their savior. Today, they lived in crude huts of woven branches on the edges of the marsh, just beyond where the mists gave way to the outside world. But I had heard enough tales to know that not all Christians lived such humble, holy lives. Many considered the religion of Avalon in direct opposition to Christianity and, like the Romans before them, sought to destroy it. That fear was what made the hairs on my neck and arms stand at attention every time I heard the word.

Octavia noticed my reaction and patted my hand. "We did what we thought was best." She sighed. "As it turned out, our good intentions only made things worse. The young priest, Father Marius, who came to our door did get your father to return somewhat to normal, but he also convinced him that his dream was a sign your father should give up the religion of his ancestors and embrace this new god, this Christ. Your father was so taken with this priest and his promises of an eternal life that he willingly agreed, intent on dragging the rest of us along with him."

She pulled me to my feet, continuing her story as we ambled back to the hall, where we would soon be expected for the evening meal. "Of course, I would not go along with this outrageous notion, and I told him so. He was not pleased and threatened not only my position in his house but the future of my child as well, decreeing she would be reared in a Christian convent as soon as arrangements could be made. It was then I determined that my little rose would be transplanted to Avalon when you returned. Anything would be better for her than being raised in this household, such as it is now."

Octavia's words tore at my heart as surely as if she had stabbed me. Not only had I lost my mother, but my father, despite his love for me, had become a stranger as well, and I now faced a life in a home that did not recognize the religion I was vowed to serve. As we returned through the yawning castle gates, for the first time, I feared my future life at Northgallis.

CHAPTER NINE

Autumn 495

Every evening, my father, Octavia, and I ate dinner at dusk in the great hall, quietly discussing our day and any news that filtered in from the village or countryside. After the trenchers were cleared, we passed the hours of early evening by sewing, writing letters, playing games, or telling stories—catching up on the lost years I was away in Avalon. I treaded carefully, still unsure of my position in this new world, but all went well. It was a quiet life, but one doing much good to heal our wounded hearts.

However, this mid-autumn evening was anything but routine; for the first time since my mother's death, we were having guests at dinner.

The household was abuzz with activity, preparing for the arrival of Lord Evrain, ruler of the kingdom of Powys, which bordered my father's lands. Though Evrain possessed only moderate power in the overall hierarchy of the country, maintaining a pleasant relationship with him was of utmost importance because of the location of his lands. Should he ever turn against my father, the proximity of his kingdom would give any enemy perfect staging grounds for an invasion of our less-fortified eastern border. This being so, I was admonished to be on my best behavior.

Even though Lord Evrain was considerably late in arriving, I was still rushing to tuck my hair beneath the cream-colored veil my father had insisted I wear low over my forehead. Apparently the visiting lord was a very religious Christian, so the sight of my sacred crescent would not make for a very good first impression. I was dismayed by having to conceal something I had worked so hard to attain and was so proud of; in my mind, the mark was a part of me, but I had no choice.

Voices carried in from the courtyard below, muffled greetings of peace. Evrain and his men were finally here.

"Guinevere, make haste!" Octavia hissed.

I turned to face her, and she scowled, pulling at the veil until it brushed my eyebrows.

"Be certain you do not let it slip," she warned. "Your father is in a foul temper as it is."

Octavia escorted me firmly by the arm as we descended the staircase into the great hall, falling into her proper place behind me only when we came within sight of Lord Evrain and his small cluster of attendants. I took a deep breath and wiped my clammy, trembling hands on the sides of my gown. Having been away in Avalon for so long, I had forgotten the rules of courtly life. *Dear Goddess, please let me make my father proud.*

I stepped forward out of the shadows, careful to stay a distance behind my father. Once the men had been formally introduced to one another, my father gracefully slid his arm behind me and gently nudged me forward.

"Lord Evrain, this is my only child, the Lady Guinevere."

I curtsied low before the silver-haired man, not daring to meet his eyes.

"Indeed, she is a beauty," he said to my father as he reached to take my hand and assist me to rise. "Lady Guinevere, I am most honored to meet you."

He had addressed me, so now I could raise my eyes. "In truth, sir, the honor is mine."

Lord Evrain released my hand and gestured to the young man on his right. "Allow me to present to you my son Fergus. He is my youngest and the only of my sons yet to take a wife."

Evrain glanced purposefully at my father as his son stiffly stepped forward. He was thin and tall, his arms and legs far more than his still-growing body could manage.

He is barely more than a boy.

Fergus roughly clasped my hand in his puppy-like paw. "I am grateful to be a guest in your home," he croaked in the uneven voice of one not still a boy but not yet a man. He shot an uncertain look at his father, who nodded in encouragement. Fergus swallowed before continuing. "And I feel most privileged to present this token to you," he stammered, fumbling to untie a pouch from his belt. "It pales in comparison to your beauty."

Out of the corner of my eye, I saw Fergus's father smile delightedly.

Oh no. This is more than a gift. Evrain is trying to make a match.

I fought to hide my fear and disgust behind a smile of surprise as Fergus removed a delicate golden chain from a small velvet bag.

I tried to catch Octavia's eye but found my father's warning stare instead. I quickly returned my gaze to the man-boy in front of me. As he struggled to fasten the golden rope around my wrist with his bulky fingers, the rubies suspended from the chain caught the torchlight, reflecting dully on the ashen surface of his face.

When the bracelet hung securely from my wrist, I clasped Fergus's hands in mine, as was expected of me. "My Lord, I am most flattered." My smile tightened to cover my true emotions as I looked into his lifeless, nervous eyes. "Your gift is truly a treasure, one that I will cherish for years to come. I only hope I will be judged as valuable to you as the gift you have given me."

Lord Evrain clapped his hands together, pleased by the exchange. "Hurrah! Now that the introductions are done, shall we sup?" He took my father by the arm and started toward the long table in the center of the room.

From somewhere behind Evrain's rust-colored cape, a man cleared his throat. Lord Evrain turned. His annoyed scowl was artfully replaced with an apologetic smile as he gestured toward a young man previously hidden in the throng of attendants.

"It appears I have forgotten someone after all," Evrain said.

The man glided forward when he was introduced, but I did not need to hear his name to know who he was. Before me stood Aggrivane of Lothian, my lover from the Beltane fires. When his dark eyes met mine, they registered the briefest moment of shock, which faded into joyful recognition coupled with a slight upturn of his lips before he could discipline his features and pretend to be introduced as a stranger.

Evrain seemed a bit embarrassed by his guest, explaining away Aggrivane's presence as an act of charity to a fellow king.

"He is the son of an inconsequential barbarian who wears a crown only by right of inheritance. He is a guest in my court, studying how to govern. Pay him no mind; he is here to learn, not to socialize." Evrain turned to me and added, "Until he wins or inherits land, he is more a servant than a noble. He is certainly not fit to be in the company of such a gracious lady."

Was I supposed to take that as a compliment? It seemed more of a veiled warning.

৩৫৫ ৩৫৫

By the time the main course was served, I was beginning to wonder if it was possible to die of boredom. My father and Lord Evrain disagreed over everything and especially seemed to enjoy arguing over the most trivial matters. I tried to force myself to pay attention to their discussion, but I kept finding every excuse possible to steal a glance in Aggrivane's direction. Judging from the way he tightened his jaw and kept his body angled away from me, he was doing everything he could to pretend to be uninterested in me, but every so often his resolve weakened and he fleetingly returned my gaze.

Perhaps it was our time apart or pure imagination on my part, but Aggrivane seemed to have grown more handsome since the last time I saw him. Everything about him made my body twinge: the way the light reflected off his glossy hair, the gleam in his dark eyes, the way his whole face lit up when he laughed. Nothing would have pleased me more than to spend the entire evening admiring him and indulging in secret memories of our night together. But I was brought back quickly to the present by a sharp pinch on my thigh. I scowled at Octavia, my lust-addled mind not yet comprehending the reason for her action.

"Guinevere," she hissed quietly, amid the din of servants changing courses and the clattering of dishes. "You'd best get control of yourself, or your father will have your hide."

"But, Octavia, he is—"

"I remember his name from your stories. I know full well who he is. But Lord Evrain does not, and it is in your best interest to keep it that way. Aggrivane is to be of no consequence to you. Do you understand?"

I nodded dumbly.

Instead of enjoying a reunion with the man I loved, I had been sentenced to the company of Lord Evrain's socially inept son. I had been attempting all night to engage the boy in some type of conversation, but he seemed just as afraid of me as he was of his father. Every time I asked him a question, he gave me the simplest possible answer and then returned to staring at his plate or at the floor. "The weather is quite fine, yes" or "I do agree that the meat is cooked perfectly." I could get no opinion or interest out of him whatsoever.

Desperate for some relief from the tedium, I tried one last topic. "How do you find living with your new guest? Do you dislike Lord Aggrivane as much as your father?"

Fergus's eyes widened, and he put down his knife. "Oh no, I like him very much. He is so kind to me."

Thrilled I had finally found a subject that interested him, I was eager to keep him talking. "How so?"

"He is the only one willing to listen to me, to teach me what he knows. I hope to be as smart and skilled as he one day. He is the best storyteller. You should hear him recite the great triads. His words are magic."

As Fergus prattled on about Aggrivane, I couldn't help but let my gaze wander in his direction. I was rewarded by a jab in the ribs from my serving maid that brought my attention back to our enamored guest, but only temporarily. I had a feeling by the end of the night, my entire side would be black and blue from Octavia's admonitions.

◦෨෬ ෨෬◦

Throughout the insufferably lengthy meal, the two lords talked mostly of things long past or those that I cared not for, but late in the evening, the subject changed to politics and I began to take notice of the conversation.

"The villagers are bursting with gossip about Uther's successor," my father noted, cutting another slice of meat as he spoke. "They say he is little more than a boy. What do you know of him, Lord Evrain? Can he be trusted to lead the country?"

Curious now, I looked up from my plate, intent on stealing yet another fleeting glance at Aggrivane. Instead of meeting his twinkling gaze, my eyes were drawn to Lord Evrain, who, now deep in his drink, was gesturing wildly as if to match his booming tone.

"So you have heard of our young king-to-be, have you? He is quite a lad," Evrain bragged as if speaking about his own son. "He is Lord Ector's son, or was," he corrected himself.

"What do you mean?" my father questioned with a wrinkle in his brow. "Has something happened to Ector?"

"Bless him, no. Oh, it is quite a tale. How is it that you have not heard? Does news not travel past the Cambrian Mountains? Surely you must know."

If the twitch of muscle in his jaw was any indication, my father was beginning to get annoyed with his drunken guest. "I assure you, my lord, we do not. Would you be so kind as to recall the events to us?"

Evrain beamed. That was just the invitation he had been waiting for.

"Father," Fergus interrupted as all eyes turned to him, shocked at the intrusion from the quiet boy. "Should not Aggrivane tell the tale? He *is* as a bard under your command." Fergus flushed visibly, squirming under his father's blazing stare. To me, he added in an aside, "He tells it so magnificently."

"Be quiet, boy," Evrain roared, gesturing violently toward his son and sloshing wine onto the table in the process.

My father grimaced. "Perhaps your son has a good idea. We have heard little from your guest this evening. It would be refreshing to hear him speak."

Evrain's eyes bulged with disbelief and anger. "He is not here to speak or to entertain. He is here to observe and to serve. I will hear of no such thing." Evrain set his jaw resolutely, as if to say there would be no budging him from that position.

Before I could cast a sidelong glance her way, Octavia had already risen and taken hold of a pitcher of wine. She sauntered over to Evrain's side and bent down to his level.

"My good lord, surely you will allow the boy to tell one simple tale." She batted her eyes flirtatiously as the liquid flowed into his cup. "What harm can it do? If he is truly as in need of learning as you say, his speech can only magnify the splendor of your own.

Besides"—she bent lower, giving everyone at the table an unob-structed view of her cleavage—"it will give you a chance to relax. All this discussion of politics must have made you weary." She ran her free hand across his shoulders, rubbing them gently.

Evrain was clearly entranced by Octavia's charms, openly ogling her. He patted her hand but then quickly recovered him-self. "I do not normally take advice from servants." He gave her a scathing, yet passionate look. "But perhaps you are right. Go ahead, Aggrivane. Tell us all of the boy who would be king." He turned to face Aggrivane, regarding him coldly, letting him know he already expected him to fail. "It is, in a way, your story to tell, after all."

For a moment, Evrain's words perplexed me. But then I remembered something Aggrivane had told me during one of our nights together in Avalon. His father was Uther's chosen succes-sor. If Uther had changed his mind at the last moment, Aggrivane would be telling the tale of his own family's undoing—how he went from being third in line to the throne of the high king to having his name struck from the possible line of succession. Of course, Evrain would use this opportunity to humiliate him. It took all of my willpower not to shoot Evrain a disgusted look.

Unfazed, Aggrivane sat up straight in his seat and cleared his throat, his eyes passing briefly over me, just long enough to let me to know he hadn't forgotten me. "The account you are about to hear comes straight from a knight who guarded King Uther and fought alongside our new king," he said, by way of preface.

Then he cocked his head slightly, as though he was listening to music only he could hear—a gesture not uncommon among bards settling into their roles—and began to weave his tale.

"It was nearing sunset in a valley near the fort of Tremontum in the wild lands of the country to the north." Aggrivane inclined his head toward me ever so slightly in acknowledgement of my lineage. "The sky was ablaze in all the colors of the dying day. The reds and oranges of evening were at war with the blue and pale yellow of day. Down on the ground, however, things were not so lively. The battle between Uther's troops and the merciless Saxons was at an impasse; both sides had retreated to camp, and it looked as if they would have to call a halt for the night and risk the possibility of defending against a sneak attack under the cover of darkness.

"The men were tired, and many were wounded. Morale was flagging under the strain of many days of fighting. Alarm spread quickly through the ranks as Uther threw down his sword in a fit of rage and retired to his tent. Most other nights he stood vigil with Merlin and his advisors, planning the next day's battle by the light of the moon. But not this night.

"The moon rose and traveled through the heavens, spreading her pale light across the camps of invader and native alike. Still there was no word from the king, no nightly orders of who was to watch and who was to sleep. The men began to grumble.

"About midnight, Merlin joined Uther in his tent. He found the king reclining on his mat, his face ashen and covered in sweat.

"'My King, what ails you? How may I be of service?' Merlin bowed low in genuine concern for his ruler and friend.

"Uther smiled slightly, the gesture barely masking his grimace of pain. 'Lord of Light, Walker between the Worlds, that is what they call you, do they not? Then indeed, you already know I am not long for this world. I suspect the spirits have told you.' He grimaced as another wave of pain racked his body and his breathing grew labored.

"'Indeed, they have.' Sorrow weighed down Merlin's voice.

"'Then we haven't much time. There is something you have long known, a secret buried deep within our hearts that must now be revealed to the one who will inherit my crown. Merlin, call my son to me and bid him bring me my sword.'

"Merlin assented with a low bow. 'As you wish, sire.'

"The night watchmen stirred as Merlin strode out of the tent and inquired of the captain the whereabouts of one of the young soldiers. He was directed to a tent on the outskirts of the encampment where the women who followed the battle slept.

"Arthur begrudgingly untangled himself from his bedmate's embrace and was directed by Merlin to a pile of boulders in a grassy patch near the king's tent. 'Your king has damaged his sword,' he said, pointing at the blade wedged between two rocks. 'He desires it returned to him, and I was told you have the strength to remove it.'

"Puzzled, Arthur regarded Merlin as one who had lost his senses and grabbed hold of the hilt. A shower of amber sparks lit up the night as the broken blade scraped against the stone. Arthur displayed the useless weapon to Merlin without a word and followed him into the king's tent.

"By this time, the whole camp had grown tense, the warriors sensing something amiss in the balmy west wind, as if it had been sent from beyond the seventh wave. Some whispered that the west wind was an omen of death, while others listened, watched, and waited for some sign from the Saxons or from their absent king.

"As Merlin and Arthur ducked below the door flap of the tent, Uther's impending death was apparent. Though the wind whistled roughly through the trees outside, the air inside had grown still. Uther's breathing was coming in shallow gasps, his face holding a mere shadow of the great power it once possessed.

"Shocked and distressed at his king's condition, Arthur knelt before him, presenting the sword. 'I have brought your sword, my lord. Tell me, what is your will of me?'

"The dying king smiled. 'It is your sword now, my son.' His eyes closed and he grasped his chest, fighting through another wave of pain. 'Take it and defend our land against those who would hold us captive, for my power is now yours.'

"Arthur knelt speechless before Uther, searching his face for meaning he could not comprehend. Finally, he turned to Merlin for explanation.

"'Uther is your father, Arthur. Soon, you will be high king.'

"Uther reached out to his son. 'I beg you bear me no ill will for concealing this from you. You'—he fought for breath—'have always had my love, and your protection was my greatest concern.'

"The king looked up suddenly, regarding them with unseeing eyes. 'My ancestors call me home, my son. I bid you farewell. May the gods be with you, and may you only die in battle.'

"One final spasm shook his body, and Uther breathed his last.

"Merlin bowed his head. 'The high king is dead,' he declared to the guards within the tent. He removed the ring of office from Uther's hand and placed it on Arthur's finger. 'And the new king is born. Hail, High King Arthur!' he cried.

"The cry was taken up by the men in the tent and echoed by those outside. Confusion reigned as word spread from one end of the camp to another. But soon the ravens began to crow, and the commotion was drowned out by shouts of the night watchmen. The Saxons were marching toward camp."

Aggrivane leaned forward and his voice grew more intense. "I tell you, it was as if the Saxons had planned the whole sequence of events themselves. Right at the moment of transition, the moment of greatest weakness, our men were being attacked. Arthur seemed unaware of this coincidence; he was strangely focused, having shaken off his shock and clothed himself in the mantle of power. Once the men were hastily armed and battle formations in place, he called them all unto him, scanning the assembled warriors with eyes of bluest fire.

"'A few hours ago, I was one of you, and now I find myself called to lead you. I do not yet ask for your loyalty, but I do ask for your trust. Allow me to lead you in this battle to secure our country's future, and then you may evaluate my worthiness to be your king. One thing I beg of you—do not allow your grief, anger, or personal grievances to cloud your minds. Think only of turning this horde of murderers away from our shores. You have all sworn an oath of allegiance to Uther. Consider victory in this battle to be his final command.' Arthur raised his father's damaged sword high over his head and, with the other arm, brandished his own. 'To arms, men of Britain! To arms!'

"Arthur's men were ready for the onslaught when the Saxons rained down upon them. Having lost the element of surprise, the Saxons were weakened, though they fought hard. Many brave men lost their lives, following Uther as his honor guard into Otherworld. But many others won great honor. As dawn brightened the sky on the first day of Arthur's reign, the Saxons were defeated, hundreds killed in all. The royal army—and the nation—were left to grieve for their fallen warriors and their dead king and to come to terms with the sudden rise of another. So began the rule of the great King Arthur."

The grand hall was silent but for the crackling of the fire in the hearth. I could not move, could not tear my eyes away from Aggrivane. Though I did not look at them, the utter stillness around me indicated everyone was as spellbound as I, living the events brought to life through Aggrivane's words.

My father was the first to stir. "Good sir, that was a fine tale. I beg you tell me where you learned such skill."

Evrain moved to interject, and Aggrivane took note.

"Truly, my lord, it is of no consequence." He dropped his gaze to the floor. "Nor am I."

Evrain seemed pleased by the show of humility, but I was not. I could not believe that Aggrivane would so willingly deny his talent and the years of Druidic training that had brought him this far. I was about to voice this thought when I caught Aggrivane's eye. He was silently begging me to keep quiet.

I slumped back in my seat as the talk returned once again to our new king.

"Now that we have heard the fantasy, what do you think to be our king's chances, eh?" Evrain asked, draining yet another cup.

"He will have a tough road ahead of him," my father said gravely. "Who upholds his sovereignty?"

"I have heard that allegiance has been sworn by Cador of Cornwall, the king of the north country, and Pellinor of Dyfed. I know he aims to gain your loyalty as well, my lord. But not all are so quick to cower before the mighty Arthur." Evrain pounded the table with his fist. "King Lot has declared war upon the whelp. He had been appointed Uther's successor long ago and rightly feels cheated of his office. He was the only lord present the night of Uther's passing who refused to kneel and swear fealty to Arthur."

Aggrivane shifted uncomfortably in his seat at the mention of his father's disloyalty. He glanced out the window and then his stool scraped loudly as he rose suddenly from his seat. "Forgive me, my lords, but the candles burn low. I must see to the horses."

Evrain motioned toward the door dismissively. "Yes, yes, be off to your duties." The tone in Evrain's voice made it clear that he was glad to finally be rid of his guest.

"We bid you good eve," my father said, rising.

"Thank you, my lords." He bowed to both kings and threw me a fleeting glance filled with longing before departing.

ours, minutes, days—I could not tell how much time passed before I was finally able to beg permission to retire for the night. A long argument about Arthur's right to the throne had followed Aggrivane's departure, and then I was subjected to the torment of a dance with the gangly Fergus. The full moon was already high in the night sky when I bid our company good night.

I turned to Lord Evrain and his son and curtsied to them. "Good sirs, I am honored to have had the privilege of your company this eve. I wish you pleasant dreams."

Evrain took my hand. "After a night such as this, how can they be anything but pleasant?" he asked with a not-so-charming implication.

"My lord, you flatter me," I whispered modestly before bidding Fergus good night.

The lanky boy kissed my hand and pawed at the bracelet

with its drops of fire dangling from my wrist. "If I had known the beauty of your eyes, I would have made these emeralds," he said with an uncomfortable grimace that betrayed the lack of confidence behind his words.

I smiled, greatly amused. "Fergus, did your father tell you to say that?"

He merely blushed wordlessly and bobbed his head in a gesture of farewell.

ം൭ 2ൟ

The drunken laughter of my father and Lord Evrain wafted out from the great hall as I slipped silently across the courtyard to the stables. I pulled my heavy cloak closer around me to stave off the cold night air, praying the tower guards would take no notice of my fleeting presence, or if they did, that they would mistake my simple garb for that of a serving girl.

My breath was coming in short, impatient puffs by the time the low, long building came into view. The sweet odor of hay mixed with the tang of the horses greeted me as I pulled open the heavy door. A faint glow illuminated one of the far stalls. My heart raced. He had waited for me.

"I was wondering when—if—you would arrive," Aggrivane said, looking up from the shining chestnut stallion whose coat he was gently brushing.

The lantern light caught the expressive gleam in his eye, and I sighed aloud, rushing toward him, eager to enfold myself in his arms. He quickly dropped the curry comb he was holding, and within moments, his lips met mine.

Pulling away, I cupped his cheeks in my hands and looked deep into his eyes. "I feared I would never see you again." Tears welled in my eyes, bringing all emotions to the surface.

"I would wait an eternity for you," he whispered softly. He pulled me slowly down to a pile of fresh hay heaped in one corner of the stable. "It is not exactly the lush grasses of Avalon." A crooked smile played across his lips, and the memory of our night together was reflected in his eyes.

I smiled in return. "My love, it will do, I assure you."

I buried my head in his chest, taking comfort in his heartbeat. For just this one moment, I longed to be back in Avalon again, to be free.

I turned my face up to him. "Why do you stay with Lord Evrain when he treats you so? Why do you not go back to your father?"

Aggrivane frowned. "I am a nobleman's son. That means I must learn to be both a warrior and a leader from a lord other than my father. My father sees alliance with Lord Evrain as crucial to future peace within our lands. Do not underestimate him; Lord Evrain is more cunning and powerful than many give him credit for. In order to prevent a feud between our two houses, I was sent to live with his family and learn from him."

I shivered in the cold. "But what can you learn from a boor such as him? Lord Evrain is evil and cruel!"

Aggrivane smirked as he pulled me nearer, leaning in so that his lips brushed my ear as he spoke in the slightest whisper. "Lord Evrain is a bitter, self-important man. He dreams of ruling the whole of this land but knows he lacks the power to do so. That is why he vehemently opposes Arthur, who is living out the dream he has secretly harbored for so long. In order to make up for his own weaknesses, Evrain uses what power he has to manipulate the other lords around him. Why else do you think he paid your father a visit? He knows that his own sons will not make strong enough rulers to continue what he has started. But if Fergus marries you and Evrain can control your father, he has indirect control of the whole of Gwynedd."

I stared at him incredulously. "Is it true?"

He nodded.

"But why does Lord Evrain hate you so?"

Aggrivane shrugged and ran his fingers through my hair, sending chills down my spine. "My mother is Arthur's sister. That makes me royalty of higher station than Evrain can ever dream. Therefore, he uses his place as my temporary superior to try to make me subservient to him. He has never allowed me to forget that I am the second of five brothers and likely will not inherit but will have to earn my lands and title." The devilish smile returned to his face. "Besides, I daresay he fancies you not so much for his son but for himself."

I swatted his chest playfully. "Do not say such things, good sir, for my innocent ears will not abide them!"

He nipped one of my earlobes. "Innocent, eh? I do not recall them being so innocent when last we parted. Perhaps I should see what can be done to refresh your memory."

All thought of the cold night air and the meeting taking place in the castle vanished as I melted into his arms, allowing their strength to refuel all that I had lost over the previous months. His kisses were like enchanted nectar; the more I tasted, the greater my desire. One of his hands caressed my breast through the fabric of my gown, while the other searched hungrily beneath the folds of my skirt.

Over the months we spent studying the stars in Avalon, I came to know every inch of Aggrivane's body by sunlight and starlight. Now, in the near darkness, I found that I could trace each scar that raised his skin and took comfort in the familiar contours of his body. His kisses grew more intense and I happily yielded my body to him, safe and content in his arms.

When the moments of pleasure had passed, we drowsed in each other's arms, dreaming of a life together as a faraway nightingale sang his nocturnal hymn.

"Why do you not ask my father for my hand?" I asked Aggrivane. "You are a lord in your own right, not a slave like Evrain would have you believe. My father would be happy to rid his house of me, I assure you."

He laughed. "I doubt that to be true." He fell into silent contemplation. "I could not ask your father in front of Lord Evrain. That would break the pact he made with my father, and Evrain would declare a war of honor upon us."

I sat up on my arms and gazed at him hopefully, my mind racing. "Perhaps you could find some reason to stay behind when Lord Evrain leaves. He would be happy to unload you into the care of my father. We both know that."

All that remained was the unanswered question—why? Why would my father allow Aggrivane to stay? I listened to the chirping of the crickets and the soft snuffling of the horses, praying for an answer. Somewhere in the distance, the low murmur of voices signaled the changing of the guard and, suddenly, I knew.

I grabbed Aggrivane by the shoulders, and the words tumbled out in a rush of excitement. "Rhys is the best swordsman in

Northgallis. My father has forbidden me to practice the arts of battle, so I know Rhys would have room for an additional student. You could study with him for a few months in exchange for teaching my cousin Bran some of the knowledge you gained on the Druids' isle. Besides, Bran would love to have someone near his age to spar with."

Aggrivane regarded me warily. "But would your father allow my teaching? He seems set against all you learned in Avalon. Plus, I hear tell of a priest that trails at your father's heels. He is not likely to accept another of the old faith into your household."

I waved a hand dismissively. "Then do not teach him the secrets of the isle, but entrust to him the knowledge of language, reading, and the written word. Every lord should have such training, but with the constant threat from the Irish, there has been little opportunity to school Bran in such things. As for Marius, I have yet to meet this deity made flesh, but no man has ever held sway over my father, least of all a priest."

Aggrivane kissed my lips softly. "You are not going to stop until I agree to present this proposal to your father, are you?"

I grinned and shook my head.

"Well then, it is settled. Upon the dawn, I will ask for a private audience with your father and tell all to him."

I kissed him hard on the mouth. "Let us then thank the Goddess for our good fortune." I pulled him down to the soft straw and closed my eyes, reveling in the joy that this man would soon be my husband.

ഛരെ ഉരൈ

"I assure you, my lord, no finer animal ever walked the earth."

Aggrivane and I froze, clasped together in fear. Had we slept? Somehow we had missed the lords' approach and were likely to be discovered. Evrain's drunken slur was unmistakable. The voices were quickly drawing near the stables.

Aggrivane's eyes had grown large, and I could tell by the tilt of his head that he was listening to sounds my untrained ears could not hear.

I slipped on my dress, looking around wildly like a trapped animal, but there was no way to escape. There was nowhere to hide, and the men were nearly at the only door.

"What do we do?" I hissed at Aggrivane, trembling in fear.

Aggrivane hastily pulled on his tunic. "Hide your face with your hair and bury your head in my chest. I will speak to them, and if the gods are with us, we will escape unharmed."

He kissed the top of my head one last time before the door swung open and Lord Evrain burst in, incoherently bragging about his horse, followed by the confident stride of my father and a lighter, shuffling footstep that I could only assume belonged to Fergus.

"Pure Eastern blood, I tell you. Sired by a Pegasus and stolen from a Saracen warrior. He was shipped here by the tradesmen in my employ. Many a lord has offered a handsome sum for his offspring, but I—"

Evrain had obviously seen us. I could imagine the look on my father's face.

"Well, what have we here?" Evrain bellowed.

I clung ever tighter to Aggrivane and willed myself to be completely still and silent.

"It appears our young ward has found himself a willing serving maid."

I felt Evrain step closer and said a silent prayer of thanks that Octavia had thought to outfit me in one of her old dresses to fool the guards in case I was seen coming here.

Evrain fingered my hair, and I could not suppress a cringe as I turned my face farther away from him.

From his tone, Evrain sounded to be appraising my worth. "Dark hair, strong body. Is she related to that Roman woman who served us at dinner?" He chuckled salaciously to himself. "If she is, then you have found yourself one fine wench, lad."

Aggrivane dropped his gaze to the floor. "Truly, I do not know, sir. We have barely spoken."

Evrain howled with laughter and gave Aggrivane a hearty slap on the back. "That's the way, my boy. The less they say, the better they are. Isn't that right, Leodgrance?"

My father cleared his throat and mumbled a polite agreement.

"My lord," Aggrivane addressed my father, "forgive this woman for not bowing to you as you deserve. She is embarrassed and fears punishment." He positioned himself between the lords and me.

"Indeed, I see no need for retribution. It is late, and we should all to bed," my father responded.

Something in his tone told me that my father knew that the woman trembling behind the curtain of black hair was no serving maid. I breathed a sigh of relief as I heard them turn toward the door. Just then, I felt something crawling up my arm, its many legs tickling my skin. Without thinking, I shook off the spider and the sleeve of my gown fell back around my elbow.

"Wait!" Evrain roared. "What is this?" Evrain stalked toward us and jerked my wrist, wrenching me away from Aggrivane's protection.

He held up my arm, and Fergus's bracelet bled ruby teardrops in the lantern light.

Damn! How could I have forgotten to remove that vile trinket?

"My lord," Evrain called, "it appears your maid is not only a strumpet, but a thief as well."

He pulled me roughly toward him. His breath stank of drink and decay as he leered at me through the raven strands that separated us. "Now, let us see what kind of creature you have trapped, Lord Aggrivane."

He yanked back my hair as if he meant to pull it out by the roots. I summoned all my courage and raised my face to him. His eyes bulged as he beheld the mark of priestesshood on my brow, and recognition spread across his face.

ഒ

"Is this how you raised your daughter to behave, my Lord Leodgrance?" Evrain spewed rage like a boiling kettle. "I knew when you married that northern savage she would be no example to your children, and then God cursed you with a daughter as your only living child."

It was nearly dawn. Evrain had been raving for what felt like hours, pacing the length of the audience chamber under the watchful gaze of Father Marius, my father's newfound savior. Aggrivane stood at a distance, his stoic silence masking the pain and fear buried deep within his troubled eyes.

"My poor son lies in his chamber, distraught by her betrayal." Evrain pointed an accusatory finger toward me.

More likely you locked him there.

"And she has disgraced me, a guest invited on your honor. My lord, she is blight on your entire house. She must be punished."

"She is also my daughter," my father said angrily.

Evrain knew he had overstepped his bounds. "I beg your pardon, my lord." He paused, steepled hands pressed to his lips in thought. "But the fact remains that these two were caught in an immoral embrace." He regarded Aggrivane coldly. "My son was openly courting your daughter. By the agreement I struck with the Lord of Lothian, this boy had no right to take what belonged to my son."

Aggrivane surged angrily toward the throne. "Guinevere belongs to no one, especially not your son." He faced Lord Evrain squarely with more fierceness than I had ever seen. "And especially not to you. If she belongs to anyone, it is me, the man to whom she swore her intention to marry and to whom she freely, willingly gave her heart."

"And her body," Evrain added with a leering snarl. "Lord Aggrivane, you have broken the agreement I made with your father, and so you will leave my house in disgrace and return to him. I will ensure your father pays dearly for your insolence." The promise of retribution lit his eyes with manic intensity. He turned toward my father. "I demand punishment of his paramour. Without it, there can be no peace between our lands."

I looked with suspicion upon the man who threatened my future. Aggrivane was right; there was more to his plan than healing a breach of honor. Evrain was fishing for something.

The morning cock crowed as my father sat staring into the distance, considering his options. Father Marius too seemed to be weighing the alternatives, his milky blue eyes hardening in meditative concentration.

"There is one solution that I believe will be pleasing to all parties," my father stated.

I jumped at the sudden breech of silence. My father motioned me forward to stand before him like a prisoner receiving her sentence.

"Lord Pellinor of Dyfed has extended an offer to allow you to live with his family. I was not going to ask you to leave so soon, but your behavior has left me no choice. Perhaps under their guidance you will learn how to behave like a lady—a *Christian* lady."

My heart was pounding, blood rushing in my ears. I could no longer contain the fury that was building inside me. "Have I no say in my own fate? When did Northgallis become a kingdom of tyranny?" I directed his attention to the sacred mark upon my brow. "I made my choice long ago, Father. I have chosen to live my life with Aggrivane, following the ways of our ancestors—of my mother's people—the way of Avalon, free from the oppression of Rome." I locked my arm possessively around Aggrivane's.

My father's face darkened with rage. "Child, I am your father, forget not that! My father was a Roman, and by virtue of that lineage, I am free to invoke Roman law, under which you are my property to do with as I please! I could have you killed or sold into slavery or prostitution if I so chose, without even the slightest question or repercussion falling on me."

He rose from his chair and bent down so he stood face to face with me, gripping my shoulders. Terrible strain marred his blood-shot eyes. "Be thankful I think so highly of you, Guinevere. All I have chosen is for you to live in the house of a kind nobleman who will see that you are well treated and well prepared for your future role as wife. Is that so much to ask, daughter?"

I should have remained silent, but the willfulness I inherited from my mother would not let me. "And who here would enforce that Roman law you threaten me with, Father? Rome hasn't given us a thought in over half a century. From whom do you draw your authority?"

That was the wrong thing to say.

"It was Rome who gave Britain an understanding of herself as a nation rather than a land of scattered tribes." My father was in his full battle fury now. "It was from Rome that Britain learned to combine her scattered forces effectively. It was by her lesson that our clans learned to live under single rule. Without Rome, our high king could not now be contemplating his united kingdom. The past glories of imperial ties spark within our family blood. You are no one to criticize Rome!"

I broke away from his grasp before he could strike me, retreating to face him from the far corner. "You never treated me like a Roman daughter when I was growing up. If you had, I could accept this now. You always gave me the freedom and respect that first drew you to my mother and her people. But now that she is dead, all that must end."

My father looked as if I had just broken his heart. He opened his mouth to speak, but no words followed.

"Leodgrance, do not forget that your wife died possessed by the devil," Father Marius said softly. He had been waiting for this very opportunity. In a flash of scarlet robes, he stood between us, bidding me be silent with wave of his hand.

"Liar!" I lunged toward him, intent on scratching out his eyeballs, but Aggrivane restrained me in a firm grip.

"Foolish child, I speak the truth." Father Marius spat his words at me with none of the compassion with which he claimed to mark his faith. "All women scream in childbirth in reparation for the sins of the flesh, but Corinna's extreme suffering could only have come from the devil, sent to punish her for giving her daughter over to the pagans instead of to the Church."

I struggled against Aggrivane's grasp, but he held me fast.

"Do not make things worse for yourself, love," he whispered.

Marius was clearly enjoying himself. "Why else would the child inside her have died? The devil runs wild in this savage country, causing old women to claim to see visions of the future and men to be morally repugnant." He cast an accusatory eye to Aggrivane before returning his attention to my father. "Why, this new king of ours is nothing more than the devil's own puppet—advised as he is by the high priest of heathens. No, Leodgrance, there was no hope for your wife. When she gave her daughter to the evil isle, she gave up her very soul. The only thing that could have saved her would have been a life of penance and austerity in the cloister. Even then she may have suffered in the afterlife."

He turned his bitter eyes toward me but refused to look into my face. "Your child here is already following the same path, wanton as she has proven herself to be. Do you wish her to suffer the same fate?"

My father suddenly looked old and weary. He sighed, the sound of a defeated man. "No, I do not." He sank back into his chair. Summoning his strength, he issued the final verdict. "Guinevere, you will live with Lord Pellinor's household until such time as a husband is chosen for you. Lord Evrain, I beg your forgiveness for any affront caused by the events of this night." He pounded his fist on the arm of his throne, sending a heavy blast echoing off the walls. "This is my will, and as I have proclaimed, so it shall be."

Father Marius regarded me with an icy stare. "I will pray that your party makes it to Dyfed before the first snowfall," he said, but there was no sincerity behind his words.

CHAPTER ELEVEN

I hardly noticed the journey south.

I had lost everything I had ever loved: my family in Avalon, my mother, my lover, and now my father. Even Octavia was forbidden to accompany me. Once again, I was alone, facing the prospect of another new home; it seemed like each time I traveled somewhere new, my heart became heavier, weighed down by another form of pain.

Life had just begun to feel normal again. The homesickness I had felt for Avalon had begun to fade; the shock and blinding grief that gripped my soul at my mother's death had begun to loosen just enough to let me breathe again; even my father had shown a flicker of his old genial nature—and then all the wounds were slashed open in a single instant.

My horse trod the miles without prodding or direction, as if he was as resigned to his fate as I was mine. The countryside passed without my knowledge. All I could see in my mind's eye was Aggrivane. The memory of him was the one thing that enabled me to draw breath—the light of his smile, the softening of his eyes each time they found mine, the warmth of his breath.

When Aggrivane and I parted in Avalon, I'd accepted it was unlikely we would ever see one another again. Of course I missed him, thought of him, dreamed of him, but that was all it was; it seemed more fantasy than reality. But when I saw him standing in the entryway of Northgallis, an unexpected beacon in my dark world, he had been real, as was our love—overwhelmingly, tantalizingly, achingly real. As our bodies came together, so did our hearts, our souls, permanently intertwined among our limbs like mistletoe in the boughs of an oak. When he whispered that he would marry me, my world was complete once again.

No matter what my father or that horrid priest said, he would always be mine. I couldn't let him go, but I couldn't be with him either, and it was tearing me apart.

The fissure in my heart seemed to expand every time I thought of him returning to Lothian. Surely his father would be merciful, would he not? Lot was widely known as a man of great integrity and strength of will. Aggrivane spoke highly of his father and it was clear that they loved one another, so he would understand; he had to. Perhaps Lot would even see the injustice that was done to us and send his men to rescue me from my prison. Then we could be together forever, just as we had intended.

Even now I could feel Aggrivane's hand in mine as we wound our ways to unknown fates. I knew with absolute certainty that as my body drew ever closer to Dyfed, a small shard of my soul journeyed northeast to Lothian with him.

෭ඁ ඁ෭

I could barely breathe as I waited outside the large oak doors of the great hall. Corbenic was a large holding, much more imposing than my own home, and standing here surrounded by guards did nothing to make me feel welcome. Inside, Lord Pellinor and Lady Lyonesse were holding court. With a murmur of voices, they attended to the room full of courtiers, common folk, and emissaries, each with their own agenda or case to plead.

The men around me shifted anxiously and stomachs rumbled audibly as the minutes ticked by. My feet were beginning to get stiff and sore when a servant emerged from the suddenly silent room to beckon us in. When I stepped through the doorway, I was greeted by a press of people on either side, strange faces peering at me with open curiosity or obvious distain. I began to sweat under the weight of their judgment, and I tried to ignore the feeling I was being paraded in front of the entire court like a criminal.

Pellinor's tall, thin frame came into view first. He was standing in front of his throne with a warm smile on his face. A few new wrinkles creased his face and less of his close-cropped black hair was visible along his forehead, but otherwise he appeared much the same as when I had seen him last, two summers before I went to Avalon.

"Guinevere, welcome." He came forward when we reached the dais and embraced me warmly. "I am so happy your father accepted my invitation. It has been far too long since we have had the pleasure of your company." He regarded me with sincere appreciation, the way I had expected my own father to receive me.

Ignoring the gaping crowd, he continued in his familial tone. "My, you have grown. You are not the only one who has come of age in the passing years." He put out his arm, and a beautiful girl about my age with long strawberry-blond hair trotted to his side. "You remember Elaine. The last time the two of you were together, you were covered in mud, do you remember?" He laughed lightly.

Elaine grinned at me, and although my body was visibly shaking, I couldn't help but be warmed by her presence. I remembered quite clearly. It was Elaine who had led us into the bog, chasing after one of her many fantasies. Time had dulled the particulars, but I remembered enough.

My heart was beginning to warm and the slightest hint of a smile tugged at my lips when I caught the eye of the woman perched in the throne next to Pellinor. She had draped herself in such a way as to appear larger, more imposing than I knew her to be. With a sudden chill, I understood it was she who was holding court and that she was simply indulging her husband's kindness. Her eyes were fixed on my forehead, and her jaw was taut. It was clear she had not been forewarned about my religious views and was not pleased.

Having held my gaze long enough to make her authority clear, Lyonesse rose and embraced me stiffly. "Welcome, Guinevere." Her words were kind, but her greeting held no warmth.

Lyonesse had never been overly affectionate, but her actions were much more formal than I recalled from my last visit. Her brief embrace threw me off balance, and I stumbled as she released me and we both returned to our places.

Pellinor too took his seat beneath a large painting in which a woman lovingly gazed on her child while the father watched serenely but protectively from behind them. In the background, an older man and woman raised their eyes skyward in silent prayer of thanksgiving. I would have thought it a portrait of Pellinor's family, if the child had not been a boy.

"Gentlemen," Pellinor said to the assembled guards, "I release you from your service. You may tell Lord Leodgrance that his daughter is safely in my care. My men will show you to the barracks, where you may dine and rest before beginning your journey back to Northgallis in the morning."

As the clamor of armor and footsteps receded, I was pleased to note the crowd had grown considerably smaller. Besides Pellinor's family, there now remained only a few people I did not recognize, among them a strikingly beautiful woman with porcelain skin and a wild curly mane of hair that was more orange than red, brighter even than Morgan's in the sunlight. She observed me with a strange mixture of emotions, as if she knew enough to pity me yet was dying to learn more. Her nearly concealed smile told me that she was amused by my situation.

I stood silently, still trembling before Pellinor and Lyonesse, unsure how to proceed. If I should speak, I could not; my throat was dry and my tongue seemed glued to my palate.

Lyonesse gazed down at me, her sapphire eyes hard and disapproving, still boring into my forehead as though she could remove the crescent by force of will. It was then that I realized she made me more uncomfortable than Argante had on my first day in Avalon. That thought sent a shiver down my spine, while beads of cold sweat made an appearance on my forehead and on the back of my neck. I looked to Pellinor and Elaine for reassurance, but Lyonesse quickly drew my attention back to her, exactly where she wanted it.

"I must admit I had serious reservations about allowing you

to live here—and I still do—but my husband promises me you will behave with the utmost decorum and mind your place. Is that correct?" Her voice was grim, as though she held little hope regarding my ability to comply.

I nodded mutely.

She seemed the tiniest bit assuaged and relaxed slightly in her chair. "I know the story of how you came to be here, the real reason why our invitation was accepted." She eyed her husband accusingly.

Pellinor was nonplussed, but I had a feeling it was all an act.

"With the addition of you to the household, we now have three mouths to feed and three husbands to find." She gestured to her daughter, who immediately blushed scarlet. "Elaine, of course, will be no problem, but I question the influence you and the other one may have on her, especially together." She threw the curly-haired woman a look of repugnance.

Why does she not call the girl by name? That simple act of disrespect rankled me.

"I do not want our home to become a house of ill repute. Given your history"—it was clear that she was speaking now both to me and the curious girl in the corner—"that could be a very difficult assumption to avoid."

"Be reasonable," Pellinor interjected. "Isolde and Guinevere have done nothing to earn your ire. Past offenses are nothing to us now. What good is it for Guinevere to have come here if she is not given a chance to begin anew? Even our Lord and Savior did not turn away the Magdalene from his companions, and he often dined with prostitutes and tax collectors. We owe Guinevere the same compassion and forgiveness."

Inwardly, I took offense at Pellinor's scriptural reference, but he meant well, so I ignored him.

"But those people were repentant of their sins, husband," Lyonesse retorted, her voice becoming higher and harsher with each word. "Guinevere has done nothing to indicate she regrets what she has done or to show firm purpose of amendment. Therefore, we must be on our guard." Her attention was back on me now. "You will be the model of righteousness while you live within our walls, do you understand? If I hear even the faintest whisper that you have done or even thought of anything that may be morally questionable, I will turn you out without a second thought." Her eyes blazed fire. "I advise you to have as little interaction with Elaine as possible until you have proven yourself to be true to the path of virtue—"

"Lyonesse, you cannot forbid two friends from being together," Pellinor interrupted, exasperated. "It is against nature, and it is not compassionate. Think how you would feel if someone did the same to you. Guinevere and Elaine are practically kin; you cannot rend the garment of family without displeasing God."

For a moment Lyonesse was speechless, thrown by Pellinor's accusation of un-Christian behavior, but she recovered and quickly changed the subject. "So be it. But your visits must be supervised."

She stood, descended two of the three steps that separated us and stood glowering down at me. Silently, she scrutinized my face, my dress, and, I suspected, my body beneath. She took a deep breath and let it out with an exaggerated sigh.

"You seem to be in good health, and you are comely enough. It *will* be a challenge finding a good Christian man willing to marry you since you are a branded woman." She started to touch the mark on my forehead with trembling fingers, but then pulled away, as if she feared being burned. "But I have faced bigger challenges in my time, and I am determined not to fail.

"The mark may mean little if we can show that you have changed and embraced the true faith," she said, more to herself than anyone else. "But the bigger problem lies in your virtue, or lack thereof." She smirked. "Normally I would call the healer and have her publicly certify your virginity, but since we all know that would be a fruitless gesture, we will have to improve your spiritual virtue instead. It will be cold comfort when a man realizes he has been bound to a used woman, but it is the best we can do under the circumstances."

Pellinor started to object once again.

Lyonesse silenced him with a wave of her hand and went on. "We attend Holy Mass at dawn every morning. I expect you to accompany us and show the proper respect. Perhaps you will even learn the meaning of true faith."

I desperately wanted to remark that my chances were better of learning it from a sermon than from her actions, but I bit my tongue.

"It is late and you must be tired from your journey," Lyonesse said, showing compassion for the first time. "You." She snapped her fingers at Isolde. "Show her to her chambers."

Isolde threw Lyonesse a look of clear distain as she emerged from the shadows near the wall and took my arm, leading me up the stairs like a lamb to slaughter.

⁕

I closed the door behind me and leaned against it, trying to comprehend what had just occurred.

"Is that their idea of a welcome?" I was trying to reconcile the warm memories of my youth with the odd greeting I had just received.

Isolde shrugged. "It's normal, if that is what you are asking. Pellinor is a just man ruling with patience and compassion, while Lyonesse is ever lording her self-importance over everyone around her. They *are* rather judgmental of those who do not conform to their standards, though." Isolde opened one of my trunks and fished around in the contents. "I dare say that an Avalonian priestess is nearly as bad as Irish royalty in their minds. But I would think you would have anticipated as much."

I shrugged. "No, I did not. I—I cannot remember them acting like this when my family came to visit." A stab of pain hit my heart at the word "family," and my brow furrowed involuntarily. "Maybe I was just too young to notice, but I think they have changed."

Isolde turned from the bed to face me. "That was nothing. When I first arrived, Lyonesse would have had me shackled and handed over like a prisoner." A sly smile spread across her face. "But she had to receive me like a second daughter, with all the pageantry and circumstance accorded to my rank, and it nearly killed her." She was grinning.

Curious now, I raised my head to meet her green eyes. "How *did* the heir to the Irish throne come to live in the kingdom of Dyfed?"

Isolde stopped unfolding my garments and looked off into space, cocking her head to one side and pursing her lips. "Actually, that is one thing we have in common. It was your father's idea."

My confusion must have been plain to read because she smiled.

"Do you not remember? You were there when my fate was sealed, or so they tell me. All of nine years old, you were sitting at your mother's knee when the council of western lords met with my mother's ambassador and agreed to trade my freedom for a promise of peace between Ireland, Gwynedd, Dyfed, and Cornwall. My presence here, and the promise of a strong marriage to some unnamed British noble, is all that stops my people from devouring this coast. Your father offered me up then to protect his seaports from plunder just as he offered you up to placate that Powys pig, Evrain."

I looked down at the floor, seeking the shadow of my feet in the firelight. "So we mean nothing to them, any of them?" I asked in barely a whisper.

Isolde snorted and I started. "Oh, we mean plenty to them. We are the most valuable currency there is to Christian men." She thought for a moment. "Well, we'd be more valuable as virgins, but you understand my point."

I met her gaze. "So you're not. . ."

"No."

"But what about Lyonesse's test?"

Isolde laughed, a hearty, throaty sound of genuine joy. "You believed that nonsense? Guinevere, did all those years on that isle rot your brain? Lyonesse is all talk, a liar determined to sell her shell of Christian perfection to everyone, including herself. But Pellinor is her biggest mark. Sometimes I think she fears he would send her away at the slightest hint of imperfection. So she overcompensates. There is no healer, no test. And even if there was, such things are easy enough to fake," she said with a dismissive wave of her hand.

I eyed her suspiciously, wondering how she came to such knowledge.

Isolde put aside the item she had picked up and looked at me purposefully. "Life in this house is one extravagant game. You will learn to play it, and I will teach you how." She wiggled her eyebrows. "It's actually kind of fun."

She sat down on the bed, motioning for me to join her. "But to win the game, you must first understand the other players." She looked impish. "You were probably too young the last time you were here to understand the details. Let's start with Pellinor. He claims to be a descendant of Joseph of Arimathea, the man in whose tomb their Christ was buried. According to legend, he was a tin trader, and after the death of Jesus, he escaped along the trade routes to Britain, where he hoped Roman law wouldn't be able to find him."

Isolde grew serious, her eyes distant as she recalled the tale she had no doubt heard countless times. "As Pellinor tells it, the prophecy of the Grail was spoken by the apostle John after Christ was laid to rest. In appreciation for Joseph's generosity, the seventh child of the seventh generation after his would bear a man of unparalleled purity, second only to Christ himself, and that man would bring the world the gift of the chalice of Christ. Some say that the one who bears it will never die, while others claim it will bestow everlasting peace on the land in which it is held."

"But that is ridiculous," I said. "It is no relic of their god but one of the treasures of Avalon. It is highly symbolic in our faith, but it has no magical properties, at least not that anyone in Avalon speaks of."

Isolde glared at me warningly. "Do not let those words, or any like them, escape your lips in this house. If you do, Pellinor will send you back to your father before you have had the chance to blink." She gripped my shoulders, looking me square in the eye. "You must understand that this prophecy is all that Pellinor has. His sons have disappointed him, so he has no hope for a stronger kingdom until Elaine marries, and given his high standards for her, that is unlikely to be any time soon."

My eyebrows knitted together in frustration. I was about to ask her to clarify when she interrupted with a question.

"Did you see the painting behind Pellinor's throne?"

"Yes, I assumed it was of his family—ancestors perhaps."

She nodded. "You are correct, in a fashion. You see, that is a painting of what the Christians call 'the holy family.' The man is Joseph, foster father of Jesus the Christ; the woman is Mary, his mother; and the child is Jesus. But what makes this painting unique is that it also contains two others: Joachim and Anne, the parents of Mary."

I stared at her, thoroughly confused, despite my basic knowledge of Christianity. I failed to see what that had to do with Pellinor.

Isolde sighed, seeing I was not making the connection. "To Pellinor, this painting represents his past, present, and future. He believes he is related to a man who performed a great service for this savior-child. He is the sixth generation since that fateful event. Elaine is the seventh child of the seventh generation, if you count all of Pellinor's children, living and dead. Therefore in Pellinor's mind, his progeny—Elaine—is fated to bear the man who will discover the Grail. That makes poor Elaine sacrosanct, for she will bear the most perfect man to live since Christ. In a way, she is to Pellinor a reflection of the Virgin Mary, which makes him and Lyonesse like Joachim and Anne."

I nodded. Somehow this was beginning to make sense. "But who then will be Joseph? You cannot mean to say that Pellinor believes Elaine will conceive miraculously? I do not think that their god would allow a wonder of that magnitude twice—if he even did once."

Isolde laughed. "No. Pellinor's mind is still partly anchored in reality. He knows she must have a husband for the child of prophecy to be born. That is why he has already begun compiling a list of possible suitors. Lyonesse says they will be brought to Dyfed to interview for her hand as soon as Elaine's monthly courses begin."

"And Elaine? What does she think about all of this prophecy? That must be a mighty weight to bear."

Isolde shrugged. "It is hard to say, really. Pellinor keeps her locked away in her room most of the time. I keep her company when I can, but that is only when Lyonesse is out. She wouldn't want her daughter associating with one such as me. Honestly, I think Elaine is a little . . . well, eccentric. If you had that pair as parents, you would be as well. All of that time alone has made her prone to mistake her imaginings for real events—although that could partly be my fault too." She smiled sheepishly, and her cheeks reddened.

"What?" I stammered, taken aback. "What do you mean?"

She ducked her head and stood, pacing to avoid my gaze. "As a good Christian lady, Elaine is not allowed any books other than those the tutor supplies her and the lives of the saints the nuns let her borrow—all rare and valuable resources that must be returned in a timely manner. I noticed when the bards come to entertain, she is enraptured by their tales of romance and

adventure, so I started sharing with her the legends of my homeland, the very same stories of tragic love and magical creatures
I was told as a child. The difference is that as I grew, I learned
what was real and what was not. I don't think Elaine has the same
ability." She paused, facing me now. Her brow was creased with
concern. "I think she believes some of the stories are true. Maybe
she has convinced herself she is one or more of the characters, I
don't know. Not long ago, she told me she had seen a vision of her
future husband in her mirror."

I cocked an eyebrow. "But doesn't that run contrary to her
faith, seeing such things?"

Isolde shook her head. "Elaine is well-versed in the extraor-
dinary abilities attributed to some holy men and women. She
believes her god has blessed her with a special gift. I believe she
needs companionship. It is good you are here. She is not a danger
to anyone, but the more you can draw her out of her fantasy world
and into her real life, the better off everyone will be."

"If Lyonesse lets me," I corrected her, grimacing at this new
responsibility.

"Oh, she will; just give her time to warm up to you. All you
have to do is be good for a while." She winked.

"Does no one else notice her behavior? Certainly Lyonesse
must be aware."

"Elaine is adept at keeping to herself anything that might
upset her parents," Isolde explained. "She knows what best suits
her strategically. Her parents love her in a way I will never understand, and she returns that love by being to them exactly what
they want—the model of virtue. But every so often, her carefully
crafted mask slips, mostly in private. Beware of her jealousy and

remember you are dealing with a mind more fragile than most," she warned darkly. "But she has been well lately, so hopefully she will not cause us any grief."

Isolde grew silent, no doubt ruminating on the slim likelihood of a peaceful winter with us all cooped up under one roof. I seized the opportunity to change the subject.

"Why do you let Lyonesse treat you like a slave?" I asked bluntly, surprised at how easily I spoke my mind around this girl.

"It is her way of teaching me humility," she answered with a deep sigh, showing no sign of offense. "I've grown used to it. I matured faster than Elaine and Lyonesse began to see me as a threat—or rather, as competition for her daughter," she corrected herself. "That was when she began insisting I walk behind her family and ordering me about." She exhaled loudly through her nose. "I'm surprised she still lets me dine at table with them. I go along with whatever she wishes—attending Mass every morning, doing tasks she finds distasteful during the day, and praying on my knees every evening with the rest of the family." She pointed a slender, pale finger at me. "You'd do well to take a lesson from me in that. The same will be expected of you. You may be a future queen, just like me, but in this house, you are little more than a servant."

I stood, crossing to stand in front of her, enraged by the future her words painted. "*I* am no servant. *You* may have accepted your fate, Isolde, but I will do no such thing! I am a priestess of Avalon, and I will *not* pretend to worship their god. I will demand the respect I deserve as an equal to their daughter in all things." My face was hot, blood boiling. "I may not have come here under my own volition, but that does not mean I will relinquish control of my life."

To my great annoyance, Isolde smirked. "To whom will you

protest? Your father? He sent you here, believing it best for you. To Avalon? They have no say in matters of family. Your life is not being threatened. You are not being harmed." She shook her head, exasperated. "You are missing my point. You do not fight them— that is what they want. Rail against them in your mind all you like, but do not show it; they sense rebellion like a falcon knows his prey. If you want to live in peace, you will keep your thoughts to yourself and go along with them until such time as someone asks to be betrothed to you."

The mention of an engagement sent another stab of pain through my heart and my eyes welled with tears, deflating my self-righteous anger. I had been engaged only a few days ago. When I looked up into Isolde's eyes, a connection formed between us, two prisoners bonded by a common fate.

"And you," I asked quietly. "When will Pellinor find you a mate?"

Her eyes grew soft, watery. I had hit a nerve. "Who knows? Elaine is his top priority and now with you here. . ." Her voice trailed off and she began to pace again, a thoughtful silence spreading out between us. "If they do not match me soon, my family will be angry."

She was so quiet I had to strain to hear, and I wondered if she was merely thinking aloud, talking to herself, but she paid me no heed.

"If I were at home, my mother would have me engaged by now," she continued in the same low tone. "That was the whole point of the peace treaty, to unite Britain and Ireland through marriage. But I have resources. My people have watchmen stationed throughout the city." She ran the knuckles of her right hand along her mouth, thinking. "Should too much time pass, any one of them could whisk me away under cover of darkness and the treaty would be void because Pellinor failed to uphold his end of the bargain and obtain for me a husband. Then I would be free to marry whomever I choose." She stopped at the window, looking out over the sea toward Ireland. Her eyes were glittering now, a plan forming in her mind. "My mother would not deny me love. Then someday, when I am Queen of Ireland, I will be able to repay what Lyonesse and Pellinor have given me. They will regret treating me so."

Suddenly, she seemed once again aware of my presence. Her attention focused on me, and she let her hand fall to her side. "I suppose we all live in a fantasy world from time to time," she said apologetically, her lips twisting into a half smile, half frown.

Gracefully, she descended into the window seat and I joined her, suddenly weary.

"We are going to cause quite a stir in their pious little world, I can feel it." There was conspiracy in her voice. "Now, if it won't cause you too much pain, I'd love to hear about the man who was worth risking your inheritance for."

◦⊙ ⊙◦

While the cold, soaking rains wrenched the last of the leaves from the trees, Isolde and I spent time getting to know one another. When I asked about her life before she came to Corbenic, she was evasive, but I learned she had a mother she practically worshiped, a younger sister she adored, and a younger brother she loathed. She, in turn, was very interested in my childhood, asking about every detail. As a result, I found myself forgetting she was

Irish—and therefore, my enemy—and telling her things I would otherwise keep to myself.

"The thing I miss the most is being able to hold a sword," I told her one quiet afternoon. "I cannot find the words to explain it, but when I do, nothing else matters. The weapon and I dance, and the rest of the world falls away." I remembered my last lesson with my mother and cousin Bran, only days before the attack that shook my life to the core. Although Bran was taller than me by an arm's span and twice as strong, I had disarmed him in only three moves. "My mother would be highly displeased if she could see how my skills have deteriorated, thanks to Avalon's policy of non-violence and my father's prohibition."

"Maybe she can." Isolde's eyes were glimmering when she looked up at me. "And I may have a solution for you." She wiggled her eyebrows at me.

Mine arched in response. "Isolde—" I said her name slowly, as though approaching an unfamiliar animal. "I don't know what you are thinking, but I know I do not like it."

She slid off her seat, graceful as a cat, wagging her index finger at me as she approached. "Don't be so quick to judge. It so happens that the son of Pellinor's weapon's master owes me a favor. I may be able to talk the master into training you. If"—she touched me lightly on the nose—"you promise to keep it a secret."

I was at a loss for words. Isolde had a solution for everything. "Of course," I croaked, eventually. "How soon do you think you can arrange it?"

Her grin signaled she was already up to no good. "I will talk with him tomorrow. My guess is you'll be sparring again before the week is out."

I still do not know what words Isolde used to charm Guildford, the weapon's master, but she was true to her word. He agreed to give me covert lessons if I agreed to teach his son to read. He didn't know what terms were specified in his own contract with Pellinor and did not want his son to suffer the same fate. He had dreams for Liam to become a warrior and win his own land one day. If he could read, his lot in life would be all the stronger.

The next evening, Isolde and I met the well-muscled swordsman and his boyishly handsome son in the barn of a farmhouse just outside the castle gates. It was close enough for us to sneak there unnoticed—it seemed Isolde knew a myriad of ways in and out of the castle—yet far enough from the prying eyes of court to evade suspicion. After all, who would question the ringing of blades on the weapon's master's property? Passersby would rightly assume someone was getting in some extra practice. What they would never guess was who.

We would occasionally vary our location so as not to arouse suspicion—one day the lower paddock, the next a clearing in the woods—but as the days went by, the barn proved to be the place with the least interruption or cause for prying eyes.

Nearly a month into my training, on a cold, clear morning, we reached the safety of the barn just as the sun broke over the horizon. I usually sparred with Liam while Guildford instructed, so I was surprised to see Guildford suited in leather armor, warming up with basic footwork and a few practice swings.

"Blessings of the day to you, ladies," he greeted us in a warm baritone.

"And to you as well," Isolde answered, sneaking a quick peck on Guildford's cheek before he could protest.

I smiled, still shy in the presence of so great a man. Guildford's name was known along the western coast of Britain from Cornwall to Rheged because he had trained most of the men who successfully fought off the Irish for the last twenty years. The irony of Isolde being my means to him now did not escape my notice.

Though his shoulder-length hair was streaked with gray and his face deeply lined, he had the agility and strength of a man half his age, and the prospect of facing off with him made my stomach clench.

Guildford must have read my expression. "Come on now, lass. We have only until the church bells toll. Get ye ready."

I threw Isolde a questioning look as I shed my cloak, tucked the hem of my tunic into my belt, and donned my own protective leather breastplate.

She read my meaning and casually asked what I had been too intimidated to ask. "I thought Liam was challenging Guinevere today?"

"Liam needs time to study what Guinevere taught him when last we met. He's been needed to help secure the last of the harvest and mind the slaughter. Isn't that right, son?"

Liam looked up from the board on which he was slowly tracing letters with a crude stylus. His cheeks and throat reddened at the attention. "Yes, Father. More hands keep the beast of winter at bay, or so Mother says."

Isolde sauntered behind him, trailing her finger across his shoulders as she passed. She bent low over his left shoulder and surveyed his work. "He's doing well. Guinevere will have him reading and writing in no time." Her breath ruffled the hair at his ear.

Liam's blush deepened.

Isolde sat down on the bale of hay next to him, guiding his hand when he struggled.

As I went through my own brief warm-up, I wondered at the nature of the favor Liam owed her. He wasn't yet old enough to join Pellinor's army and I hadn't seen him about the castle, so how had they met? It really could have been anywhere, given that Isolde had lived here for so many years, and by her own admission, Lyonesse's guard was not always as close as it was now. But since he was obviously attracted to her, I could only assume she had used that to her advantage.

Guildford skimmed the tip of my sword with his own, a subtle bid for my attention. As we did with each new technique, he took me through the whole sequence once, explaining both offense and defense as we flowed through the movements.

I began with my shield outstretched, sword drawn high as I readied to strike. I brought down my sword, aiming for Guildford's head, but he stepped forward, blocking me with his shield, and putting me on the defensive. He held my sword fast, pushing against it with his shield so that I could not release it to strike again. Quickly, he raised his own blade, thrusting at my face, and I instinctively raised my shield arm to deflect. The jolt shot down my arm and into my teeth as the sword glanced off. Guildford took advantage of my momentary shock to change tack, using the motion of my defense to propel his sword toward my thigh, while also swatting aside my sword with his shield.

"That is only half the sequence, but I want you to learn both sides of it now. Once you've practiced, we'll put it together with the pattern I showed you at our last instruction and see if you can disarm me."

Leaving me to practice as both fighters in this duel, Guildford sat on a barrel, halfway between Isolde and me, so he could correct my technique as I practiced.

"Do you really mean what you said last week?" Without preamble, he resumed the conversation they let fall last time we scurried back to the castle. "How could it possibly be done?"

"Of course." She waved a hand airily as if swatting away a fly. "I would not offer if I was not intending to keep my word. When I return home, at least one of you will come with me. I will send for the others as I can."

I wanted to stop and consider the implications of what Isolde was saying, but to do so was a potentially dangerous distraction. I tried to focus on my training as their conversation whirled around me like so many dragonflies.

"But how will you do it while keeping Lyonesse in the dark? You know if she found out, she would lash out in ways you cannot even imagine."

Isolde shook her head. "She need not know. I have connections in the kitchens, the stables, even in her own bedchamber. The family will not discover my plan until it is too late to stop it."

Liam paused in his studies. "You will break Pellinor's heart, you do realize that."

I stopped then, sword mid-swing, and turned to the boy, surprised at his astute interjection. He was gazing at her with a strange combination of infatuation and concern for his father's master.

Isolde, for her part, appeared shaken, a tiny line of worry marring the space between her eyes. She bit her lower lip as if the thought hadn't crossed her mind. "I know," she finally responded in a small voice. She swallowed hard. "It pains me to betray him so, but I cannot let years of injustice go unpunished." She looked up at Liam, eyes seeking his approval—or maybe it was his forgiveness she wanted. "I put no one in danger by what I am planning to do. I could easily wage war, but instead I chose a more subtle form of revenge."

Guildford made a sarcastic sound. "Yes, how noble of you. You merely rob their household of the best servants and craftsmen, weaken them from within."

I went back to dueling with my shadow then, uncertain whether Guildford meant his words in jest.

"Do you wish me to send for you or no?" Isolde's tone was haughty. She clearly thought him serious and was hurt by the thought.

"I do, I do." Guildford sighed. "I simply wish I did not have to betray my master in the process."

He must have stood silently, for in the next moment, I heard the crunch of his boots as he came toward me.

"Ready?" He picked up his sword, assuming a standard opening stance.

I nodded, mirroring him.

We went through the sequence again, in the same roles. When we reached his jab for my thigh, I blocked it and brought up my sword, forcing him back. I swung horizontally around my right side, and Guildford lifted his sword and shield in response, using both to absorb the brunt of the blow. Stepping to my left, I repeated the strike on the other side, harder, forcing his defenses upward, exposing his now vulnerable groin area. I touched the tip of my blade to the area just below his armor to signal where my thrust would have landed.

Guildford clapped his hands together. "That was well done indeed."

Isolde put an arm around me as I bent to examine Liam's writing, my chest still heaving from the exertion of the fight. My eyes had made it only halfway down the page before a bell tolled in the distance, signaling the beginning of the morning prayer that preceded Mass.

"We must be off. There is little time to change before we meet Lyonesse and Elaine for daily devotions," I said. No matter how many times we did this, I would never lose the fear of being caught, the sheer panic at the thought of Lyonesse's reaction to my forbidden activity.

But Isolde was as calm as ever. While I stripped off my armor and did my best to straighten my wrinkled dress, she tousled Liam's hair and pecked him on the cheek. "Be a good boy and practice your letters—for me."

Liam smiled self-consciously. "Anything for you."

I embraced Guildford. "Tomorrow, then?"

He nodded. "Indeed."

"Remember, I keep my promises," Isolde called over her shoulder.

That's what I'm afraid of. I began my morning prayers then and there, begging the gods as I ran toward the castle that whether Isolde left for Ireland as a new bride or struck out on her own as she had threatened to do, it would not bring calamity on Pellinor's house. For I was part of that house now, and as much as I was growing to love her, I did not want to see her thirst for vengeance bring pain to those who held my future in their hands.

Chapter Twelve

Winter 496

Snow was gently falling from the pre-dawn sky, covering man and beast alike in a thin film of white powder. We were gathered in the courtyard outside Pellinor's castle in the early morning darkness, along with the rest of the village, to celebrate Candlemas, the first day of spring, though it came in what felt like the depths of winter. In my religion, it was a day dedicated to the goddess Brigid, who was the patroness of women's mysteries, especially childbirth, as well as fire and all forms of poetry and inspiration. In the Christian world of Corbenic, however, the feast commemorated the day the Virgin Mary, obedient to the laws of her own religion, went to the temple to undergo ritual purification after giving birth and present her son to God and the temple elders.

"Why, oh why, must this tradition be conducted outdoors?" I muttered to myself through chattering teeth. I stomped my frozen feet on the equally frozen ground and noted a little less feeling in them. I had been cold all morning, for we woke to find all of the fires in the house extinguished. As was custom, they would not be lit again until after Mass.

"Mortification, is that what they call this?" I asked Isolde, who was nearest to me in the long line of white-cloaked, half-frozen women.

She smiled. "Appropriate, is it not? We are liable to catch our death out here."

I knew she was only commiserating with me; Isolde did not even seem to feel the cold, so great was her excitement. She hadn't slept more than an hour last night; this was her favorite feast—mainly because it was the only one performed nearly the same as it was in her homeland. It was the one time of year she could erase the miles separating her from her family.

"Wait until you see it, Guinevere; it is truly beautiful. The ritual may be Christian, but the actions and the words are practically the same. Only at home, we don't carry a statue of stone. We fashion a likeness of Brigid out of straw and carry her in a litter made of rushes."

Isolde was practically bouncing in place as she spoke, her eyes wild with passion and memory as she watched the cluster of people at the front of the line struggling to lift a heavy stone statue. Lyonesse, for her part, tried to squelch Isolde's enthusiasm and make her display the proper demeanor. But Isolde didn't even hear her. To her, reverence and happiness were one and the same; her joy was her prayer.

Among the small crowd were Pellinor and Elaine, who was dressed in white like the rest of us, but her head was veiled in lace and crowned with rushes.

Isolde looked at Elaine with a mixture of envy and sadness, an expression I recognized from my Beltane competition with Morgan.

"I always wanted to be that girl," she said wistfully.

Her words surprised me. "Did you not take her role in your homeland? You are the eldest royal daughter, so I thought that would be your right."

A small, bitter laugh escaped her blue lips. "It would have been had I stayed. My mother insisted the representative of the goddess be at least twelve years old so she would be mature enough to understand the ritual and treat the office with respect. I would have been the most devoted Bride anyone had ever seen." Her eyes searched the western horizon. Did she see the castle walls or the mountains or the icy ocean in between? No, she was searching for home.

Isolde sighed and she was present once again. "Of course, here, Lyonesse would sooner accept the Goddess before she would let me lead the procession." She paused, looking impish. "Although I hear she came from a pagan family, so there may yet be hope!"

"So if even *you* have a chance, does that mean it is not always a member of Pellinor's family who is chosen?" I could practically see my words formed by my icy breath in front of me.

Isolde's eyes widened and her face shaped into the expression I had come to associate with frustration when she had to explain something to me that she took for granted. "Oh, no. This is Elaine's year because she is fourteen, marrying age." She sniffed, a haughty sound that I couldn't be sure was caused by the cold. "Sadly, rather than treat this holy day as a source of devotion,

Pellinor and his princes use it as an excuse to parade their eligible daughters through the streets." She rolled her eyes.

A slight pain tugged at my heart for Elaine as I watched her take her place in line, reverently balancing the cross and the candle with which she had been entrusted. The poor girl thought she had been chosen for her virtue, when really it was her body on display, not her soul.

The bells tolled, announcing the dawn of the day. The line lurched forward, led by Elaine. Following close behind were Pellinor and three of his lords, each holding one corner of a heavy stone statue depicting the Virgin Mary seated with her divine child in her lap.

The snow crunched softly beneath our feet as we walked in silence, each bearing a candle lit by the priest. We wound our way out of the castle gates, through the village, and into the countryside beyond. People lined the streets, waving rushes, peculiar equal-armed crosses, and dolls made of straw. As the procession passed, many fell to their knees, crying out "thrice be blessed, noble lady!" or asking for the blessing of the goddess Brigid or the Virgin Mary.

By the time we arrived at the church, my hair was wet with matted snow and I scarcely felt the floor beneath me. The litter on which the statue rested was covered in evergreen boughs, seeds, and bowls of milk, offerings of the devotees.

As the church doors swung open to admit us, the small cluster of monks began chanting in Latin.

Pellinor and his companions placed the statue and its offerings on a special altar near the front of the little church. After giving the cross to the priest, Elaine deposited her candle directly in front of the statue, and each of us followed suit, forming a circle around the tall center candle. When Isolde stepped forward to make her offering, her face was glowing with reverent love. I did not miss the slight inclination of her head or the soft bow she made before the statue, and neither did Lyonesse. The latter nodded approvingly, not comprehending the true source of Isolde's devotion.

The priest swung a censor around all sides of the statue, filling the room with a sweet, pungent odor that seemed out of place in the bitter cold. Elaine came forward and stood next to the statue, her face now completely obscured by her veil. She held the bowl of cold, clear water the priest had just blessed and sprinkled each member of the assembled crowd as they came forward to pay their respects.

Slaves, servants, and poor workers laid their tools at the feet of the Virgin, along with the seeds they would begin planting once the earth thawed. Finally, one member of each household—a female servant, slave, or the eldest daughter—came forward and lit a candle from the one Elaine had held, carrying with it the Virgin's blessing. From this one light, each hearth fire and lamp in Pellinor's kingdom would be lit; the light had come once again to the earth to melt its frozen soil.

As Mass began, I wished it could also thaw my frozen feet.

৵৹৻ ৻৹৵

The great hall was warm, the air thick with smoke and the scent of mingled food, wine, and ale, and buzzing with the sound of merry chatter and the tinkling of dishes. Each year, on the evening of

Candlemas, Lord Pellinor held a great feast for his subjects. It was another of his rituals of penance. To atone for the sins his wealth brought upon him and to imitate as closely as possible the generous heart of Christ, on this night, he feasted the poorest of his people. Farmers, tradesmen, orphans, homeless, thieves, and prostitutes, all were welcome with open arms. Each was given a sumptuous meal, and if they lived far away or had no homes to return to, he paid the nightly fee at a nearby inn so they could slumber free of worry or fear.

Although this was not an entirely new idea—many lords held similar celebrations on Christmas or Easter—I had to admire Pellinor for doing it, and not just out of obligation; he seemed to truly enjoy himself. He went around to each table, speaking freely with every guest, asking about their wants or needs. A scribe followed quietly behind, noting what was said so it could be acted upon at daybreak. Many times I saw him discreetly press a fistful of coins into a needy hand, to be met with stunned silence, a whispered blessing, or tearful gratitude.

This is the definition of Christian love and mercy, not the doctrine of fear and guilt Father Marius proclaims in my father's house.

I had been thinking of them both a great deal lately, and as I wrestled the meat from a chicken bone, I wondered at my father's welfare. There had been no news, which was not surprising, given the bitter winter weather, but still I worried for him, alone in Northgallis with only his memories and that wretched priest to keep him company.

Elaine too looked preoccupied. She stared at her plate, mindlessly pushing at her food with her knife rather than eating it. She looked tired and very apprehensive. Perhaps Isolde had told her of her father's intentions of showing her off, or maybe she had figured it out. One thing was certain—something weighed heavy on her mind.

Isolde appeared to be enjoying herself, chatting merrily with one of the household servants. She was only a few seats down from where I sat, so I could hear snippets of their conversation. Earlier she had explained to the baker's black-haired daughter that this was the only day of the year she felt at ease; despite the title she held in her native land, it was the only time she'd felt equal to everyone else in the room. Now, a few cups into the evening, they were apparently discussing lovers past and presently desired, and were in the midst of a lengthy discussion about the physical merits of the blacksmith's son.

I turned away, embarrassed to overhear some of their more unguarded comments. I said a quiet prayer of thanks that Lyonesse was seated at the opposite end of the long wooden bench, where Isolde's drunken discourse could not reach her ears.

My eyes followed my thoughts, involuntarily seeking out Lyonesse's face. There was no head table tonight, no dais, as all were to be equal at this feast, so Lyonesse had nowhere to which she could escape. She looked absolutely miserable, sitting rigidly amidst the wives of the innkeeper, the blacksmith, and some of the soldiers, all of whom were raucously celebrating. Her pale hair was piled high and tight on her head, making her look harsh, an effect only magnified by her scowl.

I bet she would crawl through her own skin if it meant she could escape the gaggle of joyful women around her. She caught my eye, and I braced myself for the dart sure to be thrown my way, but to my surprise, rather than glare, Lyonesse smiled. It was just a twitch of her lips, but it was the first positive gesture she'd shown me since I arrived.

Pleased and shocked, I grabbed the nearest serving girl and instructed her to keep watch over Lyonesse's cup. Perhaps the atmosphere was finally rubbing off on her. Or maybe it was the wine. Whatever the solution, I wanted to keep her happy for as long as possible.

After the dishes were cleared, the court minstrels struck up a lively tune, giving everyone the chance to dance for a bit before the evening drew to a close. The baker's daughter had found a dance partner and so had Isolde—the blacksmith's son, judging by her earlier description. She whooped audibly as he spun her past my table. I couldn't help but smile. Even Elaine had timidly accepted the hand of a young soldier. I had seen him earlier today during the procession. Tall, strong, and dark-skinned, he was the son of one Pellinor's underlords, one of the many who had turned out to see Elaine on display. Now, as she hesitantly held his hand and let him lead her through the steps, she looked to Lyonesse for approval. The latter nodded encouragingly.

I had no desire to dance, and fortunately, no one seemed to notice me. As the night went on and the candles burned low, my thoughts turned to Aggrivane, as they so often did when my mind was not otherwise occupied. He would have loved an evening such as this, where one was free to be at ease, where customs and rules did not apply. He might even have taken the idea as a model back to his father in Lothian. We certainly would have done the same in our kingdom, had we married.

My brooding was interrupted by the sight of Pellinor approaching Lyonesse and softly taking her hand. She blushed at whatever he said and rose from her chair, smiling. They too began to dance, whispering in one another's ears whenever the steps brought them close. I had to look away; the intimacy of their exchange made me feel as though I was intruding on a private moment.

I rested my head on my arm to avoid seeing any of the dancers. Instead, I focused on the music and indulged my thoughts of Aggrivane. How I would have loved to have joined in the dancing were he my partner. I imagined him guiding me assuredly across the dance floor, pulling me close and then spinning me around until I dizzily fell into his waiting arms.

The Goddess brought us together twice. I had to trust she would do so again. It was the only thing keeping me from losing my mind in this strange house of piety and politics, where I was forced into a mold that I did not fit because it could never contain my soul.

But the Goddess also took him from you twice, answered a dark voice somewhere in the recesses of my mind.

But I am her priestess and must adhere to her will, no matter how loathsome it may be, I reminded myself.

Then you must realize you may never see him again, it answered, sending an icy fissure through my heart.

CHAPTER THIRTEEN

I didn't know when I fell asleep, but the next thing I knew, the hall was quiet, nearly empty. It must have been well after midnight. I rubbed my aching head—perhaps I had one glass too many—stretched, yawned, and looked around. Elaine and Isolde were having an animated conversation in the corner. From their wide grins and excited eyes, I guessed they were discussing their respective dance partners. Lyonesse was flitting about, loudly directing the servants who had stayed behind to clean up, her good mood having faded along with the effects of the wine. In another corner, Pellinor was gently removing the last of the loitering guests, a particularly troublesome man who it appeared would need more than persuasive words to convince him to leave.

"My good sir, the night draws late and snow falls deep. Will you not please accept an escort back to your home from one of my men? If you have no lodging, I will provide one night's rest for you in town," Pellinor was saying, his voice tender with compassion.

"A generous offer, my lord," the hooded man replied, looking up for the first time. "But would Christ turn his own kin out into the cold?"

As the man removed his hood, Pellinor turned a sickly shade of gray, and I gasped, recognizing Merlin at once.

"Come now, brother," he continued. "Has it been so long that you have forgotten me?"

Pellinor struggled to regain his ability to speak. "Taliesin— Merlin," he corrected himself from Merlin's given name to the Archdruid's official title with much effort. He gulped and staggered backward onto a bench. "You come only when there is news." He looked worried, aging well beyond his years in only a few moments. "What news?"

Lyonesse, Elaine, Isolde, and I rushed to Pellinor's side, blinking dumbly at one another, unsure of what to do.

Merlin held Pellinor's gaze, obviously enjoying his discomfort. "Greetings of peace to you as well." He almost laughed, extending out a strong hand to Pellinor. "Please, you must introduce me to your extended family. Your company has grown since last we met."

Once the introductions were made, Pellinor dismissed the servants and we all took seats, eager to find out the cause of Merlin's unexpected visit. Lyonesse was on my left, Isolde on my right, and Merlin took the seat directly across from me. His bronze hair gleamed in the low light of the fire that cast shadows over the planes of his face and accentuated his high cheek bones and smooth, unwrinkled skin.

While the men exchanged pleasantries, I leaned over to Lyonesse, who finally had managed to close her mouth and was now clenching her jaw as if foresworn never to open it again.

"Why does Merlin call him brother?" I asked.

"They are kin—cousins, I think, related through the maternal line. They have spoken to each other as brothers as long as I have known them," she whispered in disgust.

I smiled to myself. So the saintly Pellinor was related by blood to the Archdruid of Britain. I could not have asked for a more interesting turn of events. I wondered how Pellinor kept this family secret quiet and what advantage the silence brought to Merlin.

"You asked if I bring news," Merlin was saying. "Indeed, I bring great news. I have come to tell you of the coronation of your high king." More quietly he added to me, "And I have a message for you."

Isolde and Elaine sat up straighter and regarded me with wonder. Lyonesse leaned forward on the table, giving me a look that could only be described as lethal. If I valued my life, it said, the message better not bring any scandal upon her house—and she silently demanded to know what it was.

Pellinor, who had missed the aside, sat back, glowering. "That was two months ago, Tali—Merlin. Why do you bring this news to us now?"

"Why were you not present to witness it yourself?" Merlin countered, his hands steepled in front of him, elbows resting lightly on the table.

"Yes, Father, why did we not attend?" Elaine asked, her face aglow with curiosity.

It was the first time I'd ever heard her speak out of turn.

"Glynis, Lord Lansdowne's daughter, said it was the grandest spectacle in three generations," she added a bit peevishly.

Lyonesse's expression had cooled from murderous to livid. "Yes, husband, tell me why I was the only tribal queen who did not witness her high king's installation."

Leave it to Lyonesse to make this about herself.

Pellinor shifted in his seat, clearly uncomfortable. "I thought it best to send a representative in my stead. The weather was beginning to turn poor," he explained feebly, "and Strathclyde is such a long journey—"

Lyonesse cut him off, fuming. "You made the journey many times when Uther had need of you. What made this time any different?"

Pellinor stood, enraged by the accusation in her voice. He brought his palm flat down upon the table. The smack reverberated around the deserted hall. "How would it look for a Christian king to attend the coronation of a man who is at best unknown and at worst a heathen bastard?" His voice was somewhere between a growl and a roar.

Merlin regarded him calmly, untroubled by Pellinor's outburst. "It would look like you were in unity with your high king, and that was all anyone was asking. Arthur does not demand that his subjects agree with all that he does or believes. He simply asks for your trust and your loyalty."

As he realized Merlin was right, Pellinor sank back into his seat. The fire in him had gone out.

"So what happened? What did we miss?" Elaine asked eagerly as though the previous exchange had not taken place.

Merlin chuckled at her enthusiasm as he reached behind his

back to remove his harp from beneath his cloak. "I will tell you everything that took place, down to the last detail, but it is better if I do so with this." He ran his fingers lovingly along the bow in the wood. "The ancients say that one note of a song is twenty times more powerful than a single word, and that only in song can truth be clearly perceived, for though words can harbor lies, music cannot abide them."

He strummed an opening note.

"Wait." Elaine put out a delicate hand to stop him. "Please. Before you begin, will you kindly tell us of our high king's appearance? No one here has ever seen him, and it would help us visualize your tale." Elaine's eyes were wide, her cheeks flushed. She was sitting so far forward on the bench I feared she would fall off. She looked happier than I'd seen her during my whole visit.

Merlin grinned, obviously amused by Elaine's interest in the subject. "Actually"—he turned to me—"Guinevere has seen him, though I doubt she remembers it."

Elaine shot me a look of pure envy.

"When did I see him, my lord?" I regretted my regression to Avalonian formality as soon as the words escaped my lips. The others did not appear to notice. They were too eager to hear the answer to the question.

"He came to the Beltane fires. Think, Guinevere, and you will remember." Merlin squinted at me as though willing my mind to give up the memory.

I slowly shook my head. When I thought of that night, all I could see were Aggrivane's loving eyes.

"No matter, you will meet him soon enough." He turned back to the others. "Your king is a man of great strength, large in build and tall. He stands a full head higher than I and is twice as strong. I have no doubt he could wrestle a pack of wolves to the ground if it came to that."

Elaine gasped and Isolde giggled, grasping my wrists with clammy palms as she listened.

Merlin's smile widened, and he held Elaine's gaze, nearly hypnotizing her. "Indeed, lass, you do well to be awed. Your king's nickname is 'the bear,' due to his great size and strength, but do not be fooled—he is not a brutish man. He is known for his grace and agility, and he is an accomplished swordsman."

His gaze shifted respectfully over Lyonesse to Isolde. "But I doubt those are the details *you* are after." His eyes lingered on her as he spoke.

Her cheeks flared in response.

"His features are fine-chiseled and strong, for he is Roman on his father's side. His mother, Iggraine, can count the generations of her people in this land back to the Belgae, who called his land home for thousands of years. He received from her a kindness of heart not commonly encountered. He is not yet seventeen years old." He'd lowered his voice just slightly and regarded the three of us. "Nearly the same age as all of you, and has yet to take a wife." He looked at each of us meaningfully.

Elaine looked like she would faint.

"Enough. We have indulged your dramatics," Pellinor groused. "Get on with your tale, for the hour grows late." He faked a yawn. Elaine threw her father a nasty look. Had either he or Lyonesse seen it, she wouldn't have been able to sit down for a week.

"Perhaps I have been a little too loquacious," Merlin apologized. He picked at the strings of the harp again and a soft melody slowly took shape. "Lords from every kingdom descended upon Arthur's ancestral home, the seat of his father, Uther Pendragon. Add to them villagers and country folk from three kingdoms in every direction, and you will begin to understand the size of the crowd. Shoulder into back, elbow to elbow, they stood crammed along passageways, craning their necks to see the king in the dim light of rows of torches as he approached the inauguration stone. The stone, larger than three men's heads, even when weathered by the ages, stood atop the same hill on which it had been deposited by the gods before time began. Some say it has been in Arthur's mother's family since before the Romans came."

His story now established, Merlin began to tap out an accompanying beat with his boot on the flagstones underfoot. "At exactly the stroke of midnight, they raised him up, the Lady of the Lake supporting one elbow, the bishop the other, and his mother behind him representing his ancestors."

I imagined Viviane – who became Lady of the Lake after Argante's passing not long after I left Avalon – in her formal robes of office, silver crown and milk-white moonstone glittering in the firelight. I knew not who the bishop was, but I surmised he was a better man than Father Marius if the king trusted him enough to request his assistance.

"The crowd went silent, eagerly anticipating the response of the gods. Some say the stone cried out, proclaiming him the true high king of Britain, while others say he glowed with the light of the gods. Some even say Uther himself appeared and gave his son his blessing."

Across the table, Pellinor rolled his eyes.

"Whatever the truth, the moment had come. The contract

between Arthur and the land had been established. I stood, and in a loud voice proclaimed his right to the throne. 'Arthur, son of Uther Pendragon, who was brother to Aurelius Ambrosuis, both of whom were sons of Imperator Constantine, you stand before us seeking to be wed to the land and henceforth hold it in your care. Is that so?'

"Arthur nodded solemnly.

"'Then I ask the goddess of sovereignty if she accepts this man as her mate.'

"The Lady of the Lake approached the stone, her gait smooth and sure, her back straight, head held high. She had called upon the Goddess, and now her face was not her own. She was youthful and carefree, the light of the stars in her eyes. She stood before him, taking his hands like a lover.

"'Man of clay and bone, you are but dust in my eyes. I am the spirit of the land you seek to rule. What is it that you offer me in exchange for my approval?'

"Arthur knelt before her, looking up into her infinite eyes, and proclaimed his vow to all. 'I pledge to you and to all my people my undying loyalty, from this moment to my very last breath. I swear to uphold the laws of this country and protect its land and its people, even with my own life. I promise to reign with justice and mercy, treating all with equanimity, and to defend this land from all who would seek to do it harm.'

"The Lady faced the assembly, her eyes closed, perfectly still. The crowd held its breath in anticipation."

I realized in that moment that I was doing the same.

"She opened her eyes and proclaimed her judgment for all to hear. 'I accept your vows, Arthur, son of Uther. You have my blessing. In exchange for your loyalty, I place upon you one geis, on pain of honor, which you may never break. You must always uphold my ways while remaining respectful of other's beliefs, for all are my children and though they may tread different paths, all return to me in the end.'

"'This do I swear,' Arthur replied.

"'Arise then, High King of Britain, and be armed for battle, for as even the most placid sea is subject to storm, your reign will not be without struggle.'

"The Lady then gave him the royal regalia, a white wand made from a sacred branch from Avalon and the sword of sovereignty—called Caliburn—its intertwined snakes a symbol of the light and dark aspects of power. From her hands he took the red cup of lordship and drank from it, his eyes watering and lips puckering, for its contents were both bitter and sweet, for so too is power. He returned to the stone, placing one foot upon it, the other firmly planted on the earth. The crown of Britain was taken up both by myself and the priest. Each whispering a blessing—his in Latin, mine in the tongue of our ancestors—we placed the diadem upon his brow.

"'Dux Britanniarum!' some in the crowd proclaimed, while others bestowed upon Arthur the ancient title of 'Arddurex' before we even had the chance to declare him high king.

"One by one, the kings in attendance came forth to pledge their service—Mark of Cornwall, Gerent of Dyfnaint, Malegant of the Summer Country, Cadwalla of the Midlands, Uriens of Rheged, Evrain of Powys, Cador of Bernicia, Guinevere's father, and Pellinor's representative. Even the lands of Gore, Dalriada, Brittany, the four northern tribes, and your mother"—he smiled at Isolde—"sent emissaries to bring the new High King greetings of peace."

Merlin stopped strumming, and with the music went all of the life in the room. His face darkened. "Noticeably absent was Lot of Lothian, who believes, as husband to Arthur's sister Ana, he is the true heir to the throne. I would advise you to have no dealings with him. He can be of a dark temper and no doubt will attempt rebellion."

Pellinor yawned—genuinely this time. "Have no fear, brother. I have no esteem for that man or his progeny."

I chose to ignore his barb against Aggrivane, still trying to pry the memory of having seen Arthur in Avalon from the recesses of my mind. Lyonesse was drowsing, chin resting on her chest. Elaine, lulled to sleep by Merlin's song, sat with her head upon her mother's shoulder, a slight smile upon her lips. I guessed she was dreaming of Arthur.

Pellinor, however, seemed in no mood to sleep. In truth, he looked like he was aching for an argument. I sat up in my chair and stretched, willing myself to stay awake despite the gnawing headache I longed to stifle with sleep.

"Merlin, you say our king was crowned by both you and a Christian priest. That is quite a break from tradition—and I must admit, more than a little confusing. To which faith is he sworn?"

Merlin regarded Pellinor carefully, fully aware the man was angling for something. "Our king," he said with great emphasis, "is Druid-trained, taught by my own hand. His foster father, Lord Ector, sent him to study with us on the sacred isle a few years ago. He was never meant to take our vows, only to learn from our wisdom. Like his father, he serves the lord of light—the one whom some call Mithras, Apollo, or Lugh. However, he refuses to disparage the Christian religion because he can see in it the same marks of his own faith, but also because his mother took the habit of a Christian nun after Uther's death. To insult Christianity would be to insult her. Therefore, he upholds both his native religion and that of his mother." Merlin sat back in his chair, clearly satisfied with his answer.

Pellinor made a pensive grunting sound. "A very well-rehearsed account, but I have my doubts. The boy seems too good to be true." He muttered his next statement, but it sounded like something about no man being able to serve two masters. "Honestly, brother," Pellinor continued his complaints a little louder now, "if he lacks the sense to embrace the one true faith, how can we be sure he has sense enough to be our king?"

Merlin sighed, looking weary of this circuitous argument. "Pellinor, we all know your views, and it is obvious that nothing I can say will appease you."

Pellinor looked hurt.

"All I can do is tell you the truth. I cannot force you to believe it. While Ector always maintained he had no knowledge of Arthur's paternity, he made certain that Arthur received an education fit for an heir apparent. In addition to his Druidic training, Arthur learned the dialects of all the native tribes, is fluent in Latin and Greek, and has even taken it upon himself to learn the language of the Saxons. He is trained in arms and military strategy and can recite the names and titles of all the ranking men of the eleven tribes, should he one day need them as allies. Does that satisfy you?"

Pellinor frowned. He obviously was not expecting the king to be so well-qualified, or at least, Merlin to have such a thorough answer. "I suppose it will do."

Elaine and Lyonesse had awoken.

"Father," Elaine jumped in, seeing a lull in the conversation. "May we go to bed now?"

Her voice was so like a little child, I had to stifle a giggle.

Pellinor seemed only then to realize the rest of us were in the room. "Why yes, of course."

As we all made our way to our chambers, Elaine's preoccupation returned. I touched her shoulder and she stopped, turning to face me. Her forehead was wrinkled with worry and her eyes were heavy, morose.

"What is wrong, dear heart? Are you tired?" Truth be told, I was feeling a little unsteady myself.

She nodded. "Of course. Are you not?" She hesitated, unsure whether to elaborate. "It is only that all of this revelry and hearing about our new king has made me sad."

"Sad?" I was shocked at her response; it was the opposite of what I expected. "Why is that?"

"It made me realize how lonely I am."

With no more explanation, she turned away and ascended the stairs, leaving me gaping behind her.

⚬෧ඁ ඁ෧⚬

As I continued toward my own room, Merlin stopped me.

"Is there somewhere we may speak in private?" he asked.

I led him back into the now-empty hall, which seemed abnormally large in the silence following the feast. I wearily sank onto an abandoned bench and motioned for him to do the same.

"Guinevere, there is something you need to know," he began.

I probed his face, searching desperately for the meaning my

heart sought. "Yes? Is it about Aggrivane?" The words tumbled out, buoyed by hope.

"No." He seemed torn between regret and amusement at my optimism. "It is about Morgan."

My heart sank into my feet. Why would he go through all of this to talk to me about the one person I never wanted to think about again?

"I know she is not your favorite person, but you need to know this. She has been banished from Avalon."

"What?" I nearly fell off my seat. "Why? What happened?"

"It is complicated." He took a deep breath and began to explain. "There was a competition among the priestesses to determine who would be Viviane's second, now that she has assumed the office of Lady of the Lake. It is a long tradition in Avalon. I wish you could have taken part. You would have done well. During the three days of the full moon before the equinox, the priestesses displayed their skill at all of the ancient arts—divination, control of the elements, spell casting, mastery of the sight, and ritual. I served as judge, so Viviane could not be accused of partiality. The final test was healing. Morgan had done the best, and everyone expected her to easily win this event as well."

I involuntarily flinched, recalling her skill in that area, and the old jealousy reasserted itself. My stomach roiled, and I tasted bile.

"But when it came time for the judging, something unexpected happened. As was custom, each priestess had to drink from the cup prepared by her partner as a sign of trust. When Rowena drank from Morgan's cup, she immediately fell to the floor in a fit."

I gasped and covered my mouth with my hand. "Is she. . . did she. . . is she well?" My eyes filled with tears at the thought of my dear friend meeting such a horrible end.

"Yes, she eventually recovered. Viviane was able to give her an antidote, but we don't know what the effects will be. No one knows if it was an accident or if Morgan did it on purpose. She seemed as shocked as everyone else and has always maintained her innocence. But she was immediately suspected of poisoning Rowena because she was the closest competition. You of all people should know how Morgan treats people whom she perceives as a threat."

My mind drifted back to the day I rescued Ailis from the tree above the lake. I could still smell the burned tapestry thread and feel the puffy red blisters. Without realizing what I was doing, I scratched at the phantom sores on my arm that had long ago healed.

"But surely you do not believe she poisoned Rowena, do you? She lived with us in the House of Nine. She was our sister. Even Morgan would not—"

"When we analyzed the contents of Morgan's brew, there was an obvious error in ingredients, two herbs that should never be mixed together. You know how talented she is. It was a mistake she would not have made."

"But even she can err." To my own amazement, I found myself defending my old rival. "Perhaps she was fatigued or distracted or maybe someone wanted it to look like—"

"What is done is done," Merlin interrupted. "It was the judgment of the council—myself, Viviane, and the elder priestesses—that regardless of her intent, Morgan broke the vows she made at her consecration. By using the arts for harm, she failed to uphold the sisterhood and therefore had to pay the price. Viviane banished her from Avalon for a year and a day. After that time, she may return, if she wishes. But they had an intense row before she left, and with Morgan's pride, I doubt she will acquiesce to return."

I could scarcely believe my ears. Merlin was so calm, he could have been telling me about the weather. I could not comprehend his attitude. "So that is it then?" The frustration I was trying to suppress burst out in a fit of rage. "You sent her off the isle with nowhere to go? She has no family to return to, no friends. Avalon was her home!" I was shaking, a cold sweat blanketing the back of my neck and shoulders.

Merlin jumped to his feet, tipping his bench backward. He towered over me with such ferocity that I shrank back, heart pounding. For the first time since he arrived, I felt like I was in the presence of the Archdruid.

"Do you really think us that unkind or uncaring? After so many years with us, do you really believe us capable of turning her out on her own? We contacted several houses—prominent families, mind you—who were willing to take her in. They expected her, but she never inquired at a single one. We sent her with a guard intended to see her safely from house to house until she found employment, but she dismissed them—or rather, escaped them."

"So where is she then?"

Merlin hung his head, an uncharacteristically humble gesture. "We do not know. We have searched everywhere we are welcome, and she is not to be found. She has simply vanished."

"Much like the fey they say she came from," I whispered to myself.

"Viviane was just trying to teach her a lesson—instill some humility." Merlin continued as if he did not hear. He was thinking aloud. "No one expected her to react so rashly."

Had they not been paying attention her whole life? Morgan had always been unpredictable. What did they expect?

Merlin righted his bench and sat back down. "Guinevere, I want to share something with you, a theory I have told no one except for Viviane. Do you swear you will not repeat it?"

My breath caught. "Of course." I willed myself to be calm. I was suddenly very hot, though whether with the intimacy of Merlin's request or my nagging need for sleep, I could not tell.

"Do you remember the strange prophecy Viviane spoke during your last full moon in Avalon?"

My brow furrowed as I tried to recall the words, but all that rose to my muddled mind was something about animals and flowers.

Seeing my difficulty, Merlin recited the three verses from memory.

"'The red dragon is poised to return to the realm of spirit, but another shall succeed him. The hallowed one has received the blessing of the land, and so shall it prosper under his guidance. Although malevolent forces threaten from without, the bear shall be victorious and all shall bow at the sound of his name.

"Soon the final passage shall be crossed by one of great power, allowing the lily to emerge from shadow and bloom in the light. An unlikely rose is transplanted to this isle and blossoms in its rich soil. But beware the rose and handle her carefully, for her thorns threaten to pierce the bud of the lily, thus causing the whole garden to die.

"These here gathered serve me well, and I am pleased. But the day *will come when sister shall oppose sister, both in this sacred place and without. Loyalties will be tested and betrayed, so heed my warning. That which is birthed in jealousy shall not give life but infect all who draw near. Therefore, act with love and not out of spite. Only then shall you escape the fate the stars foretell.'"*

He continued breathlessly. "I believe I know to whom it was referring. We now know the red dragon was Uther and the Goddess foretold his passing and the rise of Arthur as king. I told you many people call him 'the bear' because of his size, and that is how he is identified in the prophecy. We also know that the final passage was Argante's death. That leads me to believe that Viviane is the lily, who has how taken her place of power as Lady of the Lake."

I nodded, amazed at how much sense that made, like pieces of a child's puzzle fitting into place. "But who is the rose? The terrible threat to Viviane?"

"We don't yet know. Only time will reveal her. But one thing we do know is the Goddess warned of enmity between priestesses. That is why I'm sharing this with you. I want you to be on your guard with Morgan. I believe you will see her again, and you should be prepared for when you do. By knowing what has happened to her, I hope you will feel a little more compassion toward her. I would hate for your jealousy to bring the prophecy to pass."

Looking into his eyes, which were now to me a scrying pool, I saw the future he feared. Morgan was standing with her arm draped protectively around a young boy, about ten years old. She sneered as though she could see me, and then the scene changed. A hooded woman delicately unlaced the praying fingers of a priest and placed a vial in his palm. He held it up to the light, and its contents glinted with malevolence. He nodded, and she turned to leave, a single stand of fiery hair betraying her identity. Morgan again. Then there was nothing but thick, choking smoke.

Merlin was still talking when I came back to myself, but I could not hear him over the shrill ringing in my ears. I grabbed the bench to steady myself as a wave of dizziness overcame me. The room swayed, and darkness beckoned. The last thing I heard was Merlin's startled cry as I collapsed at his feet.

Chapter Fourteen

*T*he images floated in and out of my view, sharper than dreams, but they were no longer of Morgan. They were of war. Men on horseback, hundreds of them, swords glittering in the fading evening light, horses braying and whinnying as the men chased something—or someone—I could not see. Before I could blink, the whole scene melted as my vision blurred.

Shapes and colors were all I could make out now. It was as if someone had draped a gauzy veil in front of my eyes. Light and darkness alternated as I struggled to get my bearings.

"She is beginning to awaken." An echoing voice spoke from somewhere across a great void.

I tried to tell the voice to leave me alone, but my mouth wouldn't work. This was all so strange. Why wouldn't my lips move? Where was the rest of my body? All I could feel was an odd tingling engulfing my other senses and the sensation that my head was on fire.

"Guinevere, love, I'm here." The voice spoke again, washing over me in waves. "You are ill, but I will take care of you, I promise."

My eyes slowly began to focus. I could now make out the form of a girl about my own age sitting next to me. Her hair looked like my head felt. I knew this girl. Who was she? I searched around in my addled mind, sifting through names that refused to attach themselves to the faces that stared back at me.

Isolde? Was that it? I must have said it out loud.

"Yes, and Elaine and Merlin are here as well. We were very worried about you."

Her smile was warm, concerned. As she spoke, something cold and comforting skimmed over the fire in my head, momentarily causing it to sputter. In that moment of relief, my mind was clear. I remembered my conversation with Merlin about Morgan and my disconcerting visions.

I looked around, seeking Merlin. He was at the foot of the bed, watching me closely.

"Guinevere," he said softly, "you fainted. I brought you to your room. It appears you are quite ill. Your illness has weakened your resistance to the sight. You've been mumbling about your visions for some time now." He rounded the bed so he stood over me and bent down close. "It is best not to fight it. Your body needs rest, and if you resist, all you will do is weaken yourself more. Just give in and let the Goddess show you what she wills."

His last words echoed in my head, pounding to the same rhythm as the pulse of my blood as I struggled to remain conscious. I was losing, and I knew it. I was being sucked into an eddy, helpless to fight the swirling disorientation that had captured my senses.

From somewhere in the back of my mind, a loose strand of memory floated free, Argante's ominous warning from the day I was called before her to demonstrate mastery of the sight.

"For the remainder of your life, the sight will come to you of its own bidding when one to whom your soul is bonded is in peril."

I fought my leaden eyelids, wanting to ask Merlin if Argante was right. I was beginning to think so. First, the vision of my mother's death. Now the nonsense about Morgan. But was the sisterhood bond enough to count? I shivered despite, or perhaps because of, my fever. The sight beckoned. What was to come?

As if she could hear my thoughts, Isolde squeezed my hand. "I will not leave you," she pledged.

It was last thing I heard before darkness dragged its cape over my eyes and the visions began again.

⁂

I could hear his thoughts, this man whose dark complexion marked him as a descendant of Britain's ancient tribes. I knew him at once. The resemblance was too certain for him to be other than Lot, King of Lothian, father of my estranged lover. And he was plotting rebellion—treason.

It had been far too easy to get to this point, simpler than anyone could have ever imagined. Clandestine meetings with others of like mind, whispered words of treachery concealed in darkness; alliances formed as gold flowed from one hand to another.

His claim to the throne was legitimate, if one followed the ancient laws of the land, which passed title and power through the matriarchal line. Because Uther had no living sisters, his wife's daughter, Ana—Lot's wife—was next in line, even though she wasn't related to the high king by blood. Through her, Lot and his sons had as much claim to the throne as Arthur, perhaps more. This, coupled with the widely known understanding between Uther and Lot that upon Uther's death, Lot would assume the throne until his eldest son came of age, was why Lot refused to swear loyalty to Arthur.

The problem was that everyone believed Merlin's account of Uther's deathbed scruples—which Lot doubted ever took place, though no one could deny Arthur's skill in guiding the bereft army to victory. On top of that, no one knew what rule Arthur followed. Being half Roman and half Belgae, he seemed to follow whatever tradition suited him best at the moment.

These young upstarts have no sense of loyalty. Lot glowered.

Lot's supporters were smart enough to stay silent, at least in public. Some had even taken oaths of loyalty to Arthur. But those taciturn allies were growing in number daily, thanks to the network of spies and mercenaries Lot had employed to sow the seed of doubt in the minds of the most powerful men from one end of the island to the other.

Those who did not join his cause willingly were subjected to harsher measures. When loyalty couldn't be bought, it was coerced. Many of the tribes' most powerful men and women had been lax in obeying their own laws. Lot smiled as he thought of the power contained in the slightest bit of shameful information. A few illegitimate children, a throng of indiscreet lovers, a couple of misplaced alliances, and a handful of murders had given him support from within almost all of the key kingdoms.

However, the most drastic measures had been reserved for Arthur's staunchest supporters. They began disappearing three days ago, taken from their own homes by brute force. The price of ransom spread across the land like wildfire: the lords would only be returned upon Lot's coronation, after they had publically declared an oath of allegiance to him.

I could see them now—Lot's soldiers. Banging on doors in the middle of the night or disrupting households at the break of dawn, dragging out by force the lords and clan chiefs who resisted Lot's cause. The soldiers were under strict orders to harm no one during their raids. Lot insisted this be a bloodless revolution. He couldn't risk the people regarding him as a tyrant. No, he would not be branded another Vortigern; he would be their savior.

The element of surprise gave Lot's men leverage, but every so often, someone would resist, and one key player had escaped. That was why they were here, hidden amidst the foliage of the forest southwest of Lothian, lying in wait for the king.

A young boy approached them from behind. Without turning to look at him, Lot grabbed the boy by the throat of his tunic, his eyes trained steadily on the road.

"What news?" he rumbled.

The boy was taken off guard by Lot's swift action and the tightness of his grip. "The king. . ."—he struggled to breathe—"approaches from the south. He—"

Lot relaxed his knuckles.

The boy sucked in air. "He will cross us as his party emerges from Eildon Pass."

Lot nodded, still fixated on the narrow path that wound its way out from between mountains. "Does he suspect?"

The boy shook his head, although he knew Lot was not watching. "No, my lord."

"And the second unit?"

"In place, sire. As soon as the king's party halts, they will surround them, cutting off any chance of escape."

"Good." Lot released his hold.

The boy quickly scampered away, deep into the trees.

A few moments later, the steady clomp of hooves and the clattering of disturbed stones broke the silence of the forest. A small posse of men had made it through the pass and spilled out into the clearing. Before I could even search their faces, Lot's men sprang out, weapons drawn like a band of robbers.

Curses and oaths filled the air as the men reeled from the surprise and took a defensive stance, their own weapons at the ready.

Fearless, Lot approached the group, his black eyes singling out the largest warrior. Thanks to Lot's ruminations, I knew without looking who this man was, but I still gasped in disbelief at the sight of him.

King Arthur looked just as Merlin had described him, but his armor and traveling cloak made him look even more imposing. His tanned face and clothes were stained with grit from the road, and the aggravated expression on his face made me fear for Lot; Arthur was not a man I would want to cross.

"Arthur, so good of you to join us," Lot purred, as if he were greeting guests at a feast.

Arthur raised a hand, and his guards relaxed their stance but left their weapons trained on the opposing party. "I remind you, Lord of Lothian, I am your king, and you would be wise to address me as such." His voice was surprisingly deep and gravelly through his tightly clenched jaw.

Lot made a show of looking around. "King, you say? I see no king here but myself."

"Then your eyes deceive you," Arthur rebutted, "for I stand right in front of you."

Lot pretended to refocus his eyes. "No. All I see is a man who stole the mantle of power from his own kin by contrived tales and trickery. This man is no king. I am the true heir to the crown of this country, and I am here to claim what is mine." Lot drew his sword and pointed it straight at Arthur.

At the same instant, Arthur mirrored the motion.

Lot's men edged in closer, itching for the battle to begin.

Arthur again signaled his men to stand down, many of whom were shuffling their feet and trembling with the effort to keep from rushing their king's aggressor.

"Lot, I do not wish to kill your men. Shedding their blood would only needlessly create widows and orphans." His rich indigo eyes scanned the opposing force, halting abruptly. "Uriens, will you too betray me?" he asked a gray-haired combatant with the intensity of a far younger man. "My brother-in-law has always opposed me, but you swore an oath to me."

"I am supporting the true claimant to the throne," Uriens stated confidently.

"Then I regret I must oppose you as well, friend." Arthur sounded truly pained. He turned his attention back to Lot. "I have heard of your plans—and of your claims. If it is a war you want, you have picked the perfect way to start one, but I doubt that is your intent." He studied Lot, appraising his opponent's every reaction. "No, you are a man of peace; despite your recent actions, you will not be satisfied if this road runs red today. It is I you desire, and so you shall have your chance. I accept your challenge of combat."

Lot snarled. This was not a turn he had been expecting. He was an excellent fighter, but to cross swords with Arthur was a dangerous proposition. He had been counting on someone else to do that part of the work. Now Arthur gave him no choice. It was either fight or lose face in front of his troops.

"Move away, men," he ordered.

Both sides fell back to give the combatants room. Arthur waited patiently, reflecting Lot's every move to give him little advantage. Lot swung first, his sword easily glancing off Arthur's shield. Arthur responded, and the dance went on. Finally, Arthur landed a blow to Lot's shielding arm, causing him to drop his defense.

The tide was turning rapidly against Lot, and he knew it. He made a pretense at following strategy, but soon struck out in desperation, slashing at any area of Arthur's exposed skin. It was the wrong move; Arthur nimbly avoided him and quickly had Lot on the ground, sword to his throat.

Lot's men shifted their weight nervously, unsure if they should rescue their fallen leader.

Arthur's back was toward them, but he understood their quandary. "If none of you make an aggressive move, you will be allowed to return to your homes in peace and without charge. Any other action will be considered treason."

Lot's men sheathed their weapons.

Arthur heaved Lot upright so that he was kneeling, facing Arthur's men. "The law states that I should take your life," he said plainly. "But I am hesitant to rush to judgment."

Lot's eyes bulged; he was incredulous that he had not already been slain.

Arthur began to pace in a circle around Lot, the point of his sword never losing contact with Lot's flesh. "You see, I am intrigued by your mind. It took an astonishing grasp of strategy to plan and execute so brilliant a coup. It seems such a waste to kill you."

Silence reigned for a long moment.

"But then again, I would be a fool to let you go outright, so I am asking myself, what is of the most value to you?" He mused aloud as he paced, clearly enjoying the tension his delay in action created. "You no longer have any money or power—I have seen to that."

"What?" Lot choked, unable to keep the requisite silence. He immediately shrank back, anticipating Arthur's violent rebuke.

But Arthur merely stopped and looked Lot square in the eye. "You did not know?" A wide grin spread across his face. "You mean to tell me that with your contingent of spies and informants, no one told you my reason for traveling north?" He gave a dubious laugh and then his face turned to granite. "I was coming to your kingdom to personally deliver your formal censure. Your treasury has been turned over to the crown for proper dispensation in light of your own misuse."

Lot's face was ashen, his mouth open wide like a drawbridge.

"Yes, I was a step ahead of you. Even if this unfortunate situation had not occurred, I was taking steps to cripple your power." Arthur looked up, like a thought suddenly occurred to him. "That reminds me, I also have in my possession a decree stripping you of all your authority and awarding it to your wife. She will rule in your place."

Lot was processing the information as fast as he could. Ana? But she was Arthur's sister—she would never betray him. The realization hit him like a bolt of lightning. That was the point.

Arthur had severed the artery that fed Lot's influence; he would never again be able to plot an insurgence without someone knowing. A string of curses and foul words flowed through his mind.

"But all of this was going to happen anyway," Arthur continued. "I am back to asking myself, what is the most fitting punishment for your crimes?" He said it almost as if he were expecting Lot to answer. Then his face lit up with inspiration. "If I do not take your life, perhaps this will illuminate for you where your loyalty should lie."

At the slight incline of his head, one of Arthur's men came forward, grazing his own blade against Lot's neck. Arthur rushed into the throng of men, disappearing from view. When he emerged, he dragged forward two men with tattooed right arms. He shoved them to the ground at Lot's knees. Two other men with identical markings were treated the same by one of Arthur's guards. The hands of all four were bound, and each now had daggers to their throats.

Had I voice in this realm between worlds, I would have screamed. One of them was Aggrivane.

"Your sons came to warn me of your treachery and voice their opposition. They accompanied me on this journey to witness your censure. Now I find they may be more useful than I expected. Perhaps the sons should indeed pay for the sins of their father."

Arthur turned his back to Lot, and one of the guards applied pressure to his blade, drawing a thin trickle of blood from Lot's eldest son, who flinched but remained silent.

"It is your choice, Lot. Your life or theirs. And by the way, I know where my sister and your youngest are staying at the moment. Tintagel, isn't it? It would be a shame if your boy had an accident."

The threat behind Arthur's words was so real I could almost see it come to life: a young boy, an untried horse, a mountainside trail, and bloodied rocks below.

Lot wrestled with himself internally, fighting two opposing instincts. His sense of self-preservation urged him to sacrifice his sons, but his impulse as a parent was to save his progeny. Compromise. There had to be a compromise.

"Is there no other way—no middle ground?" he finally said, and as he did so, his demeanor cracked.

Arthur only watched impassively as tears seeped from his prisoner's eyes. Behind him, Lot's sons bowed their heads, sharing in their father's anguish.

"So be it then." The words were the last breath escaping from a dying man. "Take me," Lot answered. "I have sealed my own fate."

Arthur approached, and as he drew his sword, Lot lowered his head. He waited, resigned, but the death blow never came. He opened his eyes and slowly looked up. Arthur stood before him, naked sword at his waist, tip to the earth.

"Lot of Lothian, I will take your life but not your mortality. Swear to me now an oath of loyalty, and you shall live."

Lot pledged his fealty, kneeling at Arthur's feet and kissing his hand. He acknowledged Arthur as the one and only high king of Britain, swore to uphold and defend him, and to remain true to him to his dying day. His words were repeated by all of the men who joined him in revolt. They had seen to what lengths their king was willing to go to preserve his title and were not willing to stand in opposition of him.

"All of my former conditions regarding your treasury and your right to rule remain in place," Arthur said. "And I will release your sons on one condition—"

"But they have done nothing wrong," Lot protested, back to his belligerent self now that the danger had passed.

Arthur silenced him with a single glance and continued as if uninterrupted. "They will take up permanent residence at my court. I know they will appreciate the opportunity, and should you ever decide to rebel again, they are easily within my reach."

Arthur's threat—or was it a promise?—weighed heavily on my mind until I finally slipped into complete unconsciousness.

CHAPTER FIFTEEN

Spring 496

Iremained in an unresponsive state for the better part of a week, alternately restless in my dreams—as Lyonesse chose to call them—or sleeping so still and silently that several times they thought me dead from fever. They had even called in Father Joseph to give me the final blessing.

"That's when the real fun began." Isolde smiled slyly at the memory as she sat at my bedside one cold, sunny morning. "Father Joseph examined you and declared you very much alive, though gravely ill. That was when I gave you the diluted drop of wolfsbane." Her tone held the slightest hint of remorse. "I know it was dangerous, but you were already more among the dead than the living..."

I gently placed my hand on top of hers. "Isolde, you did very well. It was probably that tiny drop that brought me out of my illness. Viviane used to tell us that wolfsbane was one of the few herbs that could draw a soul back through the veil and release it from the grip of death." As if on cue, a rumbling cough welled up in my chest, leaving me breathless.

Isolde looked away, embarrassed, and continued with her story. "Anyway, Lyonesse had received word that morning that what you were seeing about Lot and the high king really was true. The letter even confirmed Arthur's bitterness at Uriens' betrayal—"

A shock raced through me. My eyes widened. "What did you say?"

Isolde cocked her head to the side and scrunched up her forehead in confusion. "That Arthur is upset Uriens sided with Lot." She continued without letting me respond. "The letter also said that when it was over, Arthur took away Uriens' right to rule the town of Carlisle. They say it will be Arthur's new capital."

I wasn't listening. As she prattled on about Arthur using the town to keep a close watch on the aged ruler of Rheged, I went through our earlier conversation in my head. I had told her about Lot's revolt and the anguish I'd felt at seeing the king threaten Aggrivane's life, but as for Uriens' involvement . . . I was still trying to figure out why he was there.

"I never told you that," I interrupted Isolde mid-sentence.

"What?"

"When I recounted my visions to you, I never told you Uriens was there." An accusatory edge crept into my voice unbidden.

Confusion clouded her face, but then just as quickly cleared into another sunny smile. "No, silly, not then. You told me that while the sight was upon you. You practically narrated everything you were seeing."

I was stunned silent. I saw the visions as clear as day, but as though I was out of my body. I had no connection to it, no way to make it work, which was why I could not scream.

I shook my head. "That is not possible. I tried several times to speak before I knew what was happening. I tried to call out to Arthur, to Aggrivane, to react to what I saw."

Isolde's eyes were bright with wonder as she tried to reconcile what she had experienced with what I was telling her. "But you did, Guinevere. You screamed like you were being murdered. That must have been when you saw Aggrivane," she whispered, almost to herself.

"But how could I have been telling you what I saw?"

"You answered every question I asked you, responded to my voice . . . did you not hear me?"

"You were questioning me? I heard nothing but the sound of my visions. I would have remembered your voice. I am sure it would have brought me back to you." As soon as I spoke, I heard the affection in my own voice. I was truly growing to love Isolde.

She caught the inflection and blushed in response. "It was the same with Islene," she said quietly.

"Who?"

She looked uncomfortable now. "Islene, my sister. She has the sight. Growing up, I used to coach her through each one of her visions, asking her what she saw, drawing more description out of her. It became so ingrained in me that when I realized you were not merely dreaming like Lyonesse thought, I automatically began asking you questions. And you responded just like Islene used to." Her words rushed out, pensive and hushed as they always were when she was thinking aloud, a frequent habit. "But your gift is different than hers. Islene can see the future. You seem to be able to see things that are happening in the moment, but far away. It's almost like you can be in two places at once." Her voice wavered with emotion.

I leaned forward hoping she would go on.

"Islene told my mother not to send me here, not to sign the treaty. But no one listened to her—no one ever did." Her eyes brimmed with tears.

I patted her shoulder gently, intending to comfort her, but she winced, distracting me from my intended question about Islene's visions. "What is wrong?"

She wiped her eyes with her hand and looked down. "Nothing. I have gotten away from my point. We were talking about Lyonesse and Father Joseph."

Isolde was forcing herself to be cheery, that much was clear, but her grimace hadn't escaped my notice. I yanked back the neck of her gown, ignoring her feeble attempt to pull away. A pattern of swollen, red flesh crisscrossed down her back.

She batted my hand away, as angry now as the patchwork of scars that marred her flesh. "It is no struggle to guess at whose hand I received these. I caught her at an inopportune moment, and she called me a witch for trying to heal you. That is all you need know." Her eyes flashed a warning that made it clear I was not to ask any more.

I opened my mouth to respond.

"Father Joseph gave you a general blessing," she said, cutting me off as she turned back to the original point of our conversation. "He was nearly out the door when Lyonesse stopped him. Since it seemed you were going to live, at least for a little while, she told him about your strange dreams and said she thought you were possessed by a demon. She demanded that he perform an exorcism on you. Naturally, Father Joseph refused. He emphatically stated that your body was ill, not your spirit, and what you needed was healing and love, not fear and paranoia. He told her she would have to find another priest if she wanted that ritual performed. This, of course, infuriated Lyonesse. She commanded him to baptize you instead." Isolde leaned toward me, her previous irritation forgotten.

I could tell she was enjoying spinning this yarn. She had a gift of being able to recount things in a way that made me feel that rather than being an unconscious presence in the room, I had actually witnessed them. I could understand why Elaine was so enraptured by her.

"I have never seen a Christian priest come so close to assaulting a woman before. In a split second, Father Joseph went from a patient servant of God to an impassioned defender of the faith."

She deepened her voice in imitation of the normally mild-mannered priest. "'My lady, I care not what title you claim upon this earth; no one can command another who has reached adulthood to be baptized. That most holy of sacraments must be conferred by free will and a genuine desire to embrace our faith.'

"He gritted his teeth and laid into Lyonesse like no one had ever dared, advancing on her without fear. 'This woman has obviously made her choice.' He gestured to the mark of priest-esshood on your sweaty brow. 'Our Lord is much more gracious and understanding than you could ever comprehend. She will be saved by her own faith, should He call her home, so you need have no concern for her soul. I advise you to pay as much attention to the state of your own spirit and leave hers to her conscience. I bid you good day!' And with that he strode out of the room."

Another coughing fit shook my body, but after a few minutes, I managed to clear my lungs enough to speak. "I am sorry I missed that."

Isolde picked up a small vial from a nearby table and shifted her weight so she was sitting fully on the bed now, facing me. She uncorked the bottle and began rubbing the pungent oil on my chest. The woody, heavy scent threatened to overwhelm me, but I immediately felt a little relief. Pine oil. Whoever taught her the healing arts had trained her well.

"Oh, but it gets better. Lyonesse tried to baptize you herself after that."

"She did?" My mouth dropped open, eyebrows knit in disbelief.

She laughed. "Yes. And you screamed at the exact moment she tried to bless you with the holy water." She was laughing so hard now she was almost in tears. "Guinevere, you could not have planned it better. You scared the wits out of her. She has not been back to visit you since."

Chapter Sixteen

Spring/Summer 496

Once it was clear I would live, life at Corbenic returned to normal, or at least what passed for normal in Pellinor's household. He went back to interviewing, berating, and sometimes forcibly removing Elaine's endless suitors one by one.

But for once, the house was quiet. In a small antechamber, Pellinor was penning a letter to my father. Lyonesse was studying her prayer book, and Elaine was humming quietly to herself as she stitched. I was toying with my own needle but not really accomplishing anything. I was wishing I could find a way to sneak out and track down Guildford for another lesson. Liam had learned to write the alphabet and spell a few simple words, and I was anxious to resume his lessons after the break caused by my illness. I also was eager to begin rebuilding the muscles that had atrophied from my time in bed.

I tried to catch Isolde's attention—the artful Irish princess always was helpful in providing an excuse or distraction when one was needed—but she was too involved in a whispered conversation with two of the lady's maids to pay me any heed.

I stood, stretching my stiff limbs, and drifted over to the window, intent on searching the grounds for any sign of Guildford's whereabouts. I hadn't taken three steps when the chamber door flew open, followed by a flushed servant who almost toppled into Pellinor in his haste.

"My lord, I told him the family was not to be disturbed. I told him to wait, but I could not stop—"

Before the puffing boy could finish speaking, a stately man appeared behind him. The visitor ambled in casually, as if he had been invited and was expected.

The intake of breath from every woman in the room was audible as we surveyed our handsome guest. Even from a distance, I could tell he was taller than Pellinor. He had dark hair and pale eyes that glinted merrily, as though they found pleasure in each and every object they took in. His complexion was clear and soft and he was finely dressed, from his polished boots to the colorful, embroidered cloak secured over his left shoulder. The circular brooch that pinned it in place was a familiar symbol to me—a stylized horse whose limbs became part of an eternal knot. It was the same symbol my mother had borne on her left shoulder blade—the one by rights I should bear—the symbol of the Votadini bloodline.

"My lord Pellinor." The elegant foreigner turned to Pellinor, who had leapt to his feet, hand on his sword, at the intrusion, and addressed him with the greatest politeness. "I am Galen of the Votadini tribe, eldest son of Chief Donel the Bold. I apologize for arriving unannounced, but I was told a messenger would precede me and be sure all the proper arrangements were in place. But obviously that has not occurred." An edge of irritation crept into his voice but was as quickly covered by cautious formality tinged with warmth. "Nevertheless, I come to your home seeking the hand of your daughter." He swept into a low bow before Pellinor.

Pellinor, clearly shocked, made a slight movement as if to speak, but before he could do so, Galen turned from him and approached Isolde. I cringed, stealing a glance at the equally transfixed Lyonesse, expecting him to make the grievous blunder of mistaking Isolde for Elaine.

Galen smiled at Isolde, taking her hand in his. At his touch, Isolde's breathing hitched, bosom fluttering as she struggled to maintain her composure. She beamed back at him, effervescent eyes and alluring smile brighter than a thousand suns.

"A wild Irish rose," he declared, clearly appreciating her beauty.

Isolde blushed violently in response and dipped her head in acknowledgement of his assessment.

Galen reached back as if to stroke her wild hair but instead produced a perfect white rose in full bloom.

Isolde gasped and took the bud tenderly, gazing, speechless, back and forth from the flower to its benefactor.

"A reminder of your homeland." Galen held her gaze.

She seemed most content to revel in it.

I rolled my eyes. *More likely pilfered from someone's garden on your way in.* As attractive as the man was, I couldn't help but wonder on how many other women he had used that trick. How long had he been watching us to know where she was from? Or had he sent a spy to gather information? I looked again at Lyonesse, but she seemed just as taken as everyone else, her left hand resting lightly over her mouth, frozen by the wonder of Galen's gift.

He approached me next, eyes glinting much like a cat playing with its prey. His smile was sly, as though he knew I suspected him. He took his time studying my face, memorizing my features. Despite the protests of my mind, I felt my body growing hot under his gaze.

"If I am not mistaken, you are descended from the same race as I," he stated seriously, followed by a chuckle at the astonishment that must have registered on my face.

It took me a moment to find my voice. "Yes, my mother was from the north, from the Votadini tribe."

"We of the untamed, ancient land always recognize our own." He winked at me and produced from beneath his cloak a flawless lowland thistle.

My jaw dropped. How had he procured this? Even making the best time, he would have had to have picked this days, if not weeks ago. Yet the flower showed not the slightest blemish or sign of wear. Its bud was strong and green, the lavender spikes within firm and straight. I was beginning to wonder if he was some sort of magus or even one of the fey.

Still chortling, he turned from me to Elaine, who was now visibly trembling. He stopped in front of her and clapped his hands together silently, bringing them up to his lips in thought.

"Dear lady, you are more beautiful than anything in nature, so I can offer you no tangible token of my admiration."

Elaine seemed not to know how to take his words, her visage wavering between joy at his compliment and disappointment that she was the only one not to receive a gift.

"However," Galen continued, "I can offer you something far more dear—my life and my heart—or if you will not accept those, accept at least my humble prayers, for I will pray for your soul until the day I die." He knelt at her feet and took her hand, kissing it gently.

Part of me knew I should be revolted by the obvious display of calculated charm and overwrought spectacle, but I could not. Galen had captured my heart despite my better instincts, and it was obvious the rest of the family felt the same.

Galen completed his circuit around the room and was now speaking quietly with Pellinor and Lyonesse, the latter of whom clutched a small wooden cross to her breast, no doubt procured from the same mysterious purse as all the rest. Pellinor had been appraising Galen's livery as he beguiled each of us and was now inspecting the papers he presented. After a few moments of consultation with his wife, Pellinor called the forgotten servant over to him.

"Erwyn, please show Lord Galen to the guest quarters in the gentlemen's wing."

The servant indicated Galen should follow him, and the maids skittered out the room behind them, no doubt off to spread the word to the rest of the castle and half of the surrounding countryside.

Elaine, Isolde, and I met each other's gaze, thrilled that the unexpected suitor had been invited to stay. While we all knew he was there to court Elaine, the tension that fizzed between us in that moment meant only one thing—the women of Caer Corbenic were at war.

CHAPTER SEVENTEEN

Although men often were considered the chief strategists and architects of war, they had nothing on the cunning of a determined woman when her heart was on the line. It didn't take long for us to figure out that although Galen was there for Elaine, Isolde and I also had a chance. Despite his protestations of love, we all knew Galen simply was looking for a well-bred wife. I was the same rank as Elaine, and perhaps more attractive due to our shared Votadini heritage and the dowry of Votadini lands near Stirling I had inherited upon my mother's death, not to mention the numerous gold mines that dotted my father's kingdom. Isolde, on the other hand, was heir to the throne of Ireland, making her the highest-ranking of all of us, and therefore, also the most dangerous.

Unfortunately, Lyonesse and Pellinor were perceptive of this as well. They did all they could to keep Elaine and Galen together and away from their less desirable wards. He accompanied the family to Mass—which Isolde and I were oddly no longer required to attend—and at other times indulged him with all manner of sport and entertainment.

The positive outcome was Corbenic was a livelier place than I had ever seen it. However, Isolde and I could do little but watch from the shadows. With the little freedom we had, the two of us angled to spend time with our charming guest. During his first months at Corbenic, I was able to grab a few disparate moments once in a while, but had little luck otherwise. Isolde fared even worse during daylight hours, being fully treated as a servant now, her time taken up with an endless list of chores. To her credit, she fulfilled them with little complaint, but the fury grew behind her eyes. Because she was absent from her bed most nights, I could only speculate that she chose to trade sleep for Galen's empty hours and perhaps fill his bed in the process.

One morning I awoke to find the castle strangely silent. Guessing the family had gone to Mass, I dressed and ventured down to the kitchen to break my fast with whatever scraps I could find. Lyonesse never allowed her family to eat until after receiving the sacrament, and by the time they returned, she likely would have some diversion for me that would not indulge my aching belly.

I had just emerged from the pantry, arms full of slightly stale bread, hardened cheese, fruit, and a half-empty flagon of wine, when a shadow fell across my path. I recognized its owner just in time to stifle my scream and save my breakfast from being ruined among the greasy rushes.

"Galen!" I gasped. "You startled me. What are you doing here? I thought you would be out with the others."

He courteously relieved me of my burden, moving it to a low table and keeping one apple for himself, tossing it in the air, a glint in his eyes, only to catch it a moment later. "Pellinor was going to take me hunting—he wanted to show off Lyonesse's new pair of hounds—but he left in haste to resolve some sort of dispute among two of the northern chieftains. The messenger who summoned him said it was likely to turn deadly soon."

I sat in silence across the table from him, eating my breakfast, still slightly unnerved at being so unexpectedly alone with him.

The quiet was broken with a crunch as he bit into the apple. "In case you were wondering, Lyonesse and Elaine are in town. They went to meet with the sisters to help with some service to the poor. I offered to join them, but Lyonesse said that the sisters would object to the presence of a man within their walls, so I was not permitted to come. She sent Isolde off to market with a list so long, two servants had to accompany her to bring it all back. I doubt they will return for several hours."

So we truly were alone then? Well, except for the kitchen maid tending the fire, who seemed greatly amused by the situation, though she pretended not to listen. I knew her well enough to know she could be trusted.

And why would she need be? It was not as though something inappropriate was going on; we were just talking. And eating. Eating was safe, right? So why were my cheeks reddening more each second?

I chanced a glance at Galen. His eyes were sparkling. He smiled when he caught me looking at him. I dropped my gaze, embarrassed. I wished I had left my hair down so that it could hide me from him, like I used to do with Aggrivane.

I cleared my throat nervously. "So how were you planning to spend your day, then?"

"Well, actually, I had hoped to go riding."

I nodded, stood, and began clearing the table.

Galen grabbed my arm, and I whirled instinctively to confront him, surprised. He glanced over his shoulder to make sure the maid wasn't listening.

"I was hoping you would join me. My horse is already saddled for the hunt."

My heart leapt into my throat, missing several beats. My mind was suddenly numb. "I—I, cannot," I stammered. "Lyonesse dislikes me enough already. If it were known I went out alone with you—"

"We needn't be alone," he answered smoothly, his hand still on my arm. "Bring your lady's maid."

"I haven't one," was all I could manage to reply. My mind was beginning to scatter at his nearness. He had a fresh, wild scent like lowland heather.

He flashed a captivating grin at the kitchen maid. "I see here with us a lady who also is a maid. Will she not for a few short hours substitute as a witness that we engaged in no impropriety?" He turned to the maid. "Do you ride?"

"Yes, sire," she responded, trying to hide her joy at this exciting turn of events.

My stomach lurched. The maid was Isolde's friend, so I knew she would find out about everything that happened—as would half the household—but Lyonesse trusted her, so she was an asset in that respect. I was taking a risk, but I did not have the strength to turn him down.

"So be it," I acquiesced.

ംരുഃ ഋരം

The early morning sun caressed my skin as we set out. Galen led us east toward the Forrest of Dean and away from town, lest we be spotted by prying eyes. The maid followed discreetly behind us, clearly enjoying a rare day out of doors. All around us life was bursting forth, from the budding trees and blooming flowers to the myriad of woodland creatures who sang in the trees overhead or, frightened by thundering hooves, cleared the path before us.

We slowed to a canter as the path grew narrower, and Galen allowed my horse to fall into step with his. I could not find the courage to look over at him, but I knew he was watching me.

Self-consciously, I tucked a loose strand of hair behind my ear. The tension that held fast between us was not the sensual pressure that boiled between lovers, but also not the awkwardness common among strangers; whatever it was, it was driving me mad. Galen, however, appeared at ease. Like Isolde, he always seemed to be playing with his environment, squeezing the most out of every situation—always in control.

The breeze rustled the tender leaves, and the jays called from the treetops. Finally, I could stand the silence between us no longer.

"How did you hear Pellinor was looking for a husband for Elaine?" I blurted out the least dangerous of the questions demanding resolution in my mind.

Galen smiled playfully. "You wound me, my lady. I hoped you would ask about me."

I glared at him. "Well, I am, in a roundabout way."

He chuckled. "You would be surprised how fast word of a young virgin bride spreads across this land, especially when she is the daughter of a lord such as Pellinor." He leaned in closely, as if confiding a secret, lips nearly grazing my ear. "We men have a spy network that runs from one tip of the island to the other, and we can track the scent of an eligible woman like a fox."

I turned to look at him, to judge his sincerity, and found his face only inches from mine. Though his tone was serious, his eyes told he was teasing. I could not help but smile, although I pulled away a bit, guiding my horse just slightly to the right.

"Forget I asked then."

"No, seriously, we do," he insisted. "I was traveling in the south of Rheged, just about to cross into Powys, when I heard about Elaine."

My skin rose to goose pimples. Something about his story did not seem right. "That would have been, what, just after Candlemas? Is that not fairly early in the season to be so far from home? Were you not worried about late season snows?"

"No. It was a warm winter in that area, and the threat of dangerous weather had long since passed." His answer was as airy as if I had asked about the trees. "And in case this was going to be your next question, I was in Rheged on an official visit for my father. He has trade relations with many of the officials in that area. They provide coal, and sometimes salt, and we give them wool from our sheep. It is much higher quality than anything than could be sheared from those sorry beasts they raise." His expression dared me to ask any more questions.

His answers, while precise, seemed a little too rehearsed.

"But if you were so far away, how did you know so much about the three of us when you first arrived? And where did you get those gifts?"

Galen stopped his horse across the track in front of me,

forcing me to a halt. "My lady inquisitor has an impressive list of questions," he observed, his jaw taut with irritation. "I will answer, but you must do the same for me first. I'll bet my life you pressed that thistle with a cold iron and have it stashed somewhere safe. Am I right?"

I glowered at him.

He gave me a sardonic look, taking my silence for agreement. "As for those gifts, a man's courtship methods are his own business, and you will get no more from me on the subject. But I will tell you this. It was not difficult to learn all I needed to know about the lot of you. The closer I drew to town, the more I heard. Have you ever slept in the common room of an inn?"

He let a few heartbeats pass, and when I didn't respond, he grinned at me. "I doubt you have. Well, cheap liquor loosens lips, especially in close quarters. Many rejected suitors stayed the night in town before returning to their homes. At first, they were reluctant to speak of their embarrassing experiences at court, but I made sure the ale flowed without interruption, and as the night wore on, they began to reveal details that eventually painted a very interesting picture. Few had actually seen Elaine, but she was rumored to be beautiful. They all agreed her father was a force to be reckoned with and her family was very religious. Then I began hearing comparisons between the chaste daughter and the amorous Irish houseguest and of their mysterious friend from Gwynedd. It was not difficult for me to determine who was who when I presented myself to Pellinor. You actually aided me by all being in the room at once—removed the guesswork." He winked.

"And what did you hear about me?" I was terrified of the answer, but vanity compelled me to ask.

He shrugged and pulled his horse around, continuing forward. "Not much really. Only that you had joined the household a few months before at your father's bidding. Rest assured that many men consider you lovely, but you need not fear for your virtue, not with the Irish one around. Of course, I knew you to be a child of the north as soon as I saw you. No one else on the whole of the island is as fair of skin as we"—he scrutinized me closely—"although you have a deeper complexion than I would have imagined."

"My father is Roman," I answered.

"I won't hold that against him."

Even the maid laughed. Her giggling filled the air a few paces behind us.

I was interested now. "I wonder if you knew my mother. She was only thirteen when she came to Gwynedd, but her family still lives near the Firth of Forth, not far from Stirling."

"Ah, so you *are* a true lowlander, then. My clan is farther west, near Loch Lomond, but still within the jurisdiction of Stirling." Galen pulled up his sleeve and extended his right arm, revealing his clan tattoo. A falcon in flight, beak open in a silent hunter's cry, deadly talons at the ready, encircled his arm, just as the dragon marked Aggrivane's family. "Who ruled your mother's clan?"

I had to think hard. It had been years since my mother and I had spoken about her family, and my time in Avalon had dulled a lot of memories. "I'm unsure of who holds power now, but when I was young, my mother spoke of a king named Culhwch. He was her half-brother."

"Culhwch?" Galen was thunderstruck. "That means your mother must have been the woman called Corinna."

I was not certain if that was a question or a statement. "Yes. Did you know her?" Then another thought sent ice down my spine. "Are we kin?"

His eyes were distant; he was lost in thought but answered anyway. "No. At least, it is not likely. But my mother lived at court in Stirling and spoke often of your mother."

He stopped both of our horses by putting out his hand. His eyes scrunched up curiously. "Do you know the story of your family?"

I was confused. "I know that my mother married my father as part of a peace treaty." The similarity to Isolde's situation suddenly struck me. "I know they loved one another very much, but that is all."

"Oh, Guinevere, there is so much more. Your parents are spoken about in lore throughout the four lowland tribes."

My mouth went immediately dry, and my stomach twisted warily. The only way so many diverse people across such a wide area could know the same tale was if the bards sang it, and the bards bestowed only two kinds of fame—heroism and infamy. The only way I was going to know which dogged my lineage was to hear their story for myself.

"Tell me."

CHAPTER EIGHTEEN

alen insisted we stop and give our mounts rest and water before continuing the story. I had the sense this was simply a ploy to keep me interested, now that he had me on the hook. The maid took charge of the horses, while we walked along the marshy shore of a small river, being certain to stay within her range of sight. Playing the perfect gentleman, Galen had even asked her to point out the farthest thing she could see so that we knew when to turn around.

I knew enough not to trust him, but that amount of precaution was insulting. It was clear no matter how much he flirted, Galen had no intentions of impropriety with me, or at least none he wanted known. I couldn't help but glower inwardly that Elaine was good enough for his heart and Isolde his bed, but all I warranted was a supervised jaunt to the river and back.

He took no notice of my foul temper as we walked among the tender shoots that would grow with summer heat into reeds and grasses, mud squishing under our boots.

"Your family is quite remarkable. I am surprised you know so little," he said.

I did not answer. So many lost years, time stolen from us by Avalon and my mother's early death. *How much more would my mother have told me, how much more would I have learned if things had been different? Or would she have said anything at all?* At the moment, all I could feel was stinging betrayal that all the tribes of the north knew my family better than I. I took a deep breath and signaled with a slight incline of my head for him to begin.

"Even before the betrayal of the Saxons, old king Vortigern was paranoid and feared any ruler who might entertain the idea of challenging him. So he ordered the men of the northern tribes to come within the boundaries of his kingdom and, hence, within his control. Vortigern used the excuse that he needed their strength and skill to defend against the Irish, which was at least partly true.

"As the story is told, your grandfather, King Cunedda, believed that complying with Vortigern's wishes would prevent Votadini bloodshed. So he made the agonizing decision to leave his wife and her newborn child—your mother—to settle in northern Gwynedd. He intended to send for them as soon as he was established in his new home. But your grandmother knew what dangers lay ahead for her husband, so she did not expect to be quickly summoned. She contented herself with remaining in her homeland, rearing her child according to the traditions of our tribe. They say she was a fierce warrior—your mother."

I smiled at the memory. "Yes, she was. It was she who taught me the arts."

"Did she now?" Galen seized my hand, turning it palm up,

examining the calluses. "Ah, yes, you have the hands of a fighter." He traced lightly over each of the darkened patches of skin worn tough by repeated grasping of the sword pommel.

"Lyonesse thinks they are from the work she sometimes makes me do," I said, feeling the nervous need to explain even though he hadn't asked.

"She is fond of treating her guests as servants," he mumbled to himself.

I winced, his words confirming intimacy with Isolde, at least in conversation; they were clearly confidants.

He was still intent upon my hand. "We shall have to have a spar to see if our people are correct that women make equal partners on the battlefield as in the bedroom."

I froze. "Please, no. It is forbidden. If Pellinor or Lyonesse knew I wielded a weapon within their walls, they would turn me out."

Galen must have seen the fear in my eyes because he relented. "Your secret is safe with me." The words were murmured softly in my ear as his arms closed around me for a brief moment, and he lifted me effortlessly over a fallen tree trunk.

It was then that I caught the veiled intention behind his quip. I lost my mind at the touch of his body. It had been so long since I had felt the heat of another that I almost collapsed in his arms.

Whether he failed to notice or was concerned about the maid watching, I knew not, but he righted me very professionally, keeping a light hand on the small of my back as we continued to pace the riverbank.

"To return to my story—or rather yours." He winked. "Once your grandfather was in Gwynedd, he realized Vortigern's deal was somewhat of a trick. No land or authority automatically came with this compliance, and what was worse, his title meant nothing in this new country. He could have returned to his family, but Cunedda was still convinced they were safer if he stayed where Vortigern wished and carried out his commands. In a show of sincerity, he went to Vortigern's court to ask some assistance in setting up a new life. While Vortigern was pleased Cunedda had acquiesced to his demands, he was not one to dole out charity and so sent Cunedda away empty-handed.

"However, several prominent lords had heard him plead his case and took pity on him as a just man. One of them was your father's father, a man of Roman stock named Lucian. Lucian wished to give Cunedda a title and some holdings in his own territory of Gwynedd, but Cunedda feared this would only anger Vortigern and bring his wrath needlessly upon Lucian's house. Instead, Cunedda asked not to be treated as Lucian's equal, though he was, but as any other unlanded soldier seeking his kindness. Lucian admired your grandfather's honesty and humility, so he took him in and gave him shelter and employment fighting against the Irish invaders.

"Years passed in this arrangement, and Lucian took your father ever deeper into his confidence. He confessed to Cunedda that, unlike Vortigern, he despised the bloodshed caused by the constant fighting among the tribes of the north and the Romans with his own people. One day he came to Cunedda with a proposal. Lucian's son, Leodgrance—your father—would marry a Votadini of royal lineage, preferably one of Cunedda's relatives. Both tribes would agree to live in peace, and Lucian would ensure Gwynedd was a place the Votadini could dwell safely under Vortigern's rule. Seeing the wisdom of this plan, Cunedda offered his only daughter, Corinna, to Leodgrance as act of gratitude for Lucian's years of protection and kindness.

"When it was announced Leodgrance and Corinna were to be married, there was much rejoicing among the tribes at the peace that would follow. However, Lucian's overlord, a powerful man named Julian who exercised control over much of the western coast, did not approve of the plan. Julian despised the thought of tainting pure Roman blood with that of our kind, so he ordered Lucian to kill Cunedda, the bride, and her immediate family when they arrived for the wedding, thus eliminating the royal Votadini line and demonstrating power over their tribe. Although Lucian loved Cunedda like his own kin, he was very much afraid of Julian and reluctantly agreed to do as he was commanded.

"But Lady Fortuna was with your family, for Leodgrance found out about the plot. Like his father, he was a man of peace, but he would do what he must to save Corinna and her family. He may not have set eyes on his bride yet, but he was beginning to love her just by her actions. She was risking much to marry him—bravely leaving her home, her title, her people, all to unite with him in a treaty that was ideal in theory but would be difficult to maintain. He couldn't let her die, especially not as an innocent victim of someone else's machinations.

"On the night before the wedding, when all of the men were gathered together in celebration, Leodgrance made certain that Lucian and Julian received poisoned cups. They died, but no one ever suspected your father. He and your mother were married, and well, I think you know the rest of the story." He fell silent, leaving me to absorb the epic that had resulted in my birth.

I halted, suddenly seeing my father in a whole new light. For the first time, I was touched with pity for him. I had always known of his affection for my mother, but I never suspected how deeply his love ran or that he was capable of murdering his own father to save her. Suddenly the broken man, half crazed with grief, I left at Northgallis made much more sense. I still could not fathom what he saw in Father Marius, but at least now I understood the reason for his desperate search for comfort and redemption. He had done unspeakable things to save my mother, and she had been taken from him as violently and as suddenly as if Julian's plan had been fulfilled so many years before.

Heartache filled me at the thought of what my return so soon after my mother's death must have done to him. There I was, a younger version of the woman he just lost; I probably appeared to him much like my mother did when she came to Gwynedd to marry him. With a shock, I realized that his coldness had not been meant for me, but as a defense against the pain caused by having to face the ghost of his dead love in my eyes.

Unable to speak, I stared at Galen like a simpleton.

"Have I said something wrong?" His features were etched with genuine worry.

"No, I am fine," I croaked, trying to recover my voice. "Your story made many things about my family very clear to me, things I never expected and could not possibly explain." I took a step forward. "Please let us speak of other things. Tell me how you like Elaine. I hardly ever get to see her anymore."

"Oh, Elaine is a wonderful girl," Galen said as we resumed our walk, the forced emotion in his voice making me wonder how he really felt about her. "She is very beautiful. I've never seen hair quite like hers before—golden, yet woven with strands of red, like silk stitched with gold thread. And her eyes are so pure, so innocent." His voice softened as he searched for an apt metaphor. "In so many ways, she is like a young doe. Her eyes hold such wonder about the world, about me, about everything. Unlike most people, she sees the good, or at least the potential for good, in everyone. I am so afraid of letting her down."

His confession caught me off guard. Did Galen really have feelings for Elaine?

"Why would you let her down?"

"I am not who she thinks I am, Guinevere."

I hadn't expected him to admit this so candidly. "What?"

The tenderness in Galen's smile was almost heartbreaking. "No one is. She sees everyone as she thinks they should be. She has in her mind this false image of me—the embodiment of her fantasies of a man who is pure, who will be her savior and her one true love. I am human. I have made mistakes—grave ones—and I will continue to do so. It is in my nature to be a bit of a knave, not a saint. I cannot possibly live up to her expectations of me."

He really did love her—that much was clear. But I doubted he loved her with the fire of a paramour or the romance of a fated soul. Galen's love for Elaine was that of a protector; he abhorred the idea of shattering her innocence, but knew, just in the course of living, that he would have to. Still, she could do worse than being paired with a man who held her in such high esteem. She need never fear abuse or cruelty by his hand or any other he could control.

"So you intend to marry her then?"

His brow creased, and he regarded me quizzically. "Of course. Why else would I be here?"

I wanted to ask him when, if he loved Elaine so much, he planned to evict Isolde from his bed—although I still had no proof of that—and stop dallying with me in the forest.

I took a deep breath. "Galen, I do not understand you. Why come all this way to court Elaine when there are plenty of noble women in your own country or in other kingdoms? Yes, Dyfed is a rich land, but it will offer you little but trouble, by way of the Irish, especially when Isolde becomes queen. Why risk that fate? You have admitted you cannot possibly be the spotless knight Pellinor expects to wed his daughter. What is in it for you? What are you really after?"

His eyes flashed with anger, and he turned on me. "Why do you suspect me at every turn? You barely know me, yet you accuse me of dishonesty. From whence does this mistrust spring? I have done nothing to wrong you, nothing to offend you, yet you insist on treating me like a criminal." He snapped his fingers. "Ah, I know what it is. You are jealous. A man who is not paying attention to you is much like a toy you want but cannot have. Do you honestly believe that simply because you are daughter of the king of Gwynedd, all men will fall at your feet? You have too much virtue to be taken as a whore, but little better probability of being chosen as a wife. Your attitude will be your downfall; no man wants a haughty, distrusting wife, no matter how beautiful."

His words stung me into silence. *Perhaps my inquires had gone a little too far.*

But Galen was so engrossed in his own anger he barely registered my lack of rebuttal.

"Did it ever once occur to you that your questioning may offend me?" he demanded. "What exactly were *your* intentions when you agreed to come riding with me today? Am I to cast aside your friend and choose you instead? If you were trying to entice me or hoping I would seduce you, you not only lack understanding of what is attractive to men, but sound judgment as well. You lost any chance at winning my heart the moment you berated me with your questions. You are worse than a fishwife!"

We had reached the horses now and the maid was watching us with open curiosity, but I cared not who heard us. I felt bound to defend myself.

"I accept no blame for you being threatened by an intelligent woman. You should be used to my kind by now—no doubt you were reared by one. I was raised according to the traditions of your homeland, which bid me speak when I suspect a liar. You may be able to charm and dazzle everyone else in this household, but you have not fooled me. I may not know exactly what you are playing at, but I know you to be untrue. Good thing you will find no resistance from Elaine, as she was raised to be the docile woman you seem to so desire. I wish you both well, but I pray we never cross paths again."

Before he could recover from my rebuttal, I grabbed the reins of my horse and mounted. The startled maid quickly followed suit. I knew those roads well but gambled that, as a foreigner, he did not. He would be dependent on me to find his way back to the castle.

"Use your charm to get you home—see how far that gets you," I called over my shoulder as we galloped off. "I have no need of you, but I doubt you can say the same."

CHAPTER NINETEEN

Summer 496

Someone had been caught, but I was not sure who.

When I retired the following night, Lyonesse locked Isolde and me into our room, promising to liberate us after they returned from Mass at dawn. For a few moments after the bolt slipped into place, we stared at each other in silent shock. I had thought we were in the clear; Lyonesse seemed pleased that Galen and I refused to exchange more words than politeness required, and he gave no indication that our tryst had ever taken place. Had the maid spilled our secret? Worse yet, had Galen told them everything? After I pushed him so far, he would have little to lose, especially if he implicated both Isolde and me while remaining an innocent victim in their eyes, a deception I had no doubt he could accomplish. Horrible as that seemed, it would explain Lyonesse's desire to keep us both under lock and key.

"What does she know?" I asked quietly.

Isolde shook her head slowly, contemplating the options. "I'm not sure."

I sank down on the bed. "We could be ruined."

"We?" Isolde scoffed. "What have you to account for? Lust within your heart is not a punishable offense, and it most certainly will not get you turned out into the street."

Isolde was rarely cross with me; her jab at my lack of success with Galen was a clear sign of how worried she really was. I turned down the bedclothes and slipped beneath them.

"And you? What have you to fear?" I asked.

Isolde blew out the candle on the bedside table. "Guinevere, you are a perceptive woman. I believe you can guess without my telling you."

"So that *is* where you were each night." I stared up at the shadows on the ceiling, my stomach twisting as my suspicions were confirmed. "But you have not left our room in nearly a month."

"He has rejected me." Her voice was small, frail.

I had been watching the life drain out of Isolde for some time now. Here in the darkness, it seemed as though she had given up completely. Sick with guilt, I wondered how much of her present pain was due to my allegations. Surely Galen had told her what had happened, what I had said. If I saw through him, it would stand to reason he would fear others would soon come to the same conclusion. Better to leave her now than be caught in a sin he could not deny.

"Isolde, I am so sorry."

"You did nothing. I knew what I was getting into when I warmed his bed. A lovers' tryst is built to destroy itself; they all end in time." She was trying to remain strong, but her voice was wavering.

"Did you love him?"

She shifted in the darkness. She was on her side, facing me, silent tears caught by the pale moonlight. "I could never fall in love. My heart is not here; it is at home with the radiant roses and emerald hills. It is chasing the deer and embracing the sweet smell of the meadows. My life here is not my own, but I take happiness where and from whom I can get it. Will you condemn me for that?"

I had no answer for her. I had done enough damage already; I was the reason she lay here in pain, imprisoned in what should have been her home. I could only assure her of my love and hold her as she cried herself to sleep.

⁖⊙⊙⁖

Our confinement lasted only a few more weeks, during which time Isolde displayed a surprising skill at being able to pick locks and move about the castle unseen so that we could continue our scheduled meetings with Guildford and Liam.

"This is not the first time they have kept me under guard. You learn what you must to survive," Isolde explained while deftly jiggling the back side of the lock on our bedroom door, which could be opened from both sides if one knew how. "This one is at least a challenge; I had a duplicate key to my former room." Her impish smile was back.

Once the danger of Beltane had passed—a night full of grief at lost love for the both of us—Isolde seemed to rally, showing incredible resilience and strength. At the same time, Pellinor began "forgetting" to lock us in until it became clear he would not do so again if we would pretend nothing had changed.

One morning, Isolde and I were playing a game of Holy Stones with a set she had brought from her homeland when Lyonesse and Elaine entered the castle below after Mass. I could not tell what she was saying, but Lyonesse was angry, honking at Elaine like a goose.

As Lyonesse chased Elaine up the stairs, their voices became clearer. Apparently Elaine's crime was to return Galen's gaze during Mass when he smiled at her.

Lyonesse was still hitting Elaine with her veil when they barreled into the room.

"How dare you, you little strumpet! During holy Mass, your eyes should only be on one of two men: the priest or God. And as I do not think you can see God—you can't, can you?" Lyonesse's tone was tinged with curiosity and hope.

Elaine shook her head, incredulous at the question.

"Blessed be God for those whose daughters can," she muttered, casting a holy glance skyward before continuing exactly where she left off. "Your actions are sure to cause scandal among the whole village."

Isolde rolled her eyes and stifled a snicker, but not in time.

"You dare mock me, you ungrateful little wretch?" Lyonesse wheeled on her, unleashing the remainder of her fury. "'Tis no wonder Elaine is showing signs of immodesty with you around. I will be dead and buried before we find a Briton willing to marry one as ill-mannered and unrepentant as you."

In the time I had been here, I had seen Isolde undeservedly bear the brunt of Lyonesse's anger many times. But she had been laying into Isolde as often as she could lately, no doubt out of frustration that she had yet to see Elaine married.

I could stand it no longer. I rose to my feet, advancing on Lyonesse in defense of my friend. "Have you no comprehension of the law? Who she marries matters not. Isolde will be Queen of Ireland one day, and that means she could destroy your whole kingdom and everyone in it." I gestured to Elaine without breaking my hold on Lyonesse's eyes. "If she put her mind to it."

"Guinevere, please. I do not need you to defend me." Isolde raised her palm in a gesture of peace and turned her attention to Lyonesse. "Lyonesse, I apologize for my lack of respect. But what Guinevere says is quite true." She held Lyonesse's gaze, daring her to continue.

At that moment, Galen and Pellinor joined us, completely unaware of what had transpired. They appeared to have been arguing as well, and their whispered disagreement continued after they settled into seats near the window. My back was toward them, but I could hear them well enough.

"It has been four months," Pellinor insisted. "You are content to eat my food and sleep under my roof, yet you make no promise to my daughter. What more time could you need to know that we are true? Surely Elaine has proven her virtue to you by now."

"That is not the issue and you know it," Galen answered. "If you will not agree to allow my tribe safe haven in Dyfed, then I will not wed your daughter."

"But you have no need of my kingdom." Pellinor was fighting to keep his voice down. "Leodgrance already assures safety in Gwynedd for all Votadini who desire it."

So that was Galen's excuse for not yet signing the marriage contract—the only step that remained before he and Elaine would be formally wed.

"Not anymore," Galen said with more than a touch of bitterness.

I considered the implications of that. If my father decided to no longer honor his agreement with the Votadini—yet another tradition that had died along with my mother—he could be courting war. It all depended on how much importance it held for the current Votadini chief and how loudly his people clamored for it.

Isolde snapped her fingers in front of my face and called my name twice to summon my attention back to her.

"Sorry," I muttered. I moved one of my archers in position to take one of Isolde's foot soldiers. "What are they squabbling about over there?" I craned my neck to see around Isolde. Lyonesse and Elaine continued to pick at one another as they both pretended to be saying their after-Mass prayers. I smiled at the irony of the situation.

Isolde's hand hovered over her king. "Lyonesse says she had a revelation while at prayer during Mass. She is worried that Galen is not the man spoken of in the prophecy because he is a foreigner. According to her, the prophecy makes no mention of the man being from another land." She advanced her king on a group of my knights, proudly defending her mother's marble queen, her most prized possession.

I gave up on her foot soldier and moved my troops in position to defend against the advancing king. "What did Elaine say to that?"

Isolde laughed. "She calmly replied that nowhere in the prophecy does it state that he must be a Briton, either."

"Good for her! I bet Lyonesse had no reply."

"No." Isolde maneuvered her queen out from among her ranks and into conquering position of my queen. "But Lyonesse has started in on any little fault she can think of. It is like listening to two little girls quarrel."

I was fairly certain there was little I could do to defend my queen. I went to move a knight in between her piece and mine but rubbed my forehead instead. I was so used to using this game as a method of divination that the sight wanted to come to me now. It was taking all the strength I had to resist it; after what I had seen while I was ill, the last thing I wanted was more visions.

When I looked up again, Isolde was watching Galen. "I think you may be right, Guinevere."

"About what?"

"About Galen. I wonder if he can be trusted."

"Isolde, you are still upset because he left you."

"No," she insisted. "He told me what you asked him, and I think you are on to something. Why *is* he here if not to marry Elaine?" Isolde reached for my queen.

I began to relay what I had overheard moments before but was cut off by a bang when the door burst open, startling everyone.

A messenger entered and strode over to Pellinor, handing him two letters. "Urgent messages for you, my lord."

Pellinor looked down at the rolls of parchment and then up at me. "Guinevere, this one is for you."

My heart leapt. This had to be the news I was longing for. It was Aggrivane—I knew it. The other would be from his father or my father, telling them I could return home because Aggrivane wanted to marry me.

I tore at the wax seal without really looking at it. As I read, my heart sank. The letter was from my father.

"My beautiful daughter, I miss you so very much. I was wrong to send you away in such haste. Please forgive me."

I wondered what had prompted his change of heart, especially given Galen's revelation that Gwynedd was no longer a safe haven for the Votadini.

"You should know that I fought with our king against the Saxons near the town of York. I am happy to report that we were victorious and are now constructing earthen dams to keep the filthy mongrels at bay.

But that is not why I send this message to you. During the battle, I was grievously wounded."

My eyes misted over, and I had to remind myself that if he had written this letter, he was not dead. I scanned the page faster.

"I would have certainly died, were it not for the heroic actions of our king. He saved my life, and I owe him a great debt."

I did not get to finish reading the last paragraph because Pellinor had finished his letter and jumped to his feet.

"The king, he is coming here," he stuttered. "He wishes to hold a tournament."

"Why? When?" Lyonesse seemed as frantic as Pellinor looked.

"He did not give reasons. He is already in Gwynedd. He will arrive just before Lughnasa."

Lyonesse clapped a hand to her mouth. "But that is in less than a month!" she exclaimed, and then began muttering to herself. "I wonder why he chose not to stay in Gwynedd. Oh, Northgallis is much too small. Thank goodness, we have much more room for accommodations. A royal visit! I must tell my sister; she will be so envious!"

Pellinor was already scribbling out a reply.

"Ladies, come, we must prepare," Lyonesse commanded.

Isolde made her winning move and grabbed my queen before leaving the room. "Don't worry. You'll have plenty of time to win this back," she teased, unfazed by the turn of events.

I looked down at the last paragraph of my letter.

> *"You will be seeing me soon, as King Arthur wishes to hold a tournament in Dyfed and I will accompany his party. He has already written to Lord Pellinor advising him of the situation. I hope to bring you good news when I arrive."*

Good news? Perhaps all had been forgiven and my hopes were not in vain. All I could do now was wait.

CHAPTER TWENTY

Autumn 496

Chaos ruled Corbenic. With less than a month to prepare for the royal visit, plus all of the guests it would entail, every person was busy, all hands valuable. Elaine and Galen's courtship was temporarily overshadowed as their attention was diverted to the tasks at hand. Lyonesse used Elaine as her right hand in overseeing preparations and training the additional servants that would be needed, while Galen assisted Pellinor in managing the lodging and security logistics that came with a royal visit. I had become a servant like Isolde, cleaning long-neglected guest rooms, scrubbing linens, baking countless loaves of bread, and doing whatever was asked of me.

The king, his lords, and other visiting nobles began arriving during the week prior to the tournament, sometimes one household at a time, other times in caravans of two and three families who had traveled the long distance together for safety. The work only increased with their arrival, as there were more mouths to feed, more people to get in the way, and children and dogs underfoot.

Time slipped away rapidly, and before any of us could catch our breath, Lughnasa dawned bright and clear. It was a beautiful morning, but the sunshine brought with it the promise of oppressive heat.

My feet and arms ached from long trips to and from the market, laden down with bushels of supplies, and my hands were red and chafed from the lye used in the laundry. The last thing I wanted to do today was stand out in the sun and watch a bunch of men attempt to kill each other; I wanted to sleep. As I dragged myself out of bed, I had to remind myself that today I would meet the king, a rare honor, one for which I should be grateful.

Isolde seemed no better off than me. Deep circles rimmed her eyes, though she had not strayed from her bed at night in months. She seemed to sleep well, yet rest had little impact on the weariness that showed in her face.

We dressed for the tournament quietly, trying to balance our display of finery with material that would not suffocate us in the stifling heat.

Isolde was ready much too quickly, full of what I assumed was nervous energy. As she waited on me, she regarded herself in polished shield that was our mirror, brushing a hand over lackluster skin, frowning at her reflection.

I caught her eye in the silver disk. "Are you unwell?"

"I am fine, merely tired," she answered with an uneven voice. "Have *you* found it easy to sleep with those men carousing all night?" When she turned to face me, her smile was forced.

"If it matters, I do not believe you," I responded to her first statement, ignoring her attempt at diversion.

"It matters." She gave me a peck on the cheek. "But you are still wrong."

Before I could answer her, she was out the door, and I was forced to follow, still fastening my belt as I ran.

༄༅ ༄༅

A meadow to the east of the castle had been cleared for the tournament. Grass stripped away, the horses pawed at the dirt, sending puffs of dust into the thick air. Clumps of early spectators milled about, angling to establish their claim on areas with the best view. We were directed to a raised dais, where we would sit with the king in a place of honor, as part of the host family.

In the oval competition ring, men of all ages practiced their skills with a variety of weapons. Each was hoping to win the favor of the king and to be invited to fight with him against the enemies of the crown, which grew more numerous with each passing day. They would be given rank today, a segregation that would determine who would be accepted into the king's inner circle of compatriots and friends, and who would be forced to curry favor from without. Those yet untested would show their skills to the king, and if they met his approval, would be invited to pledge their loyalty and be trained as knights. The younger boys, whose families wished them to be trained under Arthur's tutelage, would fight in a cordoned area with wooden swords and blunted spears.

I eyed Pellinor as he watched his own warriors sparring on the borders of the ring. Although it was an honor, this royal visit came at great cost to him. The expense to replace the candles, torches, and rushes, and build up the stocks of food, wine, ale, hay, and other items for the guests and their horses must equal, if not exceed, his yearly household expenses, yet he did not seem troubled. Though Lyonesse had nearly lost her voice by shouting orders at everyone, including him, Pellinor had never seemed more serene. I suspected that he expected something from the king in return for his generosity—and I had a feeling it somehow involved Elaine.

While Lyonesse fretted over the cost of the visit and what such a high capacity of guests would do to her home, the surrounding town was thriving under the increase in revenue. Only the highest lords and their families were invited to stay at Corbenic; the others were taken in by lesser nobles from the surrounding countryside or lodged in one of the town's many inns. This meant much needed income not only for the honest innkeepers and merchants, but for the thieves, beggars, and prostitutes of Dyfed as well. Pellinor's security battalion was doing their best to keep order in the town, but even now, purses no doubt were being picked and unsavory propositions made.

I spotted Guildford among the growing crowd of warriors. He was giving last-minute pointers to Liam, who caught my gaze and waved. I returned the gesture. I was surprised to see with him my cousin Bran, now a grown man I barely recognized, and a few of the boys with whom I had sparred as a child under my mother's tutelage. With a smile, I wondered what the king would think if I stepped out into the ring and took up my own sword. The thought of Lyonesse's horrified face made me laugh out loud.

"What are you giggling at?" Isolde wanted to know.

"Nothing." I was struggling to catch my breath. "Only an amusing thought."

"And you are not going to share?" She stuck out her lower lip in an adorable pout.

From far below, a voice carried on the wind.

"Lothian, do not think victory will be yours this day. I shall not fall to your sword a second time." The speaker was a tall, dark-haired man with tan skin and imposing features.

"Who is he?" I asked Isolde.

"Accolon, son of Uriens of Rheged. He is cousin to Lothian royalty. He is very handsome."

Rather than scrutinizing Accolon, my eyes eagerly sought out the object of his taunt, desperate to know to which of the brothers it had been addressed. Another tall, dark-haired man gave Accolon a rude gesture in response. It was not Aggrivane.

"Oh heavens," Lyonesse groaned. "Must those Lothian men be so coarse? Savage barbarians." She turned to the ladies seated around her. "I wonder why Accolon is fighting for his father instead of Owain. After all, Owain is the elder son. It is his duty."

The ladies tittered in agreement. Lyonesse's lips curled up in a slow smile as she began gently flapping a small hand fan of swan feathers, not so much to cool herself as to show off her latest purchase and the wealth it implied.

Isolde rolled her eyes and whispered an answer to me. "Owain is the strategist in the family; Accolon prevails with the steel." She explained this as plainly as if she was a member of their household.

"Isolde, how do you know all of this?"

She cast a sidelong glance at me. "I have my ways."

"You have your spies, you mean."

"Call it what you will," she said airily.

The sun was nearly overhead now; the competition was soon to begin. I swept the ring one final time, looking for Aggrivane. I finally spotted him with his father and brothers. Aggrivane's back was toward me, but I breathed a sigh of relief knowing he was there, hale and whole despite whatever may have passed since we parted. I wanted to run down to him and wish him luck, but I knew better than to make such a foolish mistake.

Seeing Aggrivane reminded me there was one other person I had not spotted in the crowd. "Elaine, where is Galen? He is supposed to compete, is he not?"

Elaine looked startled that I had spoken to her.

"I am certain he is here somewhere," Lyonesse cut in. Her tone was cold and carried a warning that I should not pursue the subject further. She craned her neck to see over the massing crowd. "I cannot even find some of our own men in this throng."

Elaine looked worried. Actually, she looked like she was going to cry, and I instantly regretted my foolish question. Maybe Galen was right. Perhaps I did assume too much.

My thoughts were interrupted as the low vibration from a trio of bronze horns announced the king's arrival. Their commanding baritone rumbled in my ribcage as I turned with the rest of the crowd toward the entrance of the ring. One row at a time, we genuflected in unison as the king and his court appeared.

I sucked in air and audibly gasped when I saw him. Even from a distance, Arthur was much more striking in person than in my visions. Towering over everyone in his party, he exuded an air of power and confidence that could not be mistaken. I fell into a deep curtsey but could not lower my eyes from his face. His high cheekbones, broad nose, and chiseled jaw were softened by kind, intelligent blue eyes framed by gently sloping golden eyebrows only slightly darker than his long, straight blond hair.

"Remind me to thank the Goddess for creating him," Isolde whispered breathlessly.

I swatted her playfully as we all rose. Arthur was handsome, I would give her that, but in a carnal way that was at odds with my personal taste. I far preferred Aggrivane's poetic soul.

Arthur stood before his place, only a few removed from my own, and gestured for everyone to be seated.

"I wish to thank every one of you for attending these games today," he began, his deep voice strong, clear, and calm. "As you know, I called this tournament to invite the best of my subjects to prove their mettle and show their desire to serve with me in defending our isle. We have enemies on many fronts, and even within our land." His eyes rested briefly on Lot. "But today we are all friends.

"The tournament will proceed as follows. To separate the wheat from the chaff, we will begin with a general melee involving all adult competitors. No blood is to be spilt; if you are hit, you are to fall to your knees, raise your hands, and yield. My men"— Arthur raised his hand, and several men on the field, each wearing a bright yellow sash, did the same—"will be assisting in judging. Anyone who violates the rules will be disqualified.

"After that round of fighting, the names of the remaining warriors will be taken down, and each will fight in single combat until only two remain. In this round, you may draw blood, but you must stop before delivering what would be the fatal blow. The final ten warriors will be awarded prizes, and the winner will have the honor of assuming the role of my second."

A murmur echoed through the crowd, and Arthur paused to let them quiet.

"On this, the feast of Lugh, the warrior god and Sun King, I wish you all blessings and the best of luck." His full lips raised into a slight smile. "For my sake, try not to kill each other."

The crowd laughed, and Lyonesse grimaced, no doubt more at the pagan reference than at the inevitable bloodshed.

Isolde and I eyed each other joyfully. This was going to be fun.

৩৫ ৩৫

The general melee was over surprisingly fast. When the horn sounded, men came at one another in a dizzying kaleidoscope that changed faster than I could follow. Oaths flew through the air, along with spears and javelins, as one after another, warriors sank to their knees and then trudged, disappointed, off the battlefield.

I was saddened to see Liam among them. He had been trapped into defending himself against two much older men, a situation even his skill could not have prevented; only experience would have saved him. When he reached the sidelines, Guildford clapped a hand on his shoulder, obviously proud despite the defeat, and led him away.

There was a lull as the remaining men lined up, the scribes recorded their names, and they drew lots to determine the order of combat. Once they were sorted, the men returned to a holding area beneath our stand to rest and tend any minor injuries. This gave us a clear view of each man, and Isolde and I amused ourselves by critiquing them.

Galen appeared, and Elaine breathed a sigh of relief.

Eventually, Aggrivane led his brothers into the pen. I wanted with all of my heart to cry out to him, but I did not dare due to the close supervision I was under. Lyonesse had stiffened, well aware of who was a mere stone's throw away. All I could do was stare at Aggrivane and pray he noticed.

He must have felt me watching him because he looked up, pausing in disbelief. Once he was sure I was who he thought, he inclined his head slightly in greeting and smiled the crooked grin that had illuminated my dreams for the last year.

Our joy was short-lived, however, as the horn sounded once again and the men lined up for one-on-one combat. The first to spar were two of Lot's sons, Gawain and Gaheris, paired by chance. Gawain was the victor.

A litany of nobles followed, most of whom I did not know. Gawain and Accolon held a lengthy duel, at the end of which Accolon was forced to concede defeat; a lanky blond from Cornwall named Tristan battled Galen and emerged the victor, much to our family's disappointment; and a brawl ensued when an unruly Parisi nearly decapitated one of Pellinor's men. Both were disqualified, the Parisi for this disruptive action, and the Dyfed warrior for his extensive, bloody injury.

Although Arthur cheered with great joy and conviction at each round, eyes bright with mounting excitement, I could not match his enthusiasm. My concentration was beginning to wane when one of the men in the next pair was called by a name I hadn't heard in years—Peredur of Gwynedd, Octavia's son.

That couldn't possibly be correct, could it?

I strained to see the features of the muscular man with curly blond hair. If I looked at him just right and peeled away the years in my mind, before me stood the young boy I had bid farewell so many years ago.

I calculated in my head. Peredur was seven when I left him and his mother behind for the isle. I was in Avalon roughly four years, and it had been almost a year since I arrived in Dyfed. That meant Peredur couldn't be more than twelve or thirteen years old, at least a year younger than the minimum age to compete as an adult. *He must possess incredible talent to be allowed an exception to the rule. Either that or whomever he fights for is very powerful.*

Peredur wielded his sword with a skill and grace well beyond his years. The crowd stilled to silence as he danced across the dirt, blade held horizontal in his gloved hand as he defended against the long reach of his opponent's spear. He barely seemed to be making an effort, while his dumbfounded opponent fought with all his energy, trying to keep Peredur at bay and land a blow. In the end, Peredur defeated him with expert precision, using an attack that began by advancing on his opponent in a series of quick, short steps, and then deflecting his spear off to the left in an arc, which opened him up for the final blow. Peredur's blade sliced a long line through his opponent's armor and into his ribs. The warrior dropped his weapon, and Peredur held him captive. The tournament advanced to the semi-final round, crowd roaring its approval as the fighters changed places.

Isolde poked me in the ribs and inclined her head toward Arthur, whose gaze was fixed in our direction.

"That is the third time he has looked this way. Who do you think has captured his attention?" she asked, hope obvious in her voice.

I almost laughed when I imagined what we must look like to him—Elaine, Isolde, and I—all sitting here in a row, prize geese for the picking. We could not be more different in appearance—Isolde, tall with flaming curls, bursting with lust for life; Elaine, the petite, blue-eyed, blond definition of demure; and me, a short, raven-haired jumble of Roman and Votadini. Whatever his taste, odds were one of us would be to his liking. Even though I probably should have felt honored by that, I could not help but feel a little like a whore on display in a brothel.

I met his eyes only briefly, but long enough to see him smile just slightly. I returned his gesture with a slight inclination of my head and a soft upturn of my lips, a pleasant expression I hoped would convey kindness and respect, before turning back to Isolde.

"I think he is watching all of us," I whispered, not wanting her to know Arthur's attention was on me. I chanced another glance at him.

His eyes had shifted to Elaine.

"Actually, he seems to be concentrating on Elaine."

"Not if I can help it," Isolde muttered under her breath and sent him a smoldering look. "Will you look at those muscles? I bet he would be fun to take to bed." Her fantasies played out in her expression.

"Behave yourself," I admonished in jest, stealing one last look at Arthur. *She is right. He is a handsome man.*

Just then, Aggrivane's name was announced, and I whipped around. He stepped into the ring to face an unfamiliar opponent. The man, a foreigner from Brittany called Lancelot, was dark-haired like Aggrivane, but his eyes were a captivating shade of blue that reminded me of the wildflowers that dotted the hillsides in this part of the country.

Isolde grabbed my clammy hand and held it so tightly I

thought she was going to break it. She was bouncing nervously beside me, an action that was not helping my anxiety any.

As the men circled each other, I took a deep breath and did not let it out. Not only was my love part of this duel, it would determine which one of the two men would go on to compete to be Arthur's second. Every sinew in my body was singing Aggrivane's name, willing him to victory.

They rounded each other for a while, posturing and testing like feral dogs. Finally, Aggrivane's sword lashed out like a snake. But Lancelot blocked him and parried with a technique I had never seen, a nimble flick of the arm he must have learned in Brittany. From that moment, Aggrivane was on the defensive, never able to regain the upper hand.

Lancelot fought with a grace I did not know possible; it was as though his sword were merely an extension of his arm. He followed Aggrivane's every move, hawk-like, calculating his next several moves in response. Whenever Aggrivane changed tack, Lancelot had a response that kept him off balance.

Lancelot eventually forced Aggrivane up against the hay bales forming the perimeter of the pitch. As they fought nose-to-nose, Aggrivane abandoned his sword for a long dagger hanging at his belt.

"Brilliant!" I whispered, quietly congratulating him on his ingenuity. There was no rule against multiple weapons, though few had brought more than one into the pitch. But before I could get too excited, Lancelot had wrenched it from Aggrivane's grasp and had his sword at Aggrivane's throat.

The breath whooshed out of me as I exhaled in disappointment. I felt terribly for Aggrivane and wished I could comfort him, resenting more than ever the shackles of propriety that bound me to my seat. Isolde rubbed the small of my back comfortingly, and I placed my head on her shoulder, ready to be done with the tournament.

The final two combatants, Lancelot and Kay, Arthur's foster brother, paced at the edge of the ring, waiting for the king to give the word.

I lifted my head from Isolde's shoulder. Beside us, Elaine was wringing her hands, a habit she had when she was trying to make a decision. She called her maid over to her, removed one of the flowers from the garland in her hair, and handed it to the woman. Elaine spoke a few words to her before the maid departed, but I could not hear them.

The maid fought her way down to the edge of the ring and attracted Lancelot's attention. She said something to him, pointed toward us, and handed him the flower. He raised his hand in our direction and smiled. Though the gift had come from Elaine, I could have sworn he was looking directly at me.

"What was that?" Isolde asked warily.

"I'm not sure, but it worries me." It was very uncharacteristic of Elaine to make any bold moves, especially in so public a venue. "Did Lyonesse or Pellinor see?"

Isolde looked over my shoulder. "No, they are deep in conversation with your father."

"Oh." I didn't know whether to be relieved that they had not witnessed the strange turn of events or worried that they were speaking with my father. The last conversation they had had brought me here, so I was fairly certain I did not want to know where this one would lead.

CHAPTER TWENTY-ONE

everal hours later, I opened the door to my chamber, expecting to find Isolde there. Before the investing ceremony, during which Lancelot turned down the position at court he had rightly won, Isolde had said she was going to try to get an audience with the king and insinuated I should use the time to find Aggrivane. She disappeared into the crowd, and no one had seen her since.

The room was empty. My heart fell, and I worried over her whereabouts as I stepped out of my sticky dress, washed, and put on a fresh garment. I was just reaching for my comb when I saw it—a small pouch lying on my pillow.

I picked it up cautiously, curiously, mind racing with who could have left it and what it could possibly contain. I slid apart the drawstrings and turned the bag upside down. Two round red stones and a small roll of parchment fell into my palm. I turned the stones over in my hand. Two queens. I knew without touching the paper who the message was from.

I sank down on the bed, tears already welling in my eyes. Reluctantly, I opened the tiny scroll and steeled myself to read its contents. It was Isolde's handwriting, as flowing as her enthusiasm but cramped on the small page.

Guinevere,

> *I am fine, and you will be too. Breathe. I know you do not understand now why I have gone, but you will.*

I smiled. It was like she was standing right next to me. The tears began to fall of their own accord.

> *I have returned home, to a place where I am loved and where my future is assured. Galen is with me, but it is not what you think. It is not what they will accuse me of. Please know that I am doing this for a very good reason, and I will explain as soon as I am able.*
>
> *As you can see, I have returned your queen—you won it back today by your strength. Please accept mine as a gift. I no longer have need of it, but I pray you will find in it—and in the memory of me—the ability to endure your circumstances. You may return it to me when we next meet. I am certain we will.*
>
> *Please take care of Elaine. She needs a companion, Guinevere, especially now that I have stolen away her love. I do not wish to break her innocent heart, but believe me when I say I had no choice. She will hate me bitterly for what I have done, but I tell you truly that by hurting her now, I have saved her from a much deeper pain.*

I may not possess the sight, but I know you are destined for greatness. It was not by accident that I chose my gift to you. Whatever the days ahead may hold, remember that you create your own happiness; do whatever it takes to make life worth living.

Thank you for your kindness and friendship. Your presence has made the last year the brightest of my life. I love you as if you were my sister. You are in my heart always.

Isolde

For a long time after I finished reading, I could not move. I could not see or think. My mind kept recalling Isolde's smiling face and replaying the events of the day. I had been by her side nearly all day. How could this have happened? How could she have just disappeared? It would take a long time for me to truly understand she was gone.

It was my duty to inform the others, so I returned the two stones to their pouch and secured it to the belt at my waist. That way Isolde always would be with me. I hurried down the stairs to the hall, where the family had agreed to gather.

Pellinor's agitated voice reached me before I entered the room. "In truth, I know not where Galen is."

I barged into the room, letter in hand. "I know where he is."

Silence greeted my confident declaration, and I looked up, noticing with a start that the family was not alone. Four burly, dark-haired men with full beards were standing in a line before Pellinor. Their colorful, richly embroidered cloaks proclaimed them from the tribes of the north—those between Hadrian and Antonine Walls—like Galen. Each wore a brooch representing one of the four tribes.

"She is one of them; maybe she can tell us if what they say is true." Lyonesse scoffed at me with unusual distain.

I had no idea what was going on or what Lyonesse meant. I was one of whom? I scanned each face in the room, searching for answers. Elaine looked pale, Pellinor was growing redder by the minute, and Lyonesse wrinkled her nose at her guests as though they emitted a foul stench.

One of the men handed me an official-looking document.

As soon as my eyes fell upon it, I understood part of the confusion. It was written in their native language, which was more a series of glyphs than letters, so no one else in the room was able to read it. It had been many years since I had studied my mother's native tongue, but I understood enough to decipher its meaning.

"It is a ban of marriage," I stated, still uncertain what this meant.

"Yes," one of the strangers replied. "You will see that the bride is Fia, daughter of Brennen of the Selgovae."

I nodded, seeing her name.

"And please tell us who is listed as the husband."

My eyes dropped to next line, and I gasped. "Galen, son of Donel the Bold, of the Votadini."

I looked up at Elaine in astonishment. For a moment, she mirrored my shock. Then she began to cry.

"He is married?" I could scarcely force the words past my lips.

"Yes, lady," the tallest of the men addressed me. "And he is a wanted man. Not only did he abandon his wife, he has impregnated and deserted at least two other women in the lands between his home and here. We have come to take him to face his punishment."

"But we do not know where he is," Pellinor interjected, his face ashen now.

"I do." I held up the letter. "He has fled to Ireland."

Elaine began to sob.

"With Isolde," I added. I couldn't bear to meet Elaine's gaze.

Elaine let out a cry so guttural and heart-wrenching, I thought she was going to collapse on the spot. I expected Lyonesse to comfort her, but instead she curled her fingers around the arms of her chair, digging her fingertips into the wood in anger, knuckles turning white. It was Elaine's maid who took the poor girl into her arms, pulling her off to the corner of the room.

"Gentlemen," Pellinor's voice was sober as he passed Isolde's note to the foreigners, "as you can see, I have no power where he has gone. I assure you that he was these many months engaged to marry my daughter, and I had no hand in aiding his escape. I suggest you take your grievances to the Queen of Ireland."

The Votadini regarded one another, jaws clenched in frustration. One of them nodded, and they all bowed to Pellinor in unison. Their leader thanked Pellinor for his time, and without another word, they departed.

The tension in the room eased, but only minutely. Elaine's sobs punctuated the silence at intervals. I quickly stashed away the note before it could be taken from me.

Lyonesse crossed the room to where Elaine stood, supported by her maid, the woman's arms the only thing keeping her upright. Lyonesse reached out to Elaine and I thought she would embrace her grieving daughter, but was startled when her hand came down full force across Elaine's cheek. The crack echoed in the silence that followed.

Lyonesse circled her daughter like a wolf. "I put my faith in you, in your virtue, and you bring me a philanderer for a son?" she thundered.

Elaine stared at her mother with red-rimmed, bewildered eyes. Her tears were silent now.

"Will you now have me believe that you still possess any shred of virtue? That you could possibly still be pure?"

Elaine raised her arms against any further physical assault from her mother and answered with a quavering, pleading voice. "I assure you I am. He did me no harm at all. I am as pure as the day you birthed me!"

"A day I will forever regret if your words are lies," Lyonesse spat.

"Stop it!" Pellinor roared. "We have a bigger problem than the question of our daughter's virtue."

Every head in the room turned from Elaine to her father.

"Isolde's departure violates the treaty. We are no longer safe from the Irish. As soon as she reaches their shores, we become vulnerable. I must speak to the king."

∙⊙⊙∙

The possibility of trouble with the Irish compelled Arthur to remain at Corbenic and, with him, a council of his most trusted nobles.

Elaine spoke to no one for days, a ghost amid the feasting and festivities that accompanied the king's extended visit. When her presence wasn't required, she remained closeted in her chambers, weeping out her pain and frustration.

Even when she began to come around, Elaine spoke only when she was addressed and kept to herself as much as possible. Judging by her past behavior, this should only be a transitory phase, yet I was concerned. A light had gone out from behind Elaine's eyes, and I was afraid it signaled some permanent destructive change in her.

One evening when we were alone—Pellinor off in council with Arthur and his men, Lyonesse entertaining the ladies—I convinced Elaine to go for a walk with me. As we wound through the village streets in the cool night air, I tried to get Elaine to talk to me.

"I have nothing to say to you," she said coldly as we passed an inn where the revelers were spilling out into the street. "Were it not for you, I would be married now."

I could hardly believe my ears. "How could this situation possibly be my fault?" Isolde's? Yes. Galen's? Certainly. But me? She was mad.

"You were the one who read the document, Guinevere. Why did you not lie and tell my father those men were imposters or that the document said something else? Anything else! I loved him!" She was in a rage again, spewing vitriol as easily as she had shed tears.

"What would you have me do, Elaine? Let this scoundrel take you as his concubine?" I raised my voice in response to hers until we were both yelling. People passing us in the lane were beginning to stare, but I did not care about creating a spectacle. "Where would that leave you three moons from now when he had taken your money and your lands and left you alone and pregnant?"

She turned on me, incensed. "He would do no such thing!"

"Elaine, you heard the men. He has done it two times before, not counting his wife. What makes you any different?"

She had no reply and so lashed out like a child. "You just don't want me to be happy! You cannot find love, so no one else will either. *That* is your plan."

I halted and stared after her, shocked. "How can a heart of so few years be so dark?"

Elaine whirled and took three steps toward me so that her face was only inches from mine, her eyes dark and menacing. "Do you not understand that lack of love can blacken a heart just as quickly as loss of it?"

Her face was strained, pulled tight by the pain in her heart. "I am never allowed to love, never free—a bird trapped in a cage. I would be happier if Father gave me to the cloister. At least then Christ could be my spouse." She grabbed my forearms with surprising force, fingers digging into my flesh as she spoke, eyes straining to shed tears her body was too weary to produce. "My heart yearns for the love my mind knows exists. Everyone but me is allowed happiness. Isolde was sent here to marry. Even you, who were exiled because of love—you know the joy of its fulfillment. I have nothing."

My heart was breaking for the poor, innocent girl before me. I pulled her out of the street and into an alleyway to give us some privacy.

"You have your God," I said, thinking that reminder would bring her comfort.

"What little good He does me," she muttered.

The bitterness in her voice took me aback.

"I have faith, yes—that His will is truly what is best—but it is cold comfort when all speak of me dying barren and alone. You have no idea of my life, Guinevere." She spat my name with such hatred, she briefly reminded me of Morgan.

"Who says such things, Elaine? I have heard nothing of the sort."

She released my arms violently, flinging them away from her. "Of course not. You live in your own little world, you and Isolde, off having your fun while I am trapped in a life not of my own making."

She turned away, her back toward me as she watched the setting sun.

"Do you really think we would have chosen the lives we live?" I asked her. "I was exiled here, torn away from the only people I ever loved. I have no one here, Elaine. What kind of life is that? Isolde had no say in her placement in your house and, from what I can tell, was never welcome. Your mother treated her as a slave, and she endured it until she was forced to flee."

Elaine turned back to me, eyes flashing dangerously. "She *chose* to leave with *my* intended. Tell me, were they having an affair the entire time, or did the whore have a last-minute flash of inspiration? I cannot make myself feel sorry for her, and I never will. She deserves everything that is coming to her, and so do you."

So much for making peace with her; it seemed I had gained another enemy.

CHAPTER TWENTY-TWO

*A*fter my confrontation with Elaine, I was restless, not yet ready to return to that empty room that may as well have been a prison cell. I needed to breathe in the night air, to feel free for however many minutes I could snatch from time's grasp.

I headed deeper into the village, seeking the open fields beyond the castle walls. I knew not where I was going, but it mattered little. Had my father not been nearby in counsel with the king, I would have run away tonight, to some distant town, back to Avalon, or maybe even boarded a ship to Ireland. Until now, I had not realized how much I missed Isolde, how much I had depended on her joy, her playful outlook on life to give me hope. The last few weeks, trapped with Elaine's anger and depression, had been horrible. I could almost feel her sadness leaching into my bones, threatening to burn away my soul and turn me into a bitter shell.

As I neared the turrets of the outer wall, I began to consider asking my father to take me back home. It would mean capitulating to Father Marius and admitting guilt I did not feel, but it was an opportunity I would not see again. Once my father returned to Northgallis, I would be stuck here indefinitely. I still had the option of running later if he sentenced me to more time in Pellinor's house. As I walked, I made my mind up to speak with him in the morning.

As I rounded the corner and turned onto the main road that led away from Corbenic, I froze. Someone was coming toward me. Someone I recognized as if from a long-forgotten dream. As the figure grew nearer, my heart picked up speed. I knew that gait, the sound of those footsteps. It was difficult to make out his features in the shadow of the tower, but I didn't need eyes to know who approached.

Aggrivane. I did not know if I thought his name or whispered it aloud, but he stopped. He seemed to be regarding me with the same disbelieving awe that emanated from every pore of my skin.

Hesitantly, we each took a step forward. That was enough for a patch of light from the dying sun to fall upon us and confirm the hopes we dared not speak. We rushed into each other's arms like the reunited lovers of a fairytale.

Arms, hair, lips, clothing all entangled like seaweed at the ocean's edge. The heat from our breath won out over the cool breeze that swirled around us as we kissed, bodies crushed together, eager hands confirming this was more than a fanciful dream.

Finally, our lips parted.

"I thought you returned to Carlisle with your brothers," I

breathed, staring into the chestnut eyes I thought I would never see again, scarcely able to believe he was here, in my arms.

"I did," he answered, "but my father called me back a few days ago. I did not know if you were still here—or if you would be able to see me."

"I am here. And I will not leave your side." I kissed him gently on the cheek. "But we should take care not to be caught—again. Lyonesse is worse than Evrain could ever dream of being."

Still locked in each other's arms, we looked around for some means of escape, a shelter in which we could hide, if only for a few stolen moments.

"I know a place. Follow me." Inspiration had struck when I asked myself what Isolde would have done. The question was not *what would she have done*, but rather, *what did she do?*

I took him by the hand and led him through a winding series of side roads to a small building huddled in the shadow of the great main keep. The front door would be securely locked, but with the right encouragement, the side door should give way.

It opened just as I expected, and we slipped inside. In the dim light, I could make out just enough of the floor to get us where we needed to be.

"You brought me to an apothecary?" Aggrivane asked as we passed rows of hanging dried herbs and racks of vials containing multi-hued liquids that glinted with sinister intent in the slats of pale light that slipped through the boards in the shutters.

I laughed. "No, silly. Thanks to Pellinor's paranoia, nearly everything in the castle is connected. The cellar of this building leads up into the main structure."

"I call that sound strategic planning, not paranoia."

In the dark, I doubted he could see the sardonic look I cast in his direction, but I did it anyway. "You don't know Pellinor."

I led Aggrivane by the arm down through a series of winding tunnels beneath the walls of the castle. We had to navigate by touch as neither of us possessed any source of light. It had been much easier the first time I made this journey; Isolde had brought with her a torch when we were forced to sneak out to meet Guildford and Liam. I could still hear her matter-of-fact answer when I asked how she knew such a place existed.

"I had a lot of free time during my first few years here. They did not know enough yet not to trust me." Her clever smile illuminated my mind's eye. "They kept Elaine so closely guarded that she was only rarely a playmate to me, so I went exploring. I found more than a dozen passages on my own. The existence of this one, however, was revealed to me by one of the guards—he is dead now—but I will be forever grateful to him. It has saved my hide many times."

"Does anyone else know this is here?" Aggrivane asked as though reading my mind, his inquiry tinged with apprehension.

I shrugged. "I suppose some of the guards know. Isolde said that Elaine knew about a few of the passages but always was too scared to go into them."

I wondered from whence Elaine's fear emanated—the dark, unfamiliar terrain or imaginings of her mother's reaction if she were caught. Probably a combination of the two.

I was so deep in thought I nearly missed the subtle change in the ground beneath our feet that signaled we were approaching the other end of the tunnel.

"Wait," I said.

We both stopped walking. I ran my hand along the wall, feeling the cold foundation of the castle. My hand hit upon a wooden support beam. "This is it." I led Aggrivane a few steps west, fingertips on the low ceiling above us. "Do you feel it?"

"I do," he whispered as his fingers trailed over the hinges on the door overhead. "Where does it lead?"

"A tiny library tucked away in the southwest corner of the ground floor. Most of the books were smuggled out of Rome generations ago or given to Pellinor as gifts from the more literate parts of the empire. Almost no one uses it anymore, but Lyonesse likes the statement of wealth the collection affords. Although with all the people here, it would not surprise me if someone sneaked away for some peace and quiet. Be careful—the door is covered by a rug, so we will have to push it clear."

Aggrivane chuckled as we heaved upward on the door. "I think we will be safe. Most of the lords cannot read or write. You and I are fortunate to be Druid-trained, remember? Other than our fathers and the king, I cannot think of another literate man on the council."

I wanted to remind him that Pellinor's family was taught by the Christian priests, but I thought better of it as both the door and its covering gave way.

"We are right below a table, so watch your head," I warned him as quietly as possible.

Once we were on our feet, I brushed a few bits of spider web out of his wavy brown locks. I let him take the lead, as he recognized where we were as soon as we peeked out into the deserted hallway. I held my breath, and within minutes, we had made it to the threshold of the old servants' quarters in which he was staying.

I let out a sigh as I stepped inside, willing my pounding heart to calm. We were safe.

Aggrivane followed close behind. He swung the door closed, but it was forcefully stopped by someone's hand before it shut.

Aggrivane motioned for me to retreat farther into the cramped room.

I looked around, searching for some means of concealment or escape. A small table with a basin and water jug stood to my left, a large storage chest just opposite, and the tiny raised bed directly in front of me, one side against the wall. There was nowhere for me to go, not even a closet. Seeing no other alternative, I wedged myself between the bed and the floor, scooting as close to the outer wall as possible.

"Retiring so early, Lothian?" It was Uriens' son, Accolon. I recognized his voice from the tournament. "I thought you may fancy a late-night gamble." He shook something that rattled like it contained tiny bones or pebbles of some sort.

"No, thank you, cousin. Another time, perhaps," Aggrivane responded politely.

"Shame. I was rather hoping to avenge my loss to your house at the tournament."

I imagined Aggrivane rolling his eyes.

"You do realize that had I won," Accolon rambled on, clearly pleased with the sound of his own voice, which was dripping bravado, "I would have challenged the king in defense of my father—fought the duel Arthur denied him during Lot's revolt."

Aggrivane's reply was muted from my hiding place, but I was grateful Accolon seemed oblivious to my presence. The hinges on the door squeaked as Aggrivane opened it to let his cousin pass through.

"In quite a hurry to be a-bed tonight, are you not?" Accolon teased. "Do you perhaps have someone waiting for you?"

A footstep too heavy to be Aggrivane's crossed the threshold in my direction. Though I was facing the wall, Accolon's presence filled the room now, the pungent oils he used to keep his black hair from hanging in his face strong. His feet shuffled as he turned around, looking for where Aggrivane's mystery woman could be hiding.

I held my breath, realizing too late that I had inhaled a lung full of dust. It tickled my throat as I fought to stay silent.

I stiffened as a draft of air passed over me. Accolon must have knelt down to get a better look. I closed my eyes, praying that my black hair and brown dress would blend into the shadows.

The moments ticked by in silence. My lungs began to burn as the dust scratched at my throat, nose, and mouth, daring me to cough and divulge my location.

Finally, Accolon's footsteps retreated and the door clicked shut.

I waited a few moments, and once Aggrivane had barred the door with the storage chest, I slowly began to scoot my way out from under the bed, careful not to hit my head amid hacking coughs.

"Did he see me?" I asked when my coughing fit had ended and I was upright once again.

Aggrivane burst out laughing and brushed a hand across the top of my head, sending a shower of dust flitting to the floor.

"At least I know what you will look like when you are old and gray." He handed me a small mirror about the size of a brick. "No, I do not think he saw you. I could barely spot you, and I knew you were there."

I held up the disc of burnished metal in front of me. My hair was indeed gray, and the left side of my face looked like I had been sweeping the chimney. I looked down. The entire front of my dress was covered in dust. I tried to wipe it off, but that only made matters worse.

"Now, this will not do." Aggrivane clucked his tongue disapprovingly, shaking his head. "I will not have a woman who frequents the dustbin in my bed." He was trying to repress a smile as he sauntered to the table and poured water into the basin.

I reached for the cloth, but he grasped my hand instead.

"Let me."

Aggrivane dipped the cloth in the water and slowly drew it across my hair, his eyes never leaving mine as he worked. The musical tinkle of water droplets told me when he submerged it and wrung it out, but I never broke his gaze to look.

Even more gently, he slid the soft, moist surface down my face and neck, smooth like a caress. Each pass was followed by a kiss, and sometimes the warm trail of his tongue, until the cloth was forgotten and we were lost in each other's arms.

After a few moments, he stopped me by placing a finger on my lips. A single word passed through his. "Tunic."

I quickly unfastened my copper belt, pulled the dirty fabric up over my head, and let it fall to the floor. I stepped toward him to remove his clothes, but he again placed a fingertip on my lips.

His hand went back into the water. I shivered as he stroked my breasts with the cloth. The water was cool, yet somehow invigorating, and I arched my back in pleasure.

Aggrivane's lips met mine as he continued to bathe my naked body. His beard burned where it grazed my skin, igniting my senses. I dug my fingers into his skin, trying to make us perma-nently inseparable. He responded with crushing kisses, and I was vaguely aware of a sense of weightlessness as he carried me across the room. Before I knew it, I was intertwined with him on the bed, his tunic and breeches long since abandoned on the floor next to my dress.

ᴥꙄ Ꙅᴥ

Hours later, we lay drowsing in the small bed. He was softly strok-ing my forehead. I felt so safe in his arms, like the past year had been nothing more than a horrible nightmare from which I had finally been awakened.

"I almost died without you," I whispered.

"I felt the same way."

We spent a long while gazing into each other's eyes. I was not even aware that I was tracing the outlines of the dragon embedded in his right arm with my fingertips until I encountered a smooth, raised line above his elbow. How many other scars had he gained while we were apart?

I propped my head up on my left arm. "What happened after my father separated us?" *How did you get this?* was what I really wanted to ask.

He made a sarcastic sound. "Which part of the story do you want? It is more complicated than a bard's tale."

"Start with yours. Where did you go?"

"Lord Evrain's men escorted me home. My father was furi-ous, although I daresay it was more aimed at Evrain's manipula-tion than at me. To placate Evrain, my father sent me to the Saxon front. I cannot begin to tell you how difficult that was—facing my first real battles against so savage an enemy." His eyes took on a strange hue at the memory, a mixture of pain and suppressed fear. "I nearly lost my life a thousand times, but there was always someone there to heal me, to take away the pain until I was strong enough to fight again."

I dropped my eyes to the homespun sheets. "Camp women."

"Yes," he answered, lifting my chin with his index finger so that I had to look at him. "But not in the way you think. The women who follow the army are more than the prostitutes common gossip would have you believe. Without them, many good men would have died, myself included. There were even a few I recognized from the sacred isle, branded as they were with the mark of the Goddess."

My eyes grew wide.

"They provide our meals, clean our clothes, tend our injuries," Aggrivane hastened to explain. "How else do you think a busy camp runs? We do not have time to mend our gear, learn strategy, and tend to our basic needs all at once. They have nowhere else to go, and we gladly pay them for their services."

He laughed at the look I gave him, only then realizing the irony of his words.

"Not those services. There were many who offered such pleasures, but I partook of none." He kissed me on the forehead. "My heart and my body belong to you and no other."

I smiled up at him. "I believe you."

The corners of his mouth turned upward briefly, but then his face hardened as the memory returned. "I tell you truly, I learned more in those months than I would have in years under Evrain's tutelage. As we fought our way southeast, it was the memory of you that kept me going. Every step, every breath that I took brought me closer to the moment when I would see you again.

"We were not far from the ancient Brigante capital when Gaheris, my younger brother, caught up to our regiment and told me of our father's traitorous plan. We knew from past experience how dangerous he could be when his mind was set on something, so we went to warn the king. Arthur was grateful for our loyalty and brought us along to Lothian to witness the sanctions he would place upon our father. But Father was waiting for us. We were ambushed just beyond Eildon Pass."

"I know. I saw it," I interrupted.

He sat up. "What?"

My cheeks flushed as I understood his confusion. "I was deathly ill at the time, and the sight took over. I saw Lot's insurrection as though I was there with you."

He gave me an incredulous look. "You did?"

I nodded and relayed to him all I had seen, while he sat motionless, unable to comprehend what I was telling him, details I had no other way of knowing.

"I was scared to death when Arthur dragged you and your brothers out of the crowd. I really thought he would kill you," I said, concluding my tale.

Aggrivane had regained some of his composure. "So did I. When he took us, Arthur whispered to each of us not to fear, said that our lives were in no danger. But when Gawain began to bleed, I questioned both his sincerity and his sanity."

I smirked. "Arthur does drive a hard bargain."

"Indeed. But it worked. I have never seen a man so loyal as my father since that day. He even fought alongside the king and your father at York."

"I heard rumors of that, but was never able to confirm your fate." I placed a hand on his temple. "I feared you died."

Aggrivane mirrored my gesture. "I am safe, love. As you can see, we were victorious, though at a high cost. Were it not for Arthur, your father would have perished at the hands of the Saxons. He owes Arthur his life."

"He mentioned that in his letter, but I have not had much chance to speak with him about it."

"I would not bring it up." Aggrivane's voice grew serious. "Your father is a proud man who does not like to be reminded of his weaknesses, much less that he is in debt to another. I have no doubt he will find a suitable way of repaying our king for his kindness."

"I suppose," I said, unable to suppress a yawn. I pulled Aggrivane back down to the covers, suddenly weary of talking. "Let us sleep now, my love. We can speak of this more upon the morrow." I gave him a long, lingering kiss. "Hold me in your arms tonight and let us dream of future happiness."

As the castle fell silent around us and dreamers took to their beds, I allowed myself to hope this time would be different. Our next sighting of the morning star would mark the beginning of our lives together, just as it had once heralded our separation. Only this time there were no Druids, no priests, to keep us apart. All we had to do was make sure we were not caught. But the more I thought about that, the more difficult it seemed, especially in a house that bred spies like lice. We would have to be very careful.

CHAPTER TWENTY-THREE

The next several weeks passed in a blur of alternating pleasure and fear, one emotion when I was with Aggrivane and the other anytime anyone else was near us. I was so frightened someone would discover our affair and tear us apart again, something my long-neglected heart, only recently stitched up by Aggrivane's love, would not abide.

Some nights I carried a change of dress with me as I prowled the halls, praying to make it safely from one bedroom to the other. On others, when Aggrivane had an early morning call to duty, I dared ferry only myself across the border between the ladies' and gentlemen's chambers. I felt like a thief in my own home, stealing minutes, hours of happiness from a family that seemed adverse to its very nature. No matter how many times I sneaked back to my room, I would never lose the fear of being met by a guard before I could get inside, or worse yet, finding Lyonesse waiting for me when I thought I had made it safely.

Each night as I sank down into the bedcovers, I resolved to apologize to Isolde the next time I saw her. During my weeks of intrigue, I developed an appreciation for what she went through each time she sought joy in this house, and slowly began to realize what a hypocrite I had been. I had condemned Isolde for exactly the same behavior with Galen that I now so willingly embraced with Aggrivane.

⚭

We lay together in the cramped bed, gazing at the flames dancing in the fireplace, casting flickering shadows on all four walls of the small room.

"I am sorry I cannot offer you better accommodations," Aggrivane said. "This is certainly no Beltane bower."

I smiled at his concern. "But it is not the stables, either."

I felt his laughter before I heard it.

"I forgot that Lyonesse is well aware of who you are," I admitted. "I should be grateful she lets you lodge here at all. There is little love for your family under this roof."

Aggrivane turned his head so he could see me. "Ah, but the king favors me, so she must, as well. But I am surprised you can get away from your chambers. I figured they would have barred the door."

I giggled. "They did that for a while when Isolde was here. But she found a way out. I would have too. Nothing can keep me from you." I kissed his nose. "Though I don't think he knew for sure we escaped, Pellinor made Lyonesse swear she would never do such a thing again. That is probably why it has not happened." I reconsidered for a moment. "That, and I doubt they think I would be so bold with my father under the same roof."

Aggrivane shook his head. "A year's time and they do not know you at all, do they?"

"My true nature has never mattered much to them. They simply cast me in whatever light suits them best at the time. Now that I am out from under Isolde's corrupting influence, they choose to imagine me more like their sainted daughter. But what they do not know is that Isolde taught me many of her tricks. After all, she *is* the reason I am here with you."

Aggrivane's eyes held a kind of wonder. "You speak of Isolde often. She must have meant a great deal to you. I wish I could have met her."

I smiled at the memory of my friend. "She seems to think we will meet again, so maybe you will still have the opportunity."

We both fell silent for a while, lost in our own thoughts. Outside, the watchman announced the midnight hour.

"You said there were many sides to the story of what happened after we parted. I know what happened to you. Now what about Evrain?"

Aggrivane sat up and stretched. "He is one man I wish I could send to the Saxons. He would not last a minute, and that would be fine by me."

I had never heard his voice so bitter.

He lay down on his back, hands supporting his head. "While I was off trying not to get myself killed, my brothers, Gawain and Gaheris, were attempting to negotiate peace with Evrain. Of course, he wanted none of it, refusing all efforts on the grounds that neither of my brothers were landed lords and therefore were beneath his dignity. Arrogant cur. One of these days I will repay his many affronts to my family. Anyway, he refused to speak with anyone other than my father, who, as you know, was busy at the time, plotting to take over the throne. As Gawain tells it, one night Father had an epiphany and stormed out of the castle well after dark, intent on visiting Evrain. The result is that Evrain is now related to the king, or so he thinks."

I turned over to face him. "Say that again?"

He grinned. "You heard me. In exchange for his loyalty and forgiveness of my offense, Father offered Evrain—a widower at the time—the hand of his daughter, Amelie."

I was confused. "His daughter? Is she not also your sister?"

"No, not fully. She is a bastard some six years younger than me and was reared by her mother in another city. Up until the tournament, I had never even met her. But Evrain does not know that. He thinks she is my mother's child and, hence, niece of the king. You see, my father figured out Evrain's weakness— his ambition. He saw that Evrain was trying to use the tension between him and Arthur as an excuse to make his own bid for power. So my father offered him something more valuable than he ever could have imagined—the chance to be related to the king. He knew that Evrain would think that having Arthur's niece in his family could be a suitable device to manipulate the king. He was right. Evrain happily joined my father's cause, all past grievances forgotten."

I was awestruck. "Does your father's ambition ever end?"

Aggrivane smiled but said nothing.

"What is it? What is on your mind?"

He turned to face me. "I spoke to my father today."

I sat up, pulling him with me, our hands clasped tightly. "And what did he say?"

Aggrivane composed his features, looking more serious than I had ever seen.

My stomach knotted.

"He is not certain of your fidelity to me."

My heart leapt into my throat. I started to defend myself.

"He wants to know," Aggrivane continued, his face like stone, "if you were the one who sent the flower to the Breton bastard who defeated me at the tournament."

Slowly, I realized he was joking. Relief rushed out of me in a spray of saliva as I exhaled.

"Sorry." I dried his cheeks with my thumbs then affected my most proper voice. "You may tell your father that it was not I who behaved so rashly, but my dear friend Elaine."

Aggrivane caught me up in his arms and showered my face with kisses. "He is very amenable to our engagement and gives his blessing. He likes you, Guinevere—"

I stopped him mid-sentence, kissing him with more force than even I anticipated.

Aggrivane submitted happily and then finished his sentence as he pulled me into his lap. "Although I think he likes your dowry more."

"The lands south of Stirling? Let him have them if it means we can be together."

"Do not speak so lightly of them just because you have never seen them," Aggrivane chided. "Those lands make you a very valuable wife because they mean you have influence over the Votadini, and through them, the whole area. You—"

I stopped his thought with a kiss whose meaning could not be misinterpreted. I wanted nothing of politics at that moment, only to be lost in him.

I lost track of time in the aching passion that followed, but soon he was holding me again, both of us breathless.

"So is it true? Are we really to be wed?" I asked.

"Yes, it is, if you will have me."

"Of course I will."

"My father promised to speak to Leodgrance and obtain his permission as soon as possible, but it may take some time. As you know, this must be approached with utmost delicacy, given the household we are in and what is known of our past transgressions. But he swore to me he will not fail, and I have complete faith in him," he said, confidence in his voice.

I smiled and reached up to stroke the thin line of hair that ran along his jaw, nuzzling my cheek into his chest. I wanted nothing more than to remember this moment forever.

CHAPTER TWENTY-FOUR

The autumnal equinox came and went without a single word from the Irish. The council formulated a plan that would go into effect if any hostility was detected, so Arthur decided it was time to return to his own lands. Pellinor, ever the gracious host, insisted on organizing one final celebration to honor the king before he left.

As the first light of dawn colored the horizon, I joined some of the servants in the kitchen to gather supplies for the hunting party. I found them speaking animatedly in hushed tones. From what I could gather, one of them had received word from Isolde, who had arrived home safely some weeks before.

"She is keeping her promise," someone said.

That was all I was to know. All conversation ceased when I entered the room, a spy in the enemy camp.

But the absence of the kitchen maid who had accompanied Galen and me on our ride did not escape my notice, nor did Liam's sudden departure, allegedly to work in another household. Isolde's conversation with Guildford during my fighting lessons so long ago drifted through my mind, and suddenly it all made sense. Isolde had begun her revenge by slowly poaching Lyonesse's servants. But how far would she go? I pushed the troubling thought from my mind and busied myself seeing to the provisions for the hunt.

By mid-morning, the sun shone brightly in the clear sky overhead and we reached the summit of the hill from which we would watch the action. The maids unpacked our wares, and Elaine and I spread a cloth over the dying grass, still damp with dew.

"You were saying your husband takes full responsibility for the breach of peace?" inquired one of the ladies, whom I thought to be the wife of Arthur's foster brother, Kay.

"Yes," Lyonesse said as she arranged herself on the blanket. "He sees now that it was through his fault that the misguided girl left. He really was hard on her—treating her like a servant simply because she was foreign, with no regard to her nobility whatsoever. It is a shame really; she could have prospered under a more charitable hand. I cannot tell you how many times over the years I said to him, 'My lord, do you not think we should accept her as a daughter and treat her with the respect accorded to her station?' But he nearly took my head off at the very suggestion."

The ladies who had gathered around Lyonesse tittered disapprovingly. I busied myself with unpacking the supplies so that my tongue would not be tempted to set her straight. As usual, she was projecting her own harsh actions onto her innocent husband.

"I tried my best to instruct her." The drama built in Lyonesse's voice as she continued. "I think she was coming along until that Pictish brute darkened our door. Oh, how he had us all fooled—a demon wrapped in the guise of an angel! I told Pellinor that had he not placed all of his attention on Elaine and Galen during that time, the girl would not have acted so rashly, but he refuses to see it."

Of course, Lyonesse refused to call Isolde by her name, and I bristled in response. She continued to disrespect her even now.

Lyonesse sighed sorrowfully. "All the poor girl ever wanted was a father, and not finding one within our walls, she took flight with the devil. I doubt God will have much mercy on her soul in her homeland, filled as it is with the stench of pagan lies."

"All you can do is pray for her soul," one of the women replied earnestly.

At that I nearly lost my composure and dropped the basket I was carrying. Lyonesse turned and regarded me coldly, but only Elaine was able to see my face. I had thought her still cross with me, especially on this subject, but to my surprise, she smiled in empathy.

"And then there is the matter of the treaty," Lyonesse continued. "I doubt her people will see it as we do. It was not a sign of antagonism on our part. We had nothing to do with the actions of a disturbed child. We have sent word to them that we still desire peace, but I dread to think what such a breach of charity will do to this house."

Yes, Lyonesse, make the entire situation about yourself. You always do.

ౚఴ ౧ౚ

Disgusted with the turn of events, I sneaked into the woods. I could listen no more to the lies that Lyonesse crafted as naturally as breathing. The sad thing was that over the past year, I had come to learn she truly believed what she said; no amount of testimony to the contrary would convince her that reality was different from what she had fixed in her mind. Therefore, she was an angel of mercy, her husband an unrepentant sinner, her daughter an innocent victim, and I of no consequence.

I followed the sound of the hunt north, the rumble of the horses and the baying of the hounds not far below. Now and again, I would catch sight of one of the men, a muted blue or burgundy cloak standing out against the dull bark of a dying tree or a patch of tangled bracken. Through the last of the season's leaves, I could see my father's hair, still bright despite a generous dusting of gray, standing out from the others. He was laughing and talking with Lot. My stomach fluttered in anticipation of what they could possibly be discussing.

With a whoop and a sudden thunder of hooves, Arthur, Aggrivane, Gawain, Kay, and Pellinor took off ahead of the others, following the trail of Kay's falcon, who was dutifully stalking their prey from the sky. As I ran to keep up with them on a parallel path, I kicked at what I thought to be a stone in the grass, only to feel a squish and a slight wetness at my toe as my boot made contact with a half-rotted apple. Cursing, I dragged my foot along the grass to clean my shoe and noticed more fruit lying on the ground. Looking up, I discovered I had stumbled upon a small copse of apple trees.

Below, the quintet of hunters slowed. I wasn't sure if they were just listening or had lost the trail. I swung myself up into one of the trees to watch them, a habit my body happily remembered from Avalon. Smiling, I recalled many afternoons spent among the branches of kin to these fragrant trees with my sisters, all of us young girls with heads full of faerie tales and dreams.

When Aggrivane removed the bow from his shoulder, I realized my dreams were coming true. If our parents were discussing what I suspected, tonight we would be able to announce our intentions publicly.

A snap reverberated through the trees, and the king's horse shifted nervously. Arthur calmed the beast and cocked his head to one side, signaling to the others to remain silent. The snap came again, followed by several smaller cracks; each seemed to be closer than the last. I listened intently, holding my breath along with the hunters.

"Guinevere! There you are."

I started and clung to the branch overhead to keep from falling. I looked down. Elaine stood at the base of the tree.

"Elaine! You startled me." My heart was pounding.

"Sorry. I saw you leave the camp and was wondering where you went. May I join you?"

"Certainly." I warily extended a hand and helped pull up her small frame onto the branch opposite me. What were her motives? As far as I knew, she was still mad at me, in spite of her earlier smile.

She rummaged in her pouch. "I almost forgot. This is for you." She handed me a small roll of vellum. "I thought you may want it, and I surely have no need of it."

I unrolled the paper slowly, uncertain what it might contain. Staring back at me was a startlingly life-like charcoal drawing of Isolde. Elaine's talent was rare for one of our people, who preferred spiraling, abstract images with no clear beginning or ending. But Elaine favored her Roman tutors in this regard, drawing in a classical style that, should her parents ever see evidence of it, would surely see her punished for putting undue emphasis on human images. By offering one of her drawings to me, Elaine was giving me the power to betray her, should I choose.

I looked up at her, speechless. I had seen drawings like this before, lining the walls of her bedroom—which no one but Isolde and I ever entered, and even then in defiance of Pellinor's orders. Most of those were images from her imagination, scenes from the epic poems of the bards. I had no idea she had been drawing us.

I suppose this means she's forgiven me for whatever role she thinks I played in Galen's escape.

Elaine was never one to offer an overt apology when she realized she'd done wrong. She preferred some small gesture of amity. I recalled a time when, as young girls, we quarreled over which of us had more royal blood and she had called my mother a series of dishonorable names she could have only learned from her mother's lips, insulting me by association. She hadn't apologized then either, just showed up the next morning with a fistful of daisies, which she thrust at me, all enmity forgotten.

"Thank you," I finally croaked, still shocked at her peace offering.

Elaine giggled and settled herself against the hollow of the branches as if nothing had ever transpired between us. "This reminds me of when we were little."

Elaine's cheerful disposition today was one in a series of fluctuating moods she had displayed in the past few months. They ranged from the bitter rage and pain she had displayed when yelling at me to such joyful optimism that I began to wonder if she had taken to drinking. No one could predict her humor; it changed with the wind, often oscillating severely in the course of a single day. She had always been a moody child, given to fits of temper, but never in such extreme.

"Do you remember the time we followed those two merchants out of town?" she asked, swinging her legs merrily.

I laughed, seeing clearly in my mind's eye younger versions of ourselves stowed away on the back of a cart. One of the merchants had a son whom we both fancied. Our plan had been to ride along unnoticed until the merchants stopped at an inn for the night. What we were going to do then, I could not recall. I doubt we had thought things through that far.

"We made it nearly to the next town before we were discovered. We are just lucky the merchants were friends with your father—who knows what could have happened to us." I shivered at the thought. "I thought your father was going to kill us when we turned up back at Corbenic at twilight."

"I think my rump is still sore!" Elaine exclaimed, rubbing her backside at the memory.

"It is not half of what we deserved."

In the valley below, the rest of the hunters caught up with Arthur's party. They seemed to be discussing what to do next.

"Guinevere, can I tell you something?"

"You can tell me anything. You know that," I said absently, plucking an apple off the branch next to my head.

When Elaine did not speak, I looked up. She was wringing her hands again. I raised my eyebrows, willing her to speak whatever was vexing her.

"I—I am not sure where to begin, how to say—" she stammered.

I bit into the apple. "Just say it, Elaine."

"I think I have met my husband."

Her words tumbled over each other so fast I had to take a moment to decipher what she said. I stopped chewing. "Tell me more."

Elaine's face was as scarlet as her dress. "Please do not think me mad, but last autumn, I was in my room praying and I happened to glance over at my mirror. The light from one of the candles caught the edge of the metal, and there was this bright spark. Then it seemed to me that a face was staring back at me." She stared off in the distance, her face placid with the memory. "I could not see him clearly, but his face shone like the sun, his eyes the color of the sea. At first, I thought it was an angel, but then I was given to understand that this man was real and that he was coming for me. Guinevere, he is the man of the prophecy."

She turned to me, her eyes lit up like a child seeing a beloved relative return safely from war.

So Isolde was serious about that. I had to respond carefully. One wrong word and she might crack, spiraling into tumult as easily as she now shone. I made sure my voice was measured and even.

"Dear heart, are you sure you were not imagining things? Or mistook your own reflection? Perhaps you fell asleep and were dreaming."

"I wondered that too. But then Galen appeared. For a long time I thought he was the one. I kept trying to reconcile his face with the image in my mind, but something did not fit right. Then when he disappeared, I knew my instincts had been right. He was not the one. But then I saw him again—the man from my vision—at the tournament."

Oh no, I think I know where this is leading. The flower. That's why she gave him the flower. I swallowed my mouth full of fruit and lowered my head, looking up at her. "And who was that?" I asked, knowing full well the answer she would give.

"Lancelot, the man who won the tournament." She looked sheepish now, much younger than her years. "On impulse, I sent one of my maids to him with a blossom from my coronet. I know it was not much, but I wanted him to have a reason to remember me."

I nodded, pretending to understand, wondering what the best approach was to take with her. "No wonder you were so upset when he refused the position in Arthur's house. Have you any idea where he went after that?"

She shook her head slowly. She was gazing off over the tree-tops again. "He probably took to the road again. He said he likes being a nomad warrior, remember? But he will come for me. Someday he will proudly take my hand, and my heart."

There was a sudden commotion from the hunting party below, and we both jumped. The dogs were baying again, chasing an animal up the hill not far ahead of where we sat. The men abandoned their horses, scrambling after the dogs on foot up the rocky terrain.

Elaine and I looked at each other. If we started running now, we would cross their path in little time. We leaped down from the tree and took off in the direction of the hunt. Excitement escaped from my heart as a whoop of joy as we ran.

Soon the shouts of men were nearby and we slowed to a walk, not wanting to disrupt the hunt or spook the animal.

I was still trying to understand all that Elaine had said. "So if you know this man—Lancelot—will return, why do you sound so worried? What is there to fear?"

"The problem is that my maid overheard Arthur and my father discussing a dowry last night." She grabbed onto my arm, forcing me to halt. "Guinevere, I think the king is going to ask me to marry him!"

I considered that. Arthur had been paying a lot of attention to Elaine, and Pellinor had looked very pleased with himself lately. If the king was planning to leave soon, it would only stand to reason he would take his future wife home with him. It also would explain the hunt and tonight's feast.

I blinked, unable to resist the grin the thought brought with it. "Elaine, I think you are right. Forget about the shadows of the past and things that have yet to be. Do you understand what this means? You are going to be queen!"

"Do you really think so?" Her expression flickered from uncertain to one of serious consideration. "Queen." She repeated the word like it was foreign on her tongue. "It is certainly a higher rank than I ever imagined." Then she laughed. "Perhaps I was wrong. Maybe *this* is my fate. My mother is going to be so proud!"

꧁ ꧂

We met up with the hunting party before they crossed the ford. Pellinor and Arthur were walking at the head, chortling at some joke we had missed. Elaine curtsied to both.

"Come, daughter, walk with us," Pellinor invited, wrapping an arm around her.

I gave her an encouraging smile.

Lot and my father followed, once again in deep conversation.

To my delight, my father paused to embrace me before continuing on. I considered that a very good sign.

As I passed on down the line, I met Kay and Gawain, who were carrying the deer, which was tied to a log by its front and back legs. A line of knights followed, merrily singing a common drinking song. No one noticed that Aggrivane and I lagged at the rear, quietly holding hands behind our backs.

"Have you spoken with your father?" I asked, keeping my voice as low as possible.

"I have." Aggrivane grinned, tilting his head in so our foreheads touched. "He reiterated his support and said he would confirm this with your father."

"Did he?" I bit my lower lip in anticipation of his answer.

"He said an announcement would be made at the celebration tonight."

I stifled a squeal by stealing a quick kiss and then made sure the proper distance was between us in case anyone thought to glance back. It took every bit of control I could muster to keep from skipping back to the castle.

෮ඬ ඬ෨

Corbenic had never seen such a feast.

As we dressed for the evening, Elaine ran in and out of the room, peeking down over the balcony every few minutes and keeping me up-to-date with constant status reports.

"Oh, Guinevere, you should see the flowers! I've never seen so many blooms in one place before. They are practically raining from the ceiling," she said breathlessly, as her maid caught her by the arm, forcing her to stand still.

"She will soon enough if you stay in one place long enough for me to dress you," her maid said sharply.

When we finally arrived in the hall, I gasped. Elaine had been right. While we were away, the servants had done a spectacular job decorating the hall for the farewell celebration for the king. Brightly colored autumn leaves, gourds, berries, and flowers of every shade lined every available surface and candles glittered merrily in between.

Lyonesse sat at the high table, looking out across the hall filled with revelers. She was practically purring with delight. Her daughter had been given a place of honor next to Arthur and was now engaging him in what appeared to be delightful conversation. Her husband sat on Elaine's other side and Lyonesse next to him. She looked every inch the queen tonight.

As a ward of Pellinor's household, I had the fortune of being seated only two places to the left of Arthur. My father sat between us, Kay and Arthur's other companions following on down the line.

Kay had just begun to recite an amusing poem one of the court bards had created about one of their less graceful courtiers when my father gently touched my elbow. He nodded toward Arthur, who stood, goblet in hand.

The room fell silent by degrees as people took note of their king. "I would like to thank Lord Pellinor for his gracious hospitality over the last several moons. I and my court placed an unexpected burden on him by coming here and then staying longer than expected, so this feast is more than I could ever have asked from anyone. You have been a most cordial host, and your generosity will long be remembered." He raised his cup to Pellinor. "Long life and many blessings to you, friend."

I repeated the toast with the rest of the assembly and drained my glass.

Arthur smiled and gazed out over the crowd. "As many of you know, there is a tradition among the people of this land that when the king partakes in a hunt, the head of the stag is awarded to the fairest lady. In this court, I find many worthy candidates, but my decision is clear."

A trio of servants wheeled out the stag's head, dressed as a trophy and adorned with chrysanthemums and garlands of rosebuds. A golden chain was wound between its horns, and from it dangled a sparkling emerald the size of a man's eye.

"Elaine of Corbenic, please do me the honor of accepting this token of your king's appreciation. Your kindness has touched my heart. I swear you will never be forgotten."

Arthur took Elaine's hand and raised her to her feet. He removed the jewel from its perch and secured it around her neck.

The crowd erupted in applause, and Elaine blushed in response.

Arthur kissed the top of her hand gently before helping her back to her seat.

As the servants began to serve the main course, I caught Aggrivane's eye. He was sitting at a lower table with his father and brothers. He smiled and winked at me, and butterflies took flight in my stomach. Tonight would be something grand.

We ate heartily, the fallen deer providing some of the best meat I had ever tasted, succulent and tender, perfectly paired with sweet squash, savory salads, and other late-autumn delights.

Throughout the meal, Elaine, more jovial and outgoing than I had ever seen her, held Arthur's attention. Her sapphire eyes, accentuated by the color of her gown, sparkled invitingly, and I was not surprised that Arthur could not tear himself away.

Only once did he look in my direction, a stolen glance that first was directed at my father, then lingered on me. I was transfixed. The power and grace that emanated from the king was palpable. I could do little but stare and drop my gaze shyly to the table when he finally looked away.

By the time the plates were cleared, my face was flushed with joy, and I was feeling the effects of the wine. For once, I partook with abandon, letting it carry away my cares on a current of heady optimism. Kay kept me in stitches throughout the meal with an endless stream of humorous remarks about everyone and everything and showed little signs of stopping. He had even managed to procure my permission for a dance later in the evening.

Amid the buzz of conversation, Arthur stood again. Someone rapped on the underside of the table, and silence fell over the hall.

"I promise, this is the last time tonight you will have to listen to me speak," Arthur said.

A smattering of laughter followed.

"Many of you have made it quite clear you feel it is time for me to take a wife. I tell you tonight that I have decided to take your advice."

Another murmur rippled through the crowd as everyone looked around, wondering who the lucky woman could be. Many eyes were fixed on Elaine, who looked like she would faint. Next to her, Lyonesse was practically bursting with anticipation.

"The woman I have chosen is not someone many of you know well, as she has modestly kept to herself these many years. But in exchange for a service I would freely render to any of my subjects, her father has offered me the most valuable of gifts, his only unmarried daughter. I believe she is well prepared to lead our land in these uncertain times and can influence those I cannot. I will admit that until recently, I was unaware such a creature of beauty and learning existed in our midst, but from the moment I saw her at the tournament, I knew I wanted her to be my queen."

My father squeezed my hand, and I looked at him, confused. Out of the corner of my eye, I saw Lot lean in toward Aggrivane and whisper something in his ear. Aggrivane's face went white and he started to rise, but Lot held him fast.

I was still watching them when Arthur's words reached my ears.

"Guinevere of Northgallis, will you do me the honor of becoming my wife?"

The world slowed. I could hardly believe what I had heard. *Me? Didn't he mean to ask Elaine? There must be some mistake.*

Frantic, I looked to my father for reassurance. He grasped both of my hands and was grinning broadly.

No, there must be an explanation. Service? What service? Oh no. No. No. No. Arthur was not referring to the counsel he gave Pellinor, but to saving my father's life. I am repayment of his debt. No, this cannot be happening.

My eyes darted to Elaine, who sat frozen in shock, a single tear dripping down her cheek. Lyonesse stared at me, murderous hatred naked in her expression.

In that instant, I could almost hear the response that was expected—nay, required—repeated in the thoughts of the hundreds of onlookers.

I scanned the room for Aggrivane, to plead with him to do something to make this madness stop, but he was already gone.

All I could see were the expectant expressions of my father and Arthur. I was alone in this trap, and there was but one way out. My response was not a choice but rather the submission of one already condemned.

My lips said yes, and cheers erupted all around.

I beamed back at my betrothed, but inside my heart was screaming, *I am so sorry, Aggrivane.*

As the commotion continued, I prayed my false expression would hold and not betray the anguish in my heart. All of my hopes and dreams had fled with Aggrivane, along with my freedom. Though others saw me as a fortunate woman, I felt like little more than a prisoner, transferred from one dungeon to another. I knew almost nothing of this man who was to be my husband, and yet I was supposed to happily accept him. My heart rebelled in painful spasms. To marry without love was to embrace the cold emptiness of the tomb, only without the sweet release of death.

I looked around the room with trepidation, suddenly realizing my assent to be Arthur's wife meant more than the loss of my maidenhood. If Arthur willed it, I would become high queen, and these people, my subjects. With a jolt of alarm, I realized Argante had predicted this very moment when I stood before her as a mere girl hoping for acceptance to Avalon.

Another crown sits on her brow, she had said, or rather the Goddess through her.

Part of me wanted to collapse in the rushes, to beat my fists on the floor like a petulant child and wail at the injustice done to me. But I had made a vow when I became a priestess that I would follow the Lady's will, no matter where it led. If she wished me to be with this man, then I had even less choice than I had imagined.

I squared my shoulders and took a deep breath before glid-
ing to Arthur's side, arranging my expression into one of pleasant
shock. I felt nothing but distain for him—and for my father—for
treating me like a brood mare, but I could not let that show. There
would be plenty of time for confrontation later, in private. Now, I
had to play the part of the future queen.

Tentatively, I took Arthur's hand, and he stepped back, presenting me to the assembly. Avoiding the malevolent glares of
Lyonesse and Elaine, I lifted my head high and willed the power
of priesthood to emanate from me. This might not have been
my choice, but it was my destiny, and I was going to face it on my
own terms.

Preview of

CAMELOT'S QUEEN

Guinevere's Tale, Book 2

P ART O NE

Fledgeling

C HAPTER O NE

Winter 497

The sigh of a reed pen across parchment, one jagged line of ink. That was all it took to betray my king and myself.

My signature, made with trembling hands, may have made me Arthur Pendragon's wife, but it couldn't change my heart. He'd asked for my assent to this marriage and I gave it to him, but it was a lie.

It was my duty. That much I had resigned myself to in the two months since Arthur had proposed marriage, shattering my dreams of a life with Aggrivane of Lothian.

From my place next to Arthur, I watched with hollow detachment as our marriage contract was sealed in the snowy courtyard of the old Roman fort of Carlisle.

Arthur stood, back to the northern gate, facing my father. Arthur's breath showed as small puffs of white in the frosty air. "King Leodgrance of Gwynedd, by the signing of this contract, I bind myself to you and your kin through the hand of your daughter, Guinevere. As proof of my fidelity, I bestow upon you the price of her honor." Arthur extended a wooden box of coins, ornately wrought gold brooches, and jewels—my bride price. The money assured my father of Arthur's sincere backing of our union, but it would become mine should we ever part ways.

"I thank you, Your Majesty," my father said with a bow. "You are now my son as well. My gift to you is a symbol of my tribe, the people who are your most loyal servants." My father held out his hand, and a servant placed reins into it, which he passed to Arthur.

At the other end of the bridle was a coal-black steed, a reminder of the days when brides were sold for cattle or land rather than gold. The stallion was muscular and strong but calm, indicating he was well trained and would be a valuable addition to Arthur's growing cavalry.

Arthur handed the reins to one of his attendants and clapped my father on the shoulder. "All of Britain is indebted to you for the most precious gift of your daughter, who in a moment, will become our queen. I thank you for giving her into my care."

My eyes welled with stinging tears. To anyone in the assembled crowd, I would appear overwhelmed now that the deed was done, but in truth, my heart burned with a mix of emotions. Some small part of me knew this was the same transaction that would have taken place had I married Aggrivane as I'd intended, but my heart said this was all wrong. I should be standing next to the man I loved, one with whom I couldn't wait to share my life, not the stranger who had stolen my dreams.

But those were the ruminations of a lovesick, petulant girl, not a level-headed ruler. As Merlin approached me with a pot of fragrant rose oil in one hand and the crown of Britain in the other, I forced myself to think like the high queen I was about to become. I was married to the high king of Britain, a position most other women would kill for, and I'd had to do nothing to obtain it, thanks to my father's willingness to use me as payment for his life-debt to the king.

I glanced at Arthur. His kind gaze held not a hint of temper or malice; he would not abuse me. Plus, since he was allowing me to be crowned queen instead of simply naming me his royal wife, we would rule as equals. Those facts had to be enough to trump whatever hurt and pain I still felt. Besides, though I would never admit it, part of me wanted to be high queen. I had been raised to rule and govern, and now I had a chance beyond my wildest imaginings.

I fell to one knee before Merlin and touched my right thumb to my forehead, lips, and heart—the sign of Avalon—in acknowledgement of his office as Archdruid.

Merlin's answering smile reflected our long friendship, forged during my years in Avalon under the tutelage of the Lady of the Lake. He leaned in close so his voice was soft in my ear. "No one is more deserving of this role than you. But take care your heart does not lead you astray."

I pulled back, regarding Merlin quizzically. I had no idea what he meant. For a moment, his eyes held the glassy, faraway look of prophecy, then he blinked and it was gone.

Before I could be sure I had really seen it, Merlin turned away as though nothing had passed between us. To the waiting crowd, he proclaimed, "Guinevere of Northgallis, priestess of Avalon, and now wife to High King Arthur Pendragon, in accordance with his will, this day I anoint you high queen of Britain."

Bowing, I willed myself not to shake, though my legs felt as if they would give way beneath me.

"May you be blessed with purity of mind and judgment by the Maiden"—he anointed my hair—"with love of your people from the Mother"—he drew small, sticky shapes on my cheeks—"and with the wisdom of the Crone"—he covered my hands in the warm, perfumed oil—"and may she of a thousand names bless you and keep you always." He placed the glittering gold circlet upon my head and knelt. "May I be the first to pledge my loyalty to you, High Queen Guinevere."

The crowd genuflected as one with a soft rustling of furs and other fine materials.

Arthur came to stand by my side then and took my gloved hand. Loud enough to be heard by all, he said, "These are your people, my lady. From this day forth, they are in your care. You are my equal in war as in peace. Will you fight by my side to defend their honor with your person and your very life?"

The full weight of responsibility was a stone in my stomach as I looked out over the bowed heads of Britain's nobility, kings and queens of our thirteen kingdoms and countless tribes, along with Arthur's most trusted warriors and advisors. A flurry of movement caught my eye, and I glanced over just in time to catch my father yanking Father Marius, his confessor and advisor, to his knees. The pious troll had never borne me any affection. In fact, he had tried to ruin my life a few years before, so it gave me no small pleasure to see him forced to prostrate himself before me.

I turned my gaze back to Arthur. "I will. From this moment on, I honor and care for them as I would my own children, for they are children of the gods. I am privileged to lead them."

A cheer went up, growing louder as the group rose to their feet. In a moment, they would come forth one by one to pledge their allegiance, but there was one thing left to do. Our union must be sealed with a kiss.

I turned to Arthur. My stomach clenched as I looked up into his deep blue eyes. I saw naught of malice there, only affection and hope, hope for the future of Britain, for us. As our lips met for the first time, I told myself the past was done. What mattered now was our future and the future of our kingdom.

ಎ๑ ๑ಎ

As the sun set on the old Roman fort, nobility from across the country and emissaries from all of the surrounding lands toasted our health and welfare. Arthur and I were seated above the rest on a dais in the center of a long table, our families trailing off like ribbons on either side.

The hours sped by in a haze of ale, music, laughter, and good cheer. Dish after dish of delicacies were placed before us and removed, finely dressed pheasant giving way to fish in pungent sauce, roasted boar with potatoes and herbs followed by sweet-meats, candied nuts, and baked apples. All the while, wine and ale flowed freely—so freely some even said the fountain in the courtyard, dedicated to the god of victory, spurted wine in our honor.

Amid the clatter of plates as courses were changed, Isolde, heir to the throne of Ireland and my dearest friend, came to my side and embraced me tightly, squatting down so we were at eye level.

"I told you my queen would bring you good fortune," she teased, referring to her piece from the game of Holy Stones we'd been playing on and off for over a year before she had disappeared to Ireland.

I reached into the pouch beneath my gown and retrieved the gleaming red orb. "Is this occasion enough to return it to you, or do you wish to win it back?" I held it out to her in my open palm.

She considered for a moment, green eyes dancing with mirth. "I believe you have better things to do tonight." As though the implication in her voice were not enough, she threw a longing look at Arthur. "It is my turn to be jealous, I suppose."

My elbow caught her ribs just as she snatched up the stone. "Speaking of jealousy, how is Galen?" Galen was the one-time betrothed of our friend, Elaine, whose heart Isolde broke when she ran away to Ireland with him.

She rolled her eyes and sighed. "It is far too long a story to relate tonight, but I will tell you this. I knew what I was doing when I agreed to let him come with me across the sea. He has proven to be valuable leverage for my family."

I wondered what fate she planned for him, slightly fearful of her thirst for justice.

She read my expression and continued, "I have plans that will benefit both his country and mine."

I shook my head, in awe of her determination and strategy. "You are a formidable ruler already, and the crown has not even passed to you yet."

She flashed her impish smile. "I learned young it is never too early to read your allies and enemies and uncover what each one most needs. If you can provide it or deny it, you hold the power."

Her gaze flickered across the room to the lanky, fair-haired warrior I remembered from the tournament as part of the house of Cornwall. "Speaking of which, I have friends to make."

I wasn't sure if she meant politically or personally. Knowing Isolde, it was probably both.

We gazed at each other for a long moment, knowing we likely wouldn't see one another again before she returned home.

"I will write as often as possible. You will be a great queen." She squeezed my hand and glanced at Arthur. "Do yourself a favor. Forget about what is past and enjoy the role fate has given you." She arched an eyebrow. "I certainly would."

Her laugher trailed behind her, and I couldn't help but echo it.

⋄⋄⋄

The long meal finished, our guests reveled in earnest. Musicians filled the hall with lively song, while jugglers, bards, and entertainers of every ilk roamed among the guests, delighting and mystifying them with colorful tricks and witty verse. The tables were pushed against the walls, creating an ample dance floor, which quickly filled with tipsy couples.

Arthur led me into a lively round where we stayed side-by-side for most of the dance. Something had been bothering me, and I took advantage of the situation to unburden myself.

"Arthur, if you intended to ask me to be your wife, why did you award the stag's head to Elaine?"

His expression showed he thought the answer was obvious. "Pellinor was my host and is a valuable subject. I could not insult him by passing over his daughter without some form of honor."

"I thought you were going to ask her to be your wife."

He laughed. "So did almost everyone else. Perhaps I was a little too charming, but she is a sweet girl and thrived on my attention. What was I supposed to do, warn her I had chosen someone else?"

I narrowed my eyes at him. "A hint would have been polite. The poor girl was crushed."

Arthur grunted, and I glanced around his shoulder at Pellinor, who certainly didn't appear upset that his daughter had been passed over.

"Her father looks to be quite recovered from the disappointment," I said.

Arthur winked at me. "Gold cures most ills, trust me."

The song ended and we milled among the crowd, accepting even more well-wishes. Within a few minutes, I felt like the false smile I had maintained all day would stiffen and set, as permanent as the crescent mark of the Goddess on my brow.

I was heading back to my chair when a voice stopped me in my tracks. "Well, well," it said.

I could almost see the cat-like smile in the lilting voice. It was a sound straight out of my nightmares. I knew the speaker even before I turned. "Hello, Morgan," I said as cheerily as I could manage.

We regarded each other coldly, each taking the other's measure. She was little changed, the candlelight making her skin glow. Wherever she had fled couldn't have given her too hard a life.

She settled into a mock curtsy. "Your Majesty." She nearly choked on the words.

I gave her a triumphant smile. "Last I heard, you slipped

Avalon's guard and went missing. What ill star directs you to darken this happy occasion?"

Morgan shook her head and clicked her tongue disapprovingly. "Still bitter about being second best, I see."

"You know my role, yet you dare call me second best?"

She was nonplussed by my outrage, which just irritated me more. "I've always been better at understanding the will of the Goddess than you."

I sucked in air to reply, but then I noticed how her hand hovered protectively over her abdomen, which, now that I looked closely, was swollen. She was pregnant.

I tried to cover my astonishment. "And who did the Goddess direct you to marry? Or do you just rut like a sow and see who the child most resembles?"

Morgan's smile was indulgent, like she was dealing with an especially simple child, but her tone was frosty, biting. "My husband is Uriens of Rheged, brother-in-law to the king. Welcome to the family, Guinevere."

Before You Go . . .

Thank you for reading this book. If you enjoyed it, please leave a review on Amazon and/or Goodreads. Word of mouth is crucial for authors to succeed, so even if your review is only a line or two, it would be a huge help.

To be the first to find out about future books in this series, other novels, and insider information, please sign up for my newsletter. You will only be contacted when there is news, and your address will never be shared.

Future releases include:

Camelot's Queen (Guinevere's Tale Book 2) – March 23, 2016

Been Searching for You (a romantic comedy) – May 10, 2016

Madame Presidentess (historical fiction about Victoria Woodhull, the first American woman to run for President) – July 25, 2016

Mistress of Legend (Guinevere's Tale Book 3) – Late 2016/Early 2017

Please visit me at **nicoleevelina.com** to learn more.

∘⫷ ⫸∘

I love interacting with my readers! Feel free to contact me on Twitter, Facebook, Goodreads, Pinterest, or by email. You can also send snail mail to: PO Box 2021, Maryland Heights, MO 63043.

AUTHOR'S NOTES

Guinevere came into my head in the fall of 1999, when I was a junior in college. I had read Marion Zimmer Bradley's *The Mists of Avalon* the winter before and, though I loved the book, I really disliked her portrayal of Guinevere. So I sought out other books about her. This led me to Parke Godwin's *Beloved Exile*, which made me wonder what happened to Guinevere before and after her life with Arthur.

I can still remember the moment Guinevere first took up residence in my head. I was sitting in a quiet stone walkway on an otherwise unremarkable morning of the fall semester when she told me she had a story to tell, one different from anything anyone else has said. It was in that moment we struck up a bargain and I decided to write my own version. Or at least that's what I tell myself. This never really was my story; it's always been Guinevere's. She's been calling the shots from the very first word.

Arthurian legend is a tough subject to write about because we don't know what is true and what is not. The Dark Ages are so named for a reason. We really don't have a lot of historical data to look at when trying to reconstruct them. What we do have, works from Ven. Bede and a Welsh monk called Nennius, are at best, a wild pottage of myth, history and legend. Separating fact from fiction is difficult, but that's also what makes it enjoyable for the historical fiction author.

Scholars and historians have been debating for years whether or not Arthur ever existed. If he did, he most certainly had at least one wife (Celtic law allowed for polygamy), and hence, some form of Guinevere would have existed as well. (Most other characters have been added over time as the stories evolved.) But in the end, does it really matter? Not to me. The legend that has arisen from the idea of Arthur has inspired countless generations, and I daresay will continue to do so. While I choose to believe that a real flesh and blood person inspired these stories, I do not ask you to believe the same, only to go with me on this fantastic voyage to the past, and I hope in so doing, learn a little about yourself. If you do, I have done my job well.

I can only separate fact versus fiction for you in the confines of this book. It began with a strong female character and so that is where I will begin my apologetics. As you read this, please remember I am not a historian (nor do I play one on TV). I am a storyteller who uses history to shape the views and customs of the world in which my stories are set.

The Picts and the Tribes of the North

The Picts are a large group of tribes who lived in the highlands of Scotland. Corinna and Guinevere descend from the British tribes directly to the south of them, those who lived between Antonine Wall and Hadrian's Wall – the Votadini, Selgovae, Novantae, and Damnonii (there were other, smaller tribes in the area, but I'm simplifying by confining the discussion to these main four). In the post-Roman period the kingdom began to be called the Gododdin and its inhabitants the Men of the North.

Little is known of the culture of these tribes, so I have taken liberties in conflating what we know about the Picts with the ways of their southern neighbors. Corinna, Guinevere and

Isolde are inspired by a matriarchal ideal that may or may not be fact. I'll let the historians hash that one out. What is true is that the Picts passed tribal leadership on through a system of matrilineal succession, meaning that the noble bloodline was counted through the female line. So if a man and woman marry but have no heirs, when the man dies, the woman's nephew (his sister's son) would inherit. We see this in *Daughter of Destiny* in Lot's eldest son Gawain being Arthur's heir, after Lot. This is because Arthur and Ana are brother and sister. This is not the same as matrilineal primogeniture, in which titles are passed from mother to daughter to the exclusion of sons, which I have chosen to have Corinna and Isolde's mother practice. There is some possibility that the Picts and the Irish (and perhaps the Celts at an earlier time in history) practiced this, but to-date evidence has not born this out.

It is true, however, that the Picts allowed their women to fight in battle. How and to what extent is lost in the pages of history. But I have allowed this fact to color the personalities of my Votadini women and give them a strength, independence and vitality that I personally believe their historical counterparts would have possessed.

Although the story of Leodgrance and Corinna is a product of my imagination, the kingdom of Gwynedd really was considered a safe haven for the Votadini tribe during this time period. Scholars debate who was responsible for such an unusual move, so I have chosen to have that role fall to Vortigern for purposes of my story.

Corinna's burial customs are based in Pictish lore and the wording of her headstone is consistent with Roman tradition.

Britain

The war-torn world in which Guinevere was raised is also based in fact. During the late fifth century, Britain was struggling to find its feet after the withdrawal of the Roman Empire. That old tribal infighting would resurface is not much of a stretch of the imagination. The influx of Saxon invaders and the raids of the western coast by the Irish are also painfully real, as was the event under Governor Paulinus that came to be known as the Rape of Mona. There is even some evidence that Vortigern could have been a historical figure.

Avalon

Avalon has long been associated with Arthurian legend. Geoffrey of Monmouth was one of the first to refer to Avallo in his *Historia Regum Britanniae* (c. 1136) and he called Avalon the Isle of Apples in the *Vita Merlini* (c. 1150). Not long after, in 1191, a group of monks on Glastonbury Tor "discovered" a grave and headstone that supposedly marked the final resting place of the great King Arthur and his wife, Guinevere. While that story has largely been discredited, it cemented the association of Glastonbury with the legendary isle of Avalon to which Arthur was born after the battle of Camlann.

The Tor exists much as I have described it and the mist really does rise at dawn and dusk, but the details of Avalon's appearance are fiction, born out of inspiration begun by Marion Zimmer Bradley and continued through my own meditation and study. Another strong source of inspiration was *The Isle of Avalon* by

Nicholas R. Mann, as well as conversations in Glastonbury with Arthurian scholar Geoffrey Ashe and Jamie George, the man who helped Ms. Bradley research for her famous novel.

The Kingmaker comet is a tradition in Arthurian legend, but I can find no factual equivalent.

The treasures of Avalon are based in the legendary 13 treasures of Britain, but again there is no proof of their existence.

I have fabricated the game/divination tool of Holy Stones. It is loosely based on a combination of chess, Chinese checkers and bird's eye view role playing games. But Druids were often consulted in matters of battle and diplomacy, so the spirit behind it is true.

The herbs which the priestesses use and the goddesses on which they call are based in historical research.

Many of the rituals and beliefs in this book were taken from modern neo-pagan and Druidic practices, which seek to recreate the beliefs of the Celts, which are largely unknown. Hence, Aggrivane's knowledge of the stars, Guinevere and Morgan's practices of divination, the story of the Oak King and Holly King, the Beltane enactment of the Great Marriage, and Avalon's consecration and full moon rituals have some basis in fact. I have, however, chosen to put my own spin on these rituals to suit my story. Ironically, the salute which the priestesses give the Lady of the Lake is loosely based on the Catholic tradition of touching one's thumb to the forehead, lips and heart before the pronouncement of the Gospel during Mass. The Candlemas ritual that comes later in the book is of my own making, based on a mixture of neo-pagan Imbolc and Catholic Candlemas customs.

One of the biggest questions about Avalon remains how it became associated with the Christians. Tradition holds that

Joseph of Arimathea, sometimes known as a tin trader, either visited the isle with his nephew, Jesus, in Jesus' youth, and/or returned there after Jesus' death, bearing vessels containing His blood and water from His side. Some say one of these vessels was the Holy Grail, while others argue it really originated with cauldron of the pagan goddess Cerridwen. Pellinor's family prophecy involving the Grail is entirely a product of my imagination.

Regardless of Joseph's involvement or lack thereof, Christians did settle on the Tor somewhere between 600 – 800 AD (although I have moved their presence back to approximately 450 AD to suit my story) and remained there until King Henry VIII dissolved its monastery in 1539.

KING ARTHUR

Arthur's lineage is based on strongly debated tradition. Read any of the dozens of books attempting to uncover his real identity and you will see how many theories there are, as well as his hundreds of supposed familial connections.

The story of Arthur's coronation, is of course, fictional, but I have based the inauguration stone on the Stone of Scone, which the Scottish used for generations in crowning their kings. The title given to Arthur, "Dux Britannium" was a real Roman title meaning "Duke or military leader of Britain" that likely would have been known to the elders during the time of my story. The title of "Arddurex" comes from Frank D. Reno's book *Historic Figures of the Arthurian Era: Authenticating the Enemies and Allies of Britains Post-Roman King*. The other factual element of Arthur's coronation is the *geis*, or limitation, laid on him by the Lady of the

Lake. A *geis* or *geisa* (plural) was common in Celtic custom and even more so in legend, and as is the case in this story, often led to the ruler's undoing or even death.

The hunt for the stag, portrayed at the end of the story, is also based in Arthurian tradition.

ഇരു ളൂ

If you would like to know more about the sources I consulted in writing this book, please visit my website, **nicoleevelina.com**, and click on the "research" tab under the section for Daughter of Destiny. You may also which to search my blog, located on the same site, for additional information on many of these topics.

ACKNOWLEDGEMENTS

I always thought of writing as a solitary venture – until I wrote a book. The people here listed have helped me bring this book to life, refine my craft, and most importantly, keep my sanity. There aren't enough words for me to thank you adequately, but I will try.

Thanks to my wonderful editor, Terry Valentine, whose patience and kind refinements made this book what it is today and to Cassie Cox who helped remove my million typos and refine my style. Thanks also to Jenny Q. for the beautiful cover and to The Editorial Department for the elegant layout.

But I wouldn't have ever gotten to know these people if it wasn't for the help of my beta readers, who helped shape my book into something worth sharing. You guys rock! So to Ben Moore, Courtney Marquez, Dawn Wheeler, Tyler Thomas, Colleen Durawski and Nancy Corbett, I say thank you. Courtney, you get a special mention as my writing partner, best friend and part-time editor. Thank you for sharing this dream with me and encouraging me to never quit. Nancy, you are the best proofreader ever. "A hundred tousand tanks!"

To everyone who encouraged me along the way, especially those with whom I lived or worked (and annoyed by incessantly talking about my "other job"), thanks for not ever giving up on me. First and foremost, thanks to my parents for their love and support, especially my mom, my very first reader and biggest fan, who had to hear every plot point and thought even remotely related to this book for the 15+ years it took to go from conception to print. To all those I've worked with, especially Jennifer,

Kacie, Angela, Dee, Dierdra, Nancy, Steve, Carrie, Clare, Chris B. and Chris M., Cathy and Ron – see, now you can say you knew me when! Thanks also to Alyson Noel, Jennifer Lee Carrell, Ann Fortier and Sarah Reinke for your words of wisdom and support, both in person and online. You are my role models. To Miss Lee Safar, this is the first of many big red feathers for me, so thank you for bringing positive energy into my world and helping me make the right choices. And last, but not least, thanks to Connor and Caitlyn for accepting there are times when my lap will be occupied by my "electronic pet."

In the area of research, I owe a debt of gratitude to Professor Jonathan Jarrett of Oxford University for his kind recommendations of research material on the Picts and the people of the Gododdin, as well as to author/historian Tim Clarkson for his research into these areas. A huge thank you to Jamie George for putting up with me for two weeks in England, including when I fell into the sacred pond at St. Nectan's Glen, and to Geoffrey Ashe for patiently answering all my questions at Glastonbury Abbey. I would also like to thank the St. Louis Country library for use of their research facilities, books and help with interlibrary loan materials.

And thank you to everyone who bought, downloaded or borrowed a copy of this book. Samuel Johnson once said, "A writer only begins a book. A reader finishes it." I believe that to be true, so thank you for completing the dream I started. I hope you've enjoyed living it as much as I did.

ABOUT THE AUTHOR

NICOLE EVELINA is St. Louis-born historical fiction and romantic comedy writer. A self-professed armchair historian, she spent 15 years researching Arthurian legend, Celtic Britain and the various peoples, cultures and religious practices that shaped the country after the withdrawal of Rome. Nicole has traveled to England twice to research the Guinevere trilogy, where she consulted with internationally acclaimed author and historian Geoffrey Ashe, as well as Arthurian/Glastonbury expert Jaime George, the man who helped Marion Zimmer Bradley research *The Mists of Avalon*.

Her mission as a historical fiction writer is to rescue little-known women from being lost in the pages of history. While other writers may choose to write about the famous, she tells the stories of those who are in danger of being forgotten so that their memories may live on for at least another generation. She also tells the female point of view when it is the male who has been given more attention in history.

Nicole is one of only six authors who completed the first week-long writing intensive taught by #1 New York Times bestselling author Deborah Harkness in 2014. She is a member of and book reviewer for the Historical Novel Society, and Sirens, a group supporting female fantasy authors, as well as a member of the Romance Writers of America, Women Fiction Writers Association, the St. Louis Writer's Guild and Women Writing the West.

When she's not writing, she can be found reading, playing with her spoiled twin Burmese cats, cooking, researching and dreaming of living in Chicago or the English countryside.

CPSIA information can be obtained at www.ICGtesting.com
Printed in the USA
LVOW11s1638030516

486488LV00008B/923/P